REECE

JENNIE LYNN ROBERTS

First paperback edition August 2022

Editor: O. Ventura at Hot Tree Editing
Cover design by Damonza.com

ISBN 978-1-7399518-5-6 (paperback)
978-1-7399518-6-3 (e-book)

www.jennielynnroberts.com

For Debbie

"You may be as different as the sun and the moon, but the same blood flows through both your hearts. You need her, as she needs you."

George R.R. Martin

Acknowledgments

A huge thank you to Olivia Ventura for her insightful editing wizardry throughout this series, as well as to Donna Pemberton and the rest of the team at Hot Tree. Thank you also to the design team at Damonza.com for this gorgeous cover.

Extra special thanks to T.K. Eldridge, Jennifer Allis Provost, and Hannah Huffelmann for taking the time to do sensitivity reads, and for all their support.

There are many amazing people who have helped me pursue my dream of being a writer, especially the wonderful FaRo authors in the Discord coven. Thank you to them, and to you, lovely reader. And most importantly, thank you (always!) to Mark, Alethea, and Michael.

Prologue

KAERLUD—FISH docks—twelve years ago

THE AIR WAS SCENTED with the clean, woody aroma of rosemary, the smell that Reece would forever associate with home. With rest and safety. But the herbal freshness was not enough to disguise the ever-present stink of fish and waste, clogged gutters, and drainage ditches slowly baking in the heat. And deeper still, the lingering bitterness of sickness. The musty odor of closed rooms and sweat-damp linens, of desperate prayers and slowly fading hope.

The stink of fish didn't really bother Reece. He'd never known anything different. They'd lived in this tiny tenement room, one narrow alley down from the fish docks, for as long as he could remember. The salty air, the cry of gulls, and the ever-present reek of the day's catch were the backdrop to his entire life. In fact, the days when the winds blew in over the harbor and the entire city stank of fish guts were always their best days.

Since Papa had died at sea—just another sailor catering to the city's voracious demand for the fish its people survived on through the winter—they'd had to rely on Mama's rosemary posies to survive. Posies that sold best when the city was hot and the smell of fish so potent it was almost alive.

Mama mended clothes when she could, but the bulk of their income was in the precious herbs growing in the rows of battered pots carefully filled with soil and lovingly planted with cuttings to be gently coaxed to life in the watery light let in by the tiny, grimy window.

They had made a good business of scrounging pretty flowers at the market, then blending them with sprigs of rosemary. Their posies were charming and aromatic. Not too expensive. And the stink helped them sell. As did a big smile, a flirtatious wink, and a compliment.

When he was little, the matrons had clucked over him, stroking his blond curls and admiring the sapphire in his gray eyes. When he got older... well, his shoulders had broadened and his voice had deepened, and he'd started to get a different kind of admiration. Now he was fifteen, tall for his age, and he'd perfected the exact right amount of heat to add to his smile. He grinned, charmed, and flattered, and sales went up. He'd learned quickly that there was always something he could find to admire. Soft hair, twinkling eyes, a new dress… all he had to do was identify it and murmur his appreciation. And then he sold more.

But, despite years of practice, Reece couldn't find one single nice thing to say to the woman standing in front of him now.

Not because she was unattractive. Under the layer of street dust and the exhaustion lining her face, she was very pretty. Not because she was unkind, either. She was a

Nephilim healer, working—for no fee—through the tenements that flanked the narrow streets leading down toward the markets and the docks, and she'd shown them nothing but compassion.

His silence was because she was packing away her instruments with a kind of grim finality. Because the lines around her mouth had tightened and her jaw was clenched. And because he already knew what she was going to say.

The healer lifted her purple-blue gaze to his and dipped her chin. She didn't prevaricate or pretend that he didn't understand. "You'll need to keep Cateline comfortable. I'm leaving you with packets of elderflower tea for her. Don't drink it." The healer gripped his shoulder, eyes focused entirely on his. "It has hemlock in it. To help with the pain and the fever."

"Okay." He wouldn't touch the tea. Wouldn't have touched it anyway. Mama needed it.

"The red plague can be contagious," the healer continued, "and you've been caring for Cateline all this time." She looked him over. A quick, professional assessment. "Have you had the rash?"

"No." And gods, he'd checked and checked.

No rash, his beast added.

"Good." She released his shoulder and patted it absentmindedly. "If you see any rawness on your skin, any raised bumps or blisters, come and find me immediately. We can help…."

She didn't finish the sentence, but he knew what she would have said. The Nephilim had learned a lot about the red plague since the terrible early days when it had spread through Brythoria, decimating whole villages. They knew how to treat it. But only if they caught the fever early enough.

But when a person was grieving the loss of her husband. When she was tired, overwhelmed, and already working eighteen hours a day—focused on keeping herself and her son alive—she might not notice yet another rough patch of raw skin. Not until it was too late.

The healer turned to go, but he grabbed her sleeve and held her back. "How—" He swallowed away the lump clogging his throat and forced the words out. "How long?"

How long until his mama was lost forever, gone back to join the gods of the earth and water, to be with his papa once more? How long until he lost his home, because how could he possibly pay the rent by himself? They had no family, and none of Cateline's friends were in any position to add a hungry teenage boy to their table. How long until he was truly, utterly alone?

You're not alone. We have each other. Always.

Gods. That's what it had come down to. Him and his beast.

"Two or three days, maybe less," she murmured. "I'm sorry."

Reece let the healer go, watching as she bustled out the door and away, on to the next patient and the next. The endless array of people who needed care.

Blankets rustled behind him and his mama coughed. She had slept through the last ten minutes of the Nephilim's visit—falling unconscious suddenly, as she did so often now —but the click of the closing door must have woken her. He stepped over pots of rosemary to find the small wooden stool beside the narrow cot and sit beside her, wishing she could comfort him somehow, but knowing that she couldn't.

Mama's face was flushed, her blue eyes over-bright while the deep indigo scales on her arms were dull. But her soft smile was full of love. She reached out a thin hand and brushed her thumb down his cheek. "Reece. You're so grown up. I close my eyes, and when I open them again, you're even more handsome than you were before."

Her slight chuckle turned into a cough, and Reece wrapped his arm around her, helping her to sit. He found the water cup he'd left beside her bed, still half full, and lifted it to her lips so that she could take a labored sip. Then she slowly, gingerly, slid herself back to lean against the wall, watching him.

She laced her fingers through his, her grip tighter than he expected, her cracked lips twitching up into a tired smile. "And you're even kinder than you are handsome."

Reece chuckled, but it sounded as forced as it felt. "Do you want to try and eat something? The healer left some tea for when the pain is bad."

Mama shook her head slowly. "Not just yet. I want my mind to be clear."

She looked at him, her gaze traveling over his face for long, silent moments before she spoke again. "I've kept this inside me for a long time, and maybe that was wrong. Or maybe I'm wrong to tell you now…. I don't know. But I do know that I don't have much time left." She broke into a hacking cough, her thin fingers twitching against his. "What is the right thing to do?" she asked, her eyes lifting to focus on the far wall.

Was she speaking to him or herself? Lost in some unhappy fever dream. It was difficult to tell.

Her gaze came back to his. "Is it better to know the truth or live with the happy lie?" she asked quietly.

He didn't know how to answer, didn't know if he even wanted to. Cold shivers settled on the back of his neck as his scales hardened. "Know what truth, Mama?"

Her shoulders hunched forward, just a little, and a wave

of tarnished scales flickered sluggishly over her arms. But her chin lifted, and Reece could tell she was bracing herself.

His own beast stirred anxiously. The last time Mama had that look on her face, she'd told him that Papa's ship had gone down somewhere in the Asherahn sea. That the big, smiling man they both adored would not be coming back. She had wept slowly sliding tears that had taken a part of his heart with them as she wiped them away.

She had held him tightly as she whispered that Papa was gone… but that they had to remember they had each other. Then she had kissed his forehead and told him they would find a way to create a better life together. But it hadn't been the truth. There had been no better life. Just a long, terrible year as all of Kaerlud suffered under Geraint's taxes for his never-ending war and they suffered even more.

Reece missed his papa with a kind of desperate misery. A misery that was interlaced with a bright kernel of anger that he kept well-hidden from Mama. Anger that only got worse as their suffering grew.

Anger at the loss of the small comforts they'd once had. Anger at the way Mama cried herself to sleep. Anger at the unfairness of it all. Maybe even some guilt-ridden, swiftly suppressed anger at Papa himself, for leaving them when they needed him so badly.

Cateline patted his cheek gently with her free hand, breaking into the dark spiral of his thoughts. Then she reached under her threadbare blanket and pulled out a small embroidered purse, and passed it to him.

By the feel of it, it held several coins. Too heavy to be groats. He opened the string and glanced inside. It gleamed softly. Gods. The purse held silver pieces, at least ten. To them, it was a fortune.

"Where did…? Why…?" Hell. He didn't even know what question to ask.

Mama cleared her throat. And then she cleared it again before she started speaking. "When I was a young woman, I worked in the palace as a maid. I made a good salary. And sometimes… sometimes, I was given gifts. I saved my coin carefully, and I've held on to that purse, all this time."

He couldn't begin to understand why. Why was she given gifts? Why would have held on to this treasure when they'd needed it so badly?

His confusion must have shown on his face, because she swallowed another slow sip of water and continued. "I was pretty then," she murmured. Reece started to argue that she was still pretty, but she cut him off with a squeeze of his fingers. "I was pretty and young and naïve. So very naïve. When an older man, a man who was powerful and handsome and so very charming… even more charming than you—" She chuckled, but the sound was scratchy and laced with sadness. "When he told me he loved me, I believed him."

She coughed, a hacking fit that brought tears to her eyes before she slumped back against the wall once more as Reece sat helplessly beside her.

"He was lonely," Cateline said. "His wife had died a few years before, and he…. He knew all the right things to say. But then I got pregnant."

Her eyes met Reece's, the ring of sapphire around the gray of her irises more muted than he'd ever seen it. "I didn't tell him… but I did suggest we marry. Or perhaps make a home together. He had a child; I thought the boy could benefit from a mother."

Her scales flickered slowly up her neck, and Reece's own

scales mirrored their movement. A slowly hardening armor to block out these words he didn't want to hear.

"He said that marriage wasn't possible," Cateline admitted in a rough voice. "He would never marry again. But even if he did, it would never be to a woman like me. His family would never accept a Tarasque. I would never raise his children or stand beside him at court. He told me he loved me, he wanted me, we could have a life together… so long as I never claimed him, or even acknowledged him, publicly. And he warned me—" She took a trembling sip of water. "—never to let his family find out."

Scales flooded up Reece's arms in a cold wave as his beast growled low in his belly. But it didn't help. The scales could only protect his skin, not his heart. If she'd had a lover at court. If she'd been pregnant….

"No." Reece shook his head, trying to block out the words. "That can't be."

"It can. It was." Mama closed her eyes for a moment, leaning heavily back against the wall, but when she opened them again, her gaze was clear and somber. "I realized then how stupid I'd been. And I realized how much danger you were in. I fled that same day. I sent back a story that I'd come down with the red plague and couldn't return. Ironic, don't you think?"

Ironic? No. Heartbreaking, yes. Soul destroying, even. Had everything in his entire life been a lie?

"But what about Papa?" The words were torn out of him, scraping against his raw throat.

"Papa was a friend. We knew each other for many years. When I ran away from the palace, he took me in. He gave me a home. He married me, knowing I already carried a child. And I came to love him, more than I could have ever imagined was possible. We were happy. I was wiser then… I knew how fortunate I was to be loved by a good man. A kind man. Brennan was your father in every way but one. We had a good life."

Reece's stomach heaved. Papa wasn't his papa. His mama had a whole different life. A lover in the palace.

Gods. A new thought wormed its way up through his consciousness. A thought driven on by misery and fear and the very real knowledge that within days he would be alone in the world. A thought that blended with the anger at the unfairness of Papa's death, Mama's illness, his own impotence in the face of so much loss, and all the hardship to come.

Maybe his real father would have wanted him after all? Maybe, if Mama just had told him she was pregnant, everything would have been different. They could have lived in the palace. Surrounded by luxury. A bigger room. Real beds, not just two hard cots. A warm cloak. New boots. Hot food. Maybe even pies! That's what those rich children had, wasn't it?

His beast turned over unhappily. *No. Wrong. We were happy. We had Papa—*

For the first time in his entire life, Reece pushed away the beast who was part of him. Ignored the words that couldn't begin to help with the pain and betrayal seething in his heart.

"Why are you telling me this?" he asked, voice breaking.

"I took you from the palace to keep you safe, but years have passed, and your blood father has long forgotten that I exist. Your papa, the man who loved you, is gone, and I will be gone soon too." She gave him an exhausted smile, her dulled scales unmoving on her pale face. But he couldn't force himself to smile back.

"Noble Apollyon blood mingles with mine in your veins,

Reece. Along with the Tarasque gifts you've inherited from me, and the kindness and decency your papa taught you. You are a direct descendent of the last drake of Brythoria. You are born to be strong and honorable. It is time for you to know your heritage." She swallowed heavily. "And I wanted you to have this purse, the last gift of your noble father. I've been saving it for when you married, but you need it now."

Mama's voice faded as she finished speaking, and she slumped back against the wall, breathing hard.

A sailor called out a crude joke in the distance, and seagulls wailed over the Tamasa, but Reece could hardly hear them past the buzzing in his ears. He wasn't who he'd thought he was. Everything was a lie. He was facing a future living on the streets, when he could have lived in a palace.

Honorable. Kind. That's our heritage, his beast whispered, but Reece ignored it. The gifts of his mama and papa would be of no use to him alone on the streets of Kaerlud.

"Who was he?" he asked, his voice rough. "The man in the palace." He couldn't bring himself to say, "your lover," but they both knew who he meant.

Mama shook her head slowly. "I can't tell you." Her grip was loosening as she tired, but she still held his hand too tightly for him to escape. "It's not safe. The stories I've heard… They would kill you for sure."

She lifted his hand to her lips and kissed it gently. "Everything I've ever done, I've done because I love you. All I ever wanted was for you to be safe. When I'm gone, remember that."

Cateline sank lower into the bed and closed her eyes, her face drawn and wan as if she'd used the very last of her energy. "I love you, Reece. Remember," she whispered.

He sat with her, holding her hand, until she was fast

asleep. And even then, he sat, stunned, frozen in place in the dark, cooling room.

He loved her, he did, and he was never going to recover from her loss. But he didn't know if he could forgive her either. Her decisions had robbed him of any kind of security. Any kind of safety. And now she was dying and leaving him all alone with the repercussions of her choices.

Mama loves us.

Reece bit back his confusion and distress and grumbled, "If you love a person, you don't lie. And you don't betray people. Not ever."

She didn't betray us! She was trying to save us.

Gods. The beast didn't understand anything. "Shut the hell up," he growled back.

The beast turned over unhappily in his belly, and Reece sighed. All he had left in the world were ten silver coins. If he lived on the street and ate one meal a day, it might last him a few months. Long enough for him to learn how to survive. Maybe just long enough to see him old enough to enlist. And enlisting was his only real option now. He would have to eke out an existence for another year and then lie about his age.

Reece sat, shivering in the darkness, holding his mama's hand as grief and guilt and anger rioted through him, and made himself a promise.

He would survive. He would fight his way back into the palace. He would sleep in the soft bed and eat the hot food that he should have had from the day he was born. One day, he would get it all back. And he would never allow himself to be betrayed ever again.

Chapter One

EVERYONE LIED.

Daena knew it. She'd always known it. And yet… she'd still somehow landed up here. Imprisoned. Accused—rightly—of being a traitor. About to dive headfirst into a pool of liars. The very thing she'd tied herself in knots trying to avoid.

Since she was old enough to understand language, she'd been able to taste lies. It was different for all the truth seekers. Some heard a hissing noise that accompanied false words, others saw clouds of color surrounding the liar—burnt mustard or poisonous green. For Daena, it was taste. Sour milk, raw vinegar, the bitterness of the tannery, foul and acidic, making her gag.

Of course, what she couldn't taste was manipulation.

Omission had no flavor at all. Neither did half a truth, or a well phrased question. No, those were things she had to discern all on her own. And that was where she'd failed. Worse… she hadn't just failed to see that she was being deceived, she'd *wanted* to believe the half-truths she was told.

Oh, it was so easy to see the truth in hindsight. But, at the time, a handsome, charming, intelligent man had turned all his attention onto her, and it had been intoxicating. It had been like standing in the summer sunshine, bubbles floating through her blood.

She'd been lonely, far from home, trying to create a future her family didn't understand, a future they said was wrong—not what she had been born to be—and then along came Andred. He had wanted her exactly as she was, or so she'd believed. He'd made her feel special and precious.

Looking back, there had been times when he'd been cold and dismissive, even angry, but those had only made her work harder to prove herself. To earn the reward of his attention. His affection. To get that addictive sunshine back.

They'd gone riding through the foothills of the Thabana Mountains and swimming in the cold lakes, his big body beside her, protective and attentive. They'd snuck through the quiet of the Nephilim temple to make breathless love in the conservatories, surrounded by the lush scents of vanilla and saffron, brought from Sasania and hand cultivated in the heated rooms. He'd given her pleasure, that was never in doubt. And he'd said all the right things.

Andred had met her in Staith and courted her at the temple. She'd slept beside him and missed him when he was gone. And then he'd saved her. He'd pulled her from the burning building like a hero from a story. When he'd kept her with him "because it would be dangerous for her to leave," she'd never considered that the danger came from him. And when he'd built his army, she'd helped him.

Only in hindsight did she hear all the omissions. *I can't tell you how beautiful you are. I never imagined I would find someone like you. Gods, Daena, you're so… move this way for me, sweetheart… that's perfect.*

Just thinking about it made her want to curl up into a ball of shame and regret and hide away forever.

He was so passionate in his defense of Brythoria. So fervent in his belief that a great wrong was being perpetrated and there was only one way to defend their people. And, if she was being ruthlessly honest, she'd believed there would be a place for her in that glorious future. They were going to save Brythoria—together—and she was going to show every single person who had told her she had to be a truth seeker, no matter how much she hated it, they were wrong. She was going to be a hero, with her lover at her side. She hadn't wanted to be the queen, not really, but she had wanted to be *his* queen. And she'd been paying for it ever since.

Daena turned over on her cot to lie on her back. Gods, she felt so stupid. So utterly pathetic. Andred had used the temple—the access *she* had given him—to stash the Verturian weapons he was stockpiling for his attack on their king at Ravenstone. And afterward, when the king was dead and the Wraiths were waiting for Ballanor to reward them, she had helped them hide in those very same conservatories.

She had always known that the temple had burned down in a reiver attack… but it was only later that she realized that Andred had brought those reivers down from the mountains in the first place. That the temple had burned after Ballanor had betrayed the Wraiths—almost certainly on Andred's orders—hiding the evidence of their treachery.

By the time she'd understood the truth, she'd been trapped in his camp, flanked by mountains and hemmed in by an icy lake, with a poorly healed ankle and a full company of guards watching her every move.

She had been helpless then, but she wasn't anymore. Tor had offered her a choice, and she had taken it. She had stood in her tiny room in the barracks at Staith, looking out toward where the temple ruins lay, and made her decision. The first decision she had made entirely for herself in months.

She would atone for the help she'd given Andred. She would fix the mistakes she'd made. Whatever the cost.

Daena stared up at the ceiling, forcing her thoughts away from their constant cycle of guilt and self-recrimination. She had something she'd never imagined possible when she was stuck in the Wraith's camp: a second chance.

As frustrating as it was to be locked in a cell with her regrets hour after hour, she was deeply grateful for the opportunity she'd been given and how kind the Hawks had been to her.

She had parchment and pens, blankets, and a soft mattress. Nim visited her as often as she could—under the guise of apothecary, helping her with her injuries—and they had slowly become something close to friends.

Nim brought creams that she promised would help the ache in Daena's ankle, oils for her cramping muscles, and she noticed when Daena smelled them, testing their feel on her fingers, asking after ingredients. They compared notes on herbs and tinctures, and eventually, they shared their stories, Nim's love for Tristan shining in everything she said.

Keely couldn't visit without raising suspicion, so she sent books for Daena to read instead, often with amusing handwritten notes hidden in their covers. Apparently, the baby had taken to kicking her in the bladder, which she blamed on Tor and his heavy legs.

Daena liked these women, and she liked the Hawks. They had welcomed her so genuinely, treating her like she was truly one of them.

She liked Lucilla too, although she'd only met her once and had spent most of the time wondering what Lucilla must think of her: the woman who had helped the Wraiths kill their king, Lucilla's father. Gods.

A noise at the end of the corridor drew Daena's attention, and she swung her legs over the side of the cot and pushed herself up to sit. Her hair was tangled, and she dragged her fingers through it, trying to look a little less like a prisoner who had spent the day lying on her bed.

Jeremiel strode up to her bars, his purple-blue eyes soft with kindness. Kindness she really didn't deserve. He and his brother Rafe had met her family in Eshcol; her family who had been mourning her death. They were also friends with Ramiel, her uncle, who had been devastated by her loss, feeling responsible for helping her find a position in Staith and supporting her in the argument with her parents. Meanwhile, she'd been alive and helping Andred plot to overthrow their queen the whole time.

"—don't you think?"

She blinked at Jeremiel. He'd been speaking quietly while her mind wandered. "Sorry, what?"

His forehead crinkled into a slight frown. He was tall and serious-looking, with the same deep gravitas as her uncle Ramiel. Both of them were truth seekers like her. But, unlike her, they'd dedicated their lives to justice. They'd used their skills for the Nephilim and for Brythoria. She, on the other hand, had run away from the path her parents had chosen, only to land up Andred's truth seeker instead.

"At least that's progress, don't you think?" Jeremiel asked, his voice low even though the Constable's tower was empty except for her, and the entrance was guarded only by the Hawks.

She pushed herself off the cot and limped over to the bars. "Say that all again, from the beginning, please."

Jeremiel leaned against the bars. "I think Tor might have mentioned Reece to you?" he asked.

Yes. She nodded slowly. There was no way she could forget Reece, not when he was the man who was going to accompany her into the Wraiths' new lair. And especially not after every single one of his friends had taken extra time to tell her all about him. How the only reason he wasn't with them in the palace was that he'd been betrayed. How he'd been tortured by Dornar and yet never gave up the Hawks. They'd told her so many stories of his intelligence and skills on the battlefield, of his wit and charm off it, that she almost felt she knew him. Or at least, knew the highly polished—probably too polished—version his friends were determined to share.

"Reece has been tracking the former councilors," Jeremiel continued, "and one of them recently visited a manor house to the north of the city, on the other side of the Tamasa."

They'd traveled through that part of the country on their way back south from Staith, past the rolling pastures of dark soil, the fat livestock being brought in for the winter, and the stately Apollyon family homes bordering the eastern fens.

Those rich pastoral lands were half the reason the

Apollyon raiders had targeted Brythoria all those generations before, and they had held onto them ruthlessly as their fortunes had grown and their kings had come to rule. It was exactly the kind of place Andred would love.

"Reece watched the house for several days." Jeremiel scratched the back of his neck, looking uncomfortable. "There's a heavily armed presence and far too much activity for this time of the year. Most of the noble families have come to Kaerlud for the coming midwinter celebrations. It should be quiet, not filled with men. Men in dark tunics, who Reece says are too well-trained and cohesive to be simple guards."

A manor home, riddled with Andred's men, far from anyone. Gods and angels. It sounded just like the camp in the mountains. It sounded like a nightmare. No wonder Jeremiel didn't want to have to tell her.

"How—" Daena's words were cut off by the sound of footsteps on the stairs leading up the tower.

Lucilla, with Mathos a pace behind her, appeared at the end of the corridor, cutting off any thought of further words Daena might have had. Her hands were suddenly clammy, and her heart thudded unevenly.

Lucilla, in her breeches and dark blue tunic embroidered with the royal fighting boars, long dark hair caught up in a messy bun, didn't look—or act—like any kind of queen Daena had ever imagined. She laughed and joked. She looked everyone directly in the eyes when she spoke. Her words were clear and unequivocal. And they tasted of nothing at all: they were the truth.

This was the woman Daena had helped Andred build an army against.

Heat spread up the back of her neck, and she rubbed her fingers down the side of her face, feeling the bumps and ridges where the skin had healed. It was a habit she needed to stop. One borne of uncertainty and vulnerability in the Wraiths' encampment. But at this moment, it soothed her. Gods. She would rather be running up the bloody gorge with Tor, flames roaring up behind them, than calmly facing Lucilla.

"Afternoon, Daena." Lucilla smiled. "How are you holding up?"

"I—" The words caught in her clogged throat, and she had to swallow before she could start again. "Thank you, Your Majesty, I'm very…. It's very comfortable here."

And it was. The sentence tasted of nothing but omission.

"I understand," Lucilla said softly, "and please don't bother with 'Your Majesty' we're all friends here."

Gods. Friends. The thought made Daena want to laugh hysterically, but she cleared her throat instead.

Lucilla probably did understand some of it. The queen had been imprisoned by her father and her brother for years, after all. But she couldn't know the rest—the shame and the guilt and the humiliation.

Mathos wrapped his arm around Lucilla and pulled her closer. He was a big man, not quite as tall as Jeremiel but more muscular, with burgundy and gold scales that flickered at his wrists, and a glint in his eye that suggested he was only ever a few minutes away from his next amusing comment. Although at this moment, his face was serious. Concerned, even. Something had changed.

Mathos dipped his chin. "Reece has met with Tor. We have confirmation; he's found the Wraiths."

Gods. Her time was up. No more visits from the Hawks. No more books or witty anecdotes; no more relaxed conversations with Nim. Now she had to step up and do what she'd promised.

Daena wiped her hands slowly down the sides of her skirt. She could do this. She *would*.

"Tor has a plan," the queen said, her voice quiet but strong, "and we're ready to make our first move." Her gaze was locked on Daena's as she continued. "We'll start by letting all of Kaerlud know you're to be tried by the Nephilim court and that you will be testifying, in detail, against the Wraiths. We will invite the former council members and make it clear to them that our goal is to expose Andred and the Wraiths, and to ensure that the entire kingdom knows them for what they really are: the king's murderers, Ballanor's cronies, and traitors to the throne."

Gods. Daena gripped the bars that separated them and let the cold iron ground her. Andred would be furious. The Wraiths would be utterly enraged at being painted as murdering traitors, and they would blame it all on her. And they wouldn't be alone—the rest of Kaerlud would hate her just as much, condemning her for supporting Andred in the first place. What kind of life would she ever be able to have after that?

She swallowed hard. She would have the life she'd earned… if she even got that far. "Okay." Her voice croaked.

Lucilla gave her a swift, approving nod before continuing. "We don't just want to humiliate Andred, however. We need to stop him completely, and that means we have to identify and arrest all the people who are supporting him too."

Daena waited, jaw clenched, knowing there was more.

"We're going to let everyone *think* there will be a trial,"

Lucilla said in a low voice. "But in reality, the trial is the bait. You and Reece will be the trap."

Hell.

"It will be dangerous," Lucilla said gravely. "The risks are very high, and it'll never work unless you're completely committed. You will need to work with Reece—give him access to the Wraiths and help him identify what is truth and what isn't—and he will do everything he can to keep you safe."

"Okay," Daena said again. What else was there to say?

"But," Lucilla said, her voice determined, "I want you to be completely clear that you don't have to do any of this. We can find another way to get Reece in with Andred. He could go in alone. If we have to, we can arrest them now and look for another way to find their accomplices."

Lucilla's dark eyes met Daena's without flinching. "I'm giving you this choice—we can sneak you out of Kaerlud, spread a story that you died in captivity, and you can go and live your life somewhere far from all of this. Or you can help us win this war before it starts. What do you want to do?"

Cold sweat slid slowly down her ribs, the iron under her palm hurt, she was gripping it so tightly. Tor's plan was dangerous. Andred would detest everything about this trial. She didn't even want to imagine the look on his face when he heard about it. Or what he might do when he got hold of her.

Lucilla was giving her a chance to run and hide and not have to face any repercussions for what she'd done, to avoid all that danger.

But what would be the point? If she ran now, she would spend the rest of her life knowing she'd failed, steeped in guilt and self-hatred.

Once upon a time, it seemed like a lifetime ago, she had wanted to work with her plants, to use them to make a difference. That seemed like a hazy dream now, something so utterly unattainable it wasn't even real. But she *could* still make a difference. She could help her queen and the kingdom they both loved. She owed a debt to Lucilla, and she would pay it. With her life, if it came to that.

"Yes. I want to do this," Daena said firmly. Her words tasted of air and honesty.

"Truth," Jeremiel agreed quietly.

"Thank you, Daena. We are all deeply grateful." Lucilla smiled at her, a warm look of thanks and genuine appreciation. Mathos murmured his agreement behind her and Jeremiel dipped his chin in acknowledgment.

Lucilla leaned forward, her eyes locked on Daena's. "This is what we're going to do…."

Chapter Two

THE AIR BLOWING across the farmlands was earthy and slightly sour, carrying the tang of the fens from just a few miles to the east. Thank the gods it was past autumn and properly into winter. In summer, the interlocking channels of still water would have attracted mosquitoes and midges in their thousands. As it was, the shrubby weeds and fen sedge were weighted down with gleaming spider webs, and the ground was cold and hard.

Not as bad as the foothills of the Thabana Mountains. Frozen and rocky and terrifying, nothing to eat, waiting for the earth to collapse around us.

Reece grunted. His beast was right, for a change. Neither of them missed life as a sapper in the border war. Undermining earthworks. Sneaking through mountain passes. Taking the first—worst—charges, tasked with destroying the Verturian fortifications ahead of the infantry. It had been dangerous, bloody work, with very low life expectancy… and the best rates of pay. Which was exactly why he'd chosen it. He hadn't cared much about dying, but he'd cared a great deal about being comfortable when he got the fuck out of that hellhole.

Of course, all that money was gone now. To be fair, he'd spent most of it as a Blue, living in Kaerlud as one of Geraint's personal guards. He'd finally had access to the most comfortable beds, invitations to the wildest parties, the newest fashions, the richest food… and Helaine. Gods.

He'd thought what they had was good. She wasn't just beautiful, she was stunning. Her sky-blue scales had complemented his deeper indigo. Her long blonde hair was as soft and gleaming as the silk dresses she filled out to perfection. She was clever and funny, but also precious and expensive, like a jewel.

They were both tall, attractive, charming, and elegant. They'd been the golden couple; invited to all the best gatherings, including parties with Andred, the Wraiths, and the array of illustrious families they relaxed with. Together, they had created a life that was the polar opposite of scrounging through the dirt of Kaerlud.

He hadn't loved Helaine. But, no matter what anyone else said—including her—he had been faithful. Never, in a million years, had he expected her to turn around and betray them all to Ballanor.

I told you. Tor told you. Everyone told you. Helaine wanted power and riches and she thought you'd give them to her… but you embarrassed her instead. You discarded her in front of her friends.

They *had* all told him, but it hadn't meant anything to him. Helaine had been a Tarasque trying to make her way in the highly politicized Apollyon Court… just like him. He had also wanted power and riches, and he couldn't see a damn thing wrong with that. He still couldn't.

And yes, he had left her. But Geraint had just died at Ravenstone, the Hawks were exiled, and it seemed sensible to break things off. He'd tried to get her in private, but the palace was in an uproar. Ballanor was hauling Val and Alanna in, and Helaine had joined the other nobles in watching them get dragged through the courtyard. She'd refused to move, refused to miss the spectacle, and he'd been out of time. He'd no choice but to talk to her then and there.

Honestly, he'd thought she would understand. He'd thought that what they'd shared would mean something. That they could continue as friends. It had never occurred to him that he couldn't ask for her help when they came back.

But he should have known better. Gods. His mother had done the exact same thing: lied to his face and then ripped the floor from under his feet right at the worst possible moment.

His gut twisted as the suffocating memories rose. Helaine's treachery had triggered something in him. He'd still been struggling with the horrors of Ravenstone, the loss of his home, his safety—all the things he'd worked so hard for—when she'd betrayed him. He'd cared for her. He'd thought she cared for him. But in the end, it had counted for nothing. And it had pushed him into the dark pit of misery he'd carried, hidden beneath the surface—beneath the banter and charm he excelled at—for so many years.

And, of course, his beast had been no help at all. Instead of complaining about Helaine or the Wraiths as it used to, it had focused all its disdain on him. He'd half expected it to be happy when he'd lost the riches and comforts it had derided for so long, but instead, it merely increased its litany of complaints, until he was prepared to do almost anything to shut it the hell up.

A sharp whistle cut through the air—and his thoughts—

and Reece focused his attention on the opulent farmhouse in the shallow valley below him. It was time for the guards to rotate.

Soldiers dropped from trees and stepped out from behind walls before making their way in a clockwise circle around the farmhouse, their eyes carefully scanning the road, grounds, and even the air.

It was a good system—especially given how under-resourced they were. Only twenty Wraiths had made it out of the northern mountains, and every one of them had been strategically positioned. There were no obvious patrols. Nothing to see, except for the few minutes once an hour when the soldiers moved.

If someone was listening, they might notice the bird calls on the quarter-hour as the guards checked in, but the first call always came from the road, confirming no one unexpected had ventured down the winding drive. And when someone did come down the road, a series of watchers—local men and boys paid handsomely for their time—reported them long before they reached the house.

It was everything Reece would have expected from the Wraiths.

He hadn't wanted to believe that it might be true. Deep in his heart, he'd hoped that Tor was wrong. But two days ago, he'd seen Andred, Caius, and Usna. The Wraiths were definitely here.

A wave of scales shivered up his arms and over his shoulders. His beast hated Andred and the men who served him—hated their betrayal—as much as Reece did. Maybe more.

His beast rattled out a low growl. *I knew who they were from the beginning.*

Reece's fingers twitched. The apple brandy in his flask

called to him. It would be so easy to reach down and take a sip. And then another. Enough to quiet down the beast and the never-ending voice in his head.

It had started when his mother died. His beast disagreed with him often and loudly, and he had started to resent it. Their relationship had improved when they were in the army. When they were focused on surviving one day at a time. When Tristan plucked him out of the sappers and gave him a home in the Hawks, it had almost been like they were a unit again. The beast was happy; Reece admired and respected Tristan and slowly formed strong bonds with the rest of the Hawks. It had been good.

But then the Hawks were called to the palace, promoted to the Blues. Reece finally had everything he wanted within his reach. But the more successful Reece was—the more he was wanted and desired, successful and comfortable—the more difficult his beast became.

It got so bad that he couldn't bear the constant snarling and complaining. That was when he'd realized that a couple of glasses of wine before a party sent the beast to sleep—if not entirely, then enough that Reece could have a good time without being bombarded by unwanted inner opinions. A few sips of brandy before meeting with the Wraiths, or Ballanor and his friends, was enough.

Then Helaine betrayed him—another betrayal by someone he'd trusted. Another betrayal that had cost him his home, his life, nearly even cost him his friends—and it brought back all those ancient feelings of hurt and rage.

That kernel of darkness he'd carried around, hidden deep in his heart, had roared to life, flaming and burning everything around him. He'd lashed out, and his beast had lashed back. It had been ashamed. And he hadn't wanted to hear it. So, he did what he already knew worked: he drank.

But the more he drank, the more he did things the beast hated. Things he knew were wrong but couldn't seem to stop himself from doing. The easy charm he'd used as a shield his entire life was gone, and all he had left was rage and misery. His beast complained, and the more his beast griped, the more he drank. Until his life was a blur of alternating drunkenness and hangovers and constant fighting with himself. A never-ending spiral of rage and guilt.

Reece dropped his forehead onto the freezing ground, his shame and disgust mingling uncomfortably with the beast's judgment. Tristan—the man who had been like an older brother to him—had been tortured because Reece had trusted Helaine. Nim had been forced to kill Grendel. Ballanor had battled Val. Dornar had…. Fuck. He couldn't think about Dornar.

Those brutal hours with the former Lord High Chancellor were like a festering wound in his soul. Reece hadn't given up his squad. He hadn't betrayed anyone. But he'd gone over a dark edge anyway. He'd realized that he couldn't be near the Hawks, not without saying and doing things that hurt them, so he'd taken himself away. Until now. Until Tor had offered him this chance at redemption.

He was doing this for the Hawks. He owed them, after everything he'd done. He was going to make sure that they were safe, that the kingdom was safe. And that meant, no matter how irritating his beast was, he had to stop drinking.

It had been hard. Much harder than he'd expected. At first, he'd felt like he had the worst hangover of his life. His stomach had churned, and his heart raced while his head thumped in agony. But that was only the start. After that came the sweats and the fever. And, gods, the feeling that the world was going to crash in on him at any moment. The utter certainty that he was going to die alone in his cheap lodging.

He'd huddled beside the narrow bed, listening to the bells in the distant Nephilim temple, counting down the hours and wondering how much time he had left. It took three days before he started to think he might survive. Several more after that before he could make it through the day.

He had done it for the Hawks. Just as he would complete this mission. After that… then he would see.

Maybe there would be a small reward, something he could use to start again. Perhaps the Hawks could find him some work in the palace, some way to get his old standing back. Then he could claw back some of those comforts he'd lost. Maybe he could even look for his real father.

I'm sick of destroying things. I want to build, his beast agreed. *But the rest… that's a fucking stupid idea.*

"Fuck off," he replied under his breath.

I'm trying to help.

Reece groaned. "You know what would help? If you would just shut the fuck up."

The beast responded with a long rumbling growl.

Reece ignored it. He was so tired of bickering with himself. Of being at war with his own thoughts.

He watched the manor home for another hour, reminding himself of everything Tor had told him about Andred and the Wraiths, all the suggestions and advice: Daena is your ticket in, and once you're both accepted, you can watch each other's back. Andred trusted her before, hopefully, he will again. She'll have access that you will never be given, and even more importantly, she'll know when Andred's lying… but we can't send her in alone. Your job is to protect her. Andred is even more arrogant than before: make him think it's all his own idea. If you need help quickly, hang a shirt somewhere visible. And don't die.

Fucking hell. How was he supposed to not die when his partner in all this was a woman whose blood ran with treachery?

His beast growled, but he didn't even bother to respond.

By the time the guards rotated again, his entire body was stiff and his face was almost numb with cold. He ignored the discomfort. He'd been a sapper in the northern campaigns. And after the hell of the last year, this was nothing. Finally, after weeks of preparations, it was time.

While the sentries were moving, distracted, he rose to a low couch. Then he slipped between the grasses, rocks, and rough shrubs. Taking care to stay off the skyline, he snuck back down the far hillside, heading away from the manor and over the neighboring farmland. Then, after waiting for long minutes, carefully checking it was empty, he stepped onto the road from the ferry.

He'd timed it to the ferry arrival; anyone who saw him would assume he'd just arrived on the northern shore. He checked his sword, two daggers—one on his thigh, another at his ankle—and hip flask, tightened his vambraces, and pulled his cloak over everything. His hair had grown long, and he pulled it back and tied it with a leather strip. Then he started to walk, whistling as he went.

He was still whistling when he turned the corner and nodded at the three old men playing dice at the side of the road. One of them lifted a hand in salute and then bent over to whisper to a young boy who was throwing a stick to a nearby dog. Reece was only a few paces past when he heard the boy and his dog take off running across the fields. Good.

A series of sharp bird calls cut through the air before he

even reached the long stone wall at the front perimeter of the manor. And by the time he turned in past the massive wrought iron gates, a pair of well-armed Apollyon guards was waiting for him. Exactly as expected.

He recognized them but didn't know either of them well. "Morning." Reece lifted his hand in a two-fingered salute and carried on walking.

If they knew who he was, they didn't show it. In fairness, he looked very different from the last time they'd seen him. Back then, he'd been cleanly shaved and beautifully dressed. Now he looked like a vagrant. Now he *was* a vagrant.

The guards glared, moving across the drive to block his entry. "This is private property."

Reece shrugged. "I have an invitation."

"No." The guard—Roy? Royn? Something like that— dropped his hand to the hilt of his sword. "You don't."

A sliver of fear trickled up his back. His recollections of Dornar were still fresh and disturbing. But the nerves somehow focused his mind. In a strange way, standing there, daring those burly soldiers to finally end him, sent a trickle of brighter awareness through him. The first tingle of interest, anticipation even, that he'd felt in months.

Reece tucked his thumbs into his belt and forced himself to grin, to find some of that glib eloquence that had kept him fed for so many years. "I bet you one hundred groats that I do have an invitation."

The guard took a menacing step closer. "Show it to me, then."

Reece laughed. "No, thanks. I will, however, discuss it with General Andred. You can pay me afterward."

The guard drew out his sword and took another step forward, lifting the blade to point it right at Reece's heart. "You need to go."

Reece took a step back, lifting his hands. His focus was riveted on that bright sword. On the gleam of light along the blade.

His beast growled menacingly, covering his skin with a thick layer of scales, for once working with him instead of against him. All his worries faded away as his attention settled entirely into this moment. Gods. He should have gone out and looked for death sooner—it reminded him that he was actually alive.

He turned toward the window and whistled loudly. "Caius! Usna! I know you're in there!"

"That's enough." Both guards lifted their swords.

Gods, he hoped this worked. The guards stepped toward him, and he dropped his hand to his own weapon, about to draw it, when the front door opened and a rough voice called a halt.

Caius stepped into the doorway. His face was cast in shade, half-hidden, but Reece had seen him in dimly lit halls and parlors many times and knew him instantly. He was lean for an Apollyon, but very strong nonetheless, hair well-cut and smoothed neatly, uniform pristine. They'd spent long hours playing blackjack and drinking together in Kaerlud. Both with a very similar taste in women and pleasure. Or so Reece had thought, anyway.

He's an asshole.

Reece grunted. That might be true, but the last thing he needed was to be distracted now.

"Caius, my friend," Reece called out, ignoring the two swords pointed at his throat.

Caius ran his eyes over Reece's old cloak, grass-stained breeches, and long, dirty hair, his nostrils flaring. Then he crossed his arms over his chest and sneered. "Fuck. Another Hawk on our doorstep. Don't tell me, I have to let you see

Andred or you'll walk away and take your family money
with you?"

Ah. So that was how Tor got in.

Clever.

Reece put on his most charming grin. The one that
worked so well in the palace and irritated the living shit out
of Tristan. "I don't know who you've been speaking to, but
my family didn't have a groat between them. And now
they're all dead." Except for his real father, whoever the hell
he was. "But I will come in, thanks."

He pushed the swords out of his way and walked past
the scowling guards, whispering as he went, "I'll take my
money in silver pieces, Royn."

Caius growled, loud enough he could almost have had a
beast. The guards' heavy swords still pointed unwaveringly
at Reece's back. Scales flickered in slow waves over his
exposed back, but it didn't make him feel any less
vulnerable.

"We've already had one Hawk try to destroy everything
we've worked for," Caius spat. "We won't tolerate another.
You shouldn't have come here."

Reece forced himself to keep his shoulders down and his
hands off his weapons. His left arm—the arm Dornar had
broken in three places—throbbed at his side. "Look at me,
Caius. Do I look like a Hawk to you?"

"Yes."

Yes.

Both answers, Caius's and his beast's, were swift and
unequivocal. And strangely, they gave Reece the strength to
do what he had to do next.

"I was never a Hawk. Of course I took the chance to get
out of the sappers. You would have done the same. But I
was never really one of them. I was one of you. I always

was. You should have given me the chance to come with you when you… left."

They hadn't left. They'd killed their own king, and now they were betraying their queen. And the Wraiths had never offered him a place, despite offering one to Tor several times. But the Wraiths did what suited them.

They always did.

Gods, he wished he'd seen it sooner.

Caius didn't even twitch. "How did you find us?"

"Let's discuss it inside."

"How. Did. You. Find. Us?"

Reece settled his stance more firmly before glancing meaningfully at the gate guards. "You don't want to hear it outside."

Caius gestured at the guard. "Cut off his arm."

A rough, almost hysterical laugh bubbled up inside him. Reece held out his left arm. "Could you take this one? It still aches. From when Dornar tortured me… and the Hawks did nothing."

Strictly true. Even if they'd found another truth seeker —which he sincerely hoped they hadn't, or Tor's plan would be fucked—they would agree that was truth.

On the other hand, if they had found a new truth seeker, he wouldn't have to work with Daena, another lying, betraying backstabber, so that would be something at least.

"What?" Caius asked, his gaze traveling down Reece's arm, genuinely interested for the first time.

"Ask anyone," Reece said. "I'm nothing to the Hawks. Less than nothing. I hate them for what they did."

That was not, exactly, the truth. The Hawks were constantly trying to get him to come back. Even Alanna had asked him to come back, and she had more reason to hate him than anyone. But if he was careful to think of himself as a Hawk and think of how much he hated himself, then it was true in a way.

And if nothing else, he was enjoying this game; pitting his wits against these men. Choosing his words carefully so that everything he said was literally true… at the same time as being a complete lie.

Perhaps this is what happened to Daena? his beast pointed out roughly. *Perhaps Andred played this exact game with her?*

Reece blocked it out. He didn't for one instant believe in a truth seeker who couldn't hear the truth. Daena had supported Andred for as long as it suited her; now she was supporting someone else. It was a fucking mystery how Tor could trust her.

"Is that a fact?" a new voice asked. "That you're nothing to the Hawks now." It was a deeper, rougher voice. The voice of a man used to shouting orders and being instantly obeyed. And Reece knew it all too well.

Andred stepped out of the house behind Caius. He was tall for an Apollyon, his arms rippling with muscles under the winding black and red tattoos. Andred's family had been extremely wealthy—they had been among the first Apollyon raiders to claim Brythoria and swear fealty to the new line of kings, and they'd been richly rewarded for it—and his noble history was marked over his flesh.

There was a time, it felt like a lifetime ago, when Reece had stood beside him at palace functions and wondered if they could be brothers. Or, if not Andred, any of the other noble sons. Perhaps even Ballanor could be his missing sibling. He could be the son of the king and not even know.

His beast turned, forcing acid up his throat at the thought of being anything to Ballanor, and he swallowed as he stepped closer.

"Ask anyone," Reece repeated. "I left the Hawks months ago."

Andred signaled to Caius, who waved for the guards to lower their swords and return to their posts flanking the gate. As soon as they were gone, Andred narrowed his dark eyes at Reece. "How did you find us?"

He was almost in. He was so close, he could taste it. Reece lowered his voice and offered another partial truth. "I needed some cash. I took work on the docks. Sometimes people need to be reminded to make their repayments on time… you know how it is."

Reece's lips twitched into a sneer. He remembered those debt collectors very personally, and he hated them all deeply. But Andred didn't need to know that the work he'd taken had been hauling cargo to pay for his nasty lodgings in smelling distance of the Fish Street Docks; nothing to do with the debt collectors.

"I was out by the northern ferry, chasing down a lead, when I saw one of the former councilors heading this way." He *had* been chasing down a lead. Tor's advice to stick close to Pellin.

Gods, that man was a bastard. Poor Tor, with a father like that. Luckily Pellin was also an idiot with a massive god complex. He'd surrounded himself with guards, worn all his jewels, and led Reece right to the Wraiths' front door.

"I thought it would be interesting to see where he got to… and look what I found."

"That was yesterday," Andred muttered.

Actually, Pellin's *second* visit was yesterday. His first visit had been the week before, but Reece had needed that time to learn the Wraiths' habits.

Reece chuckled. "I didn't think you'd appreciate me arriving in the middle of dinner."

Andred didn't laugh. But he didn't order him killed either, so that was something. "What do you want, Reece?" he asked.

"To join you."

Now Andred did laugh. "We don't need you. Or want you."

Reece grunted. "Rumor is that only twenty of you made it out of the Thabana Mountains. You need all the help you can get. Especially if you want to get into the palace…." He forced himself to put all the arrogance he'd once had into his voice. "Breaking down walls and undermining fortresses is my special skill, after all."

Andred and Caius watched him, eyes sharp, and Reece waited. The first thrill of danger was draining away, and now he just felt tired and slightly sick. He was alone, far from his squad—former squad—and he wanted this to be over.

I'm with you, his beast murmured. It was so unexpected. The first supportive thing that his beast had said in so long, he didn't know how to react and it took him a moment before he could continue. "You know what," he muttered, "I don't care. Go fetch your truth seeker and ask her. She can clear everything up for you." He glowered first at Andred and then at Caius. "Fuck, I forgot, you seem to have lost yours. Last I heard, she was about to stand in front of the entire kingdom and tell them all about you. Long stories of cruelty and deception, all validated by the Supreme Justice. Good luck with your little rebellion when every single person in Brythoria hates you."

He counted to five, listening to the seagulls screeching over the distant fens, and then he turned to go.

"Wait." Andred's annoyed tone stopped him.

Reece turned to look at him over his shoulder. "Yes?"

Andred scowled at him. "Yes, General, sir."

"Yes, General, sir," Reece repeated, doing his best to sound sincere.

Fuck this asshole, his beast rumbled in his head, rolling its eyes, and Reece had to agree.

"I accept," Andred declared.

"Accept what?"

"Your offer to fetch my truth seeker." Andred grinned at him, but there was no humor in it whatsoever. "Fetch her, and then we can have this conversation again."

"Absolutely not," Reece replied. "That's not why I'm here. And why would you want her anyway? She's been held in the Constable's tower for weeks. She's told them everything she knows." He took an ostentatious step back, shaking his head. "Her trial will be held in the Nephilim courts by the end of the week, and then she can look forward to a very short life in Gatehouse Prison or, more likely, being hung for treason. Even if she had anything to offer you, it's impossible."

"Agreed," Caius mumbled, looking highly irritated.

"You're both fools," Andred stated coldly. "Leaving her to denounce us in front of the Nephilim would be a disaster when we take control of the palace. The Nephilim will find her guilty, but they'll find us guilty at the same time. We can't fight a civil war. Not yet."

"Fine. Let me kill her for you then," Reece said firmly. "You got what you could out of her already. You don't need a pet truth seeker, not anymore."

Andred grunted. "Daena helped build our army, and she will again. That she's been held as a prisoner and is about to be condemned will make her even easier to control than before." His grin widened, and for the first time, Andred looked genuinely amused. "This works perfectly.

Reece will prove that he really can undermine the palace, and we get our truth seeker back just in time to vet all the nobles swearing up and down that they've never supported Lucilla and would gladly give their fortunes to have a real king back on the throne. And," he added, lip twitching, "if you both die, we haven't lost anything."

"I don't—" Caius started, but Andred gave him a quelling look. "This will work in our favor. You'll see."

Fucking hell. It had actually worked. Reece didn't know whether to be impressed or terrified.

Yes. But now we have to get Daena and bring her here. Into this wasps' nest.

That wasn't an issue. Daena had betrayed her family. Then she'd betrayed her queen. Then she'd betrayed the traitors she was betraying everyone else with. Daena was only coming back to the people she'd chosen once already.

"I think this is a mistake," Reece grumbled, looking Andred in the eye and being entirely honest. "But I'll do it."

Chapter Three

THIS WAS A TERRIBLE PLAN. A horrible plan. And she was probably going to die without having got anywhere near to Andred. Damn it all.

Daena had spent days sitting in her cell, looking up to the sky through the tiny, barred window and wishing she was out in the air. That she could see trees and feel the wind on her face. But now that she had all those things, she wished she was back in her cell where it was warm and comfortable and safe.

The long, slow walk through the palace grounds and out to the waiting carriage was bitterly cold, and the crowds watching her were silent enough that she could hear the rasp of her breath, loud in her ears.

Crews of workers stopped putting up midwinter decorations to stare at her. Her shackles dragged against the roughly set bones of her left ankle, adding weight and instability. The wind was biting and sour, her cloak made her itch, and every doubt she'd ever had about herself was screaming in her head. But even worse than all of that was the condemnation pouring over her in waves. There was no jeering, no catcalls. Tristan had glared out at the throngs and demanded respect, and they had given it… to him. Not to her. They *hated* her.

They knew about Ballanor's lies and treachery. They were coming to like—if not love—their new queen. Lucilla was rebuilding their city and their homes. She had ended the war and given their families a chance at a better life. She too had suffered at the hands of Ballanor and Geraint before him, and her people knew it. And they knew that Daena had betrayed Lucilla.

It was a relief to reach the closed carriage. Jos helped her climb in, doing what he could to ease the heavy weight of the shackles. Daena stared down at her hands and tried to ignore the angry gazes. She'd known it would be like this. It stung like a handful of nettles, but it was no more than she deserved.

The carriage ride to the Nephilim temple was a jarring, miserable journey. She sat alone in the back while the Hawks rode beside her—guards to the prisoner. Low clouds spat out dirty flurries of sleet and rain, and she huddled into her threadbare, reeking cloak. Lucilla herself had apologized, but they couldn't give her any better; Daena had to walk to her trial in the clothes she'd been wearing when she climbed out of Andred's camp. They still smelled of smoke and ash and fear sweat. A dark stain showed where Keely had bled over her. It was like pulling on a dirty old skin. One she'd been so grateful to shed and had sincerely wished never to see again.

The carriage trundled down a long cobbled avenue, past the fabric market. The colored awnings were dark with rain, bolts of cloth stacked carefully inside to keep them dry.

People were browsing, visible through the rain-streaked windows. They were shopping and laughing. Going about their lives.

It was almost impossible to imagine such a thing from within her strange gray bubble inside the carriage, with its utter isolation and the reek of smoke, the smell she hated more than anything else in the world.

Finally, they reached their destination and the carriage slowed. Daena peered out the window at the temple. It was so much like courts at Eshcol, the home she'd grown up in, if she hadn't been so frightened, it would have hurt. Geometric tiles formed swirling mosaics in reds and yellow-brown ochres, while mullioned windows held stained glass that would cast jewel-toned rainbows over the interior ceramic floors, illuminate the polished oak of the latticework screens, and turn the water in the fountains to diamonds.

A long walkway was flanked by statues of the archangels, lush gardens spreading out around them. At the far end of the path, a series of broad steps led up toward the heavy oak doors of the main entrance of the courts. And to the panel of truth seekers waiting for her.

For a moment, everything was still. Only the drifting rain moved. Then Tristan called his orders, soldiers spread out, and she was pulled briskly from the carriage onto the street.

The motion kicked her trepidation up to outright fear. Her breath came in sharp pants, and she fought to slow it, digging her nails into her palms for some kind of balance. Gods and angels. She couldn't panic now. She had to keep it together.

Garet and Jos—both Mabin—flanked her, while Mathos and Tristan led the way, Jeremiel at the rear. They spread out, watching the crowd, keeping everyone well back.

Daena lifted her eyes to look along the path, up the stairs, all the way to the huge wooden front doors. At the top of the steps stood Uncle Ramiel. His hair looked grayer than she'd ever seen before. His face was more lined. And he watched her with an intent, concerned focus. The Hawks had warned him; he knew what was about to happen, and he looked like he was only just holding himself back from putting an end to it all.

She met his eyes and dipped her chin a fraction. Reassuring him and herself. She was doing this. The tension around her ribs eased, and she took in a deeper breath.

They crossed the last of the cobbles. Tristan and Mathos stepped onto the path between the statues, leading the way. She reached the edge of the road and stepped onto the tiny white dot of paint she'd been told to look for, Garet and Jos beside her.

Then, exactly as she'd promised, she paused.

She counted to ten, then took a breath and let it out slowly. And then the bells in the temple began to ring, just as she'd known they would.

Jos and Garet each took one of her arms as if to guide her along the last crucial steps into the court. And a second later, the world shuddered.

A loud, creaking groan reverberated around them all. Cracks spread out over the cobbles. The ground she was standing on shivered, and her stomach lurched uncomfortably.

Jos and Garet tightened their grip. Ramiel took a massive step closer, his hand reaching out, almost as if he could stop this. Stop her. But it was too late. There was a sharp, grinding crack. And then the road collapsed in on itself right under her feet.

There was a moment of breathless weightlessness. A huge yawning sinkhole opened beneath them, everything crushing and tilting. Her stomach dropped, and then she was falling, screaming as she plummeted, utterly helpless to save herself.

Clouds of dust poured up around them and her ears rang with the earth's roar. She flailed, her entire body flooded with the terror of smashing into the ground below…. But the devastating blow never came. She forced her eyes open, forced herself to look, and breathe, and see that she wasn't dead.

Her shoulders howled where Jos and Garet held her, but they never let her go. They were hovering just feet above the stinking waters of the sewer that ran beneath the road. Their wings beat hard, and their faces were pale in the dim light, but they had kept her safe. Protecting her through the explosion and the horrendous fall.

A sob bubbled up, but she swallowed it away. She knew what it would sound like. Hysterical and out of control. And she couldn't risk anyone above hearing.

"Are you ready, Daena?" Jos whispered.

No. She wasn't ready. But it was time, nonetheless. Reece had done what he had promised and undermined the path. The Hawks had done what they had promised and kept her safe. Now she would do what she had promised and give her life to save the kingdom from Andred. "Yes," she whispered.

"Good luck," Jos replied, "and thank you." Then, with a quick glance toward Garet, some silent communication, they let her go.

She fell the last few feet into the waist-deep freezing

muck, stumbling when her shackled feet landed on the sewer bed. She staggered heavily, only just managing to right herself before her face went under. Gods. The smell. Nothing could have prepared her for the acid foulness or the icy cold, but she didn't have time to think about it; she had to move.

Above her, Jos and Garet were shouting up, and soldiers were calling down. Tristan was bellowing for lights and a search party. Someone was cursing the Wraiths, blaming them loudly for everyone to hear.

She blundered forward and took the first right turn, as she'd been instructed. It was darker here, away from the rays of dusty light filtering in through the sinkhole. The hazy gloom surrounded her as she muttered to herself, urging herself faster. There was no time. She had to *move*.

Her shackles dragged and caught. Her left leg was cramping, and her feet were growing numb, but she couldn't stop. Soon they would have a search party in the sewers.

She took the next left turn, staying close to the edge of the foul waterway, her eyes searching the almost darkness. A light flared a few yards farther down the tunnel, and she almost wept with relief. There he was. The man who had promised to guard her back. Thank the gods.

She wanted to run to him. He was a Hawk. His friends had told her so many times that he was a good man. And he was her only point of safety left in the world.

But before she could, he looked her up and down... and sneered. He crossed his arms over his chest, his expression cold and suspicious.

She froze for a long moment. This was the man she was supposed to trust with her life. The man who would be her partner. But he looked just like the crowds she'd passed in the palace: he'd judged her and found her guilty. He didn't even know her, but he hated her anyway.

Gods. Suddenly she was so very tired. She was right back where she'd started, surrounded by enemies, alone and unwanted. With no choice—

No. She couldn't let herself think like that. She did have a choice, and she'd made it. She was no longer a tool to be used and discarded. She was a person. Fuck him.

She stood straighter, fighting the cold and urge to retch as she pulled herself to the edge of the sewer and waited. He had to give her the signal.

Eventually, he whistled, a short, sharp repeating pattern. The one the Hawks had taught her. It was him. She nodded, then murmured, "You must be Reece." Thank the gods, her voice came out firm and confident.

Reece grunted, not even bothering to reply, and gestured toward a half-submerged paving stone. "Sit. I need to see your shackles."

Hell. She stared at him for a long moment. He was objectively very attractive. Golden-brown hair, clear gray eyes, tall and lean, his skin flickering in the dim light with burnished deep-blue scales. But she'd had experience with handsome, ruthless men, and she knew better than to fall for that again.

She didn't want to sit in front of him. She didn't want him to see her leg or know she had any kind of vulnerability. But she'd committed to this plan, and so far, everything Tor had promised had been true. She didn't trust Reece, but she did trust the Hawks.

She sat on the paving stone. Her heavy gray woolen dress stuck to her legs in a stinking mess, and her teeth had started to chatter, but he didn't seem to notice as he knelt in front of her, produced a key from his pocket, and opened the lock. The heavy iron ring clicked open, and he moved it aside. The movements were perfunctory, but his hand on her leg was gentle.

He lifted her foot and turned it this way and that before grunting to himself and moving on to the next lock. Once again, he checked her leg, his fingers hot as they brushed carefully at her skin. "You'll be fine," he murmured. "Nothing broken. Maybe some bruising. If you need help, tell me."

He pulled a pair of thick gloves from his back pocket and handed them to her. "Wear these; we don't know what's down here."

The thoughtful act was so utterly at odds with his obvious disdain that she didn't know what to say. He slid the shackles into the water, taking care not to splash, and pushed himself up and away, the hard look settling back over his face.

He led her toward a smaller pipe and gestured for her to climb in. The opening was the size of a small carriage wheel. Big enough to crawl through, but tight enough to be close and dark and awful. She stretched her neck from side to side, and then dragged herself up. "How far must I go?"

"I'll tell you when we get there," Reece grumbled from behind her. "I can see better than you." And then he blew out the light.

Her body started to shake. Shock and fear and confusion churned through her. And then, rising through the fear, came anger. Of course he could see better; he was Tarasque. But he didn't have to be so bloody rude. "Why don't you go first, then?" she hissed.

"Because the soldiers will be behind us, and I can hear better too."

Gods save her from arrogant assholes. She considered

replying, but she was too cold and tired to bother. She swallowed her retort and turned away. She had come this far; she just had to keep going, one step at a time.

It felt like they clambered through the slime for hours, although it was probably far less. Her body ached, her skin crawled, and her throat burned with the smell of sewerage. And it was utterly dark. She had felt isolated before; now she felt entirely detached from the world. There was only her, the slosh-slosh as she pulled herself through the tunnel, and the slowly growing pain as she dragged her ankle through the cold.

Eventually, when the entire world had focused down to the throbbing from her hip to her toes and the shuddering gasp of each next breath, Reece grunted, calling her to a stop.

"Ahead of you, the pipe opens up. There's a ladder on our left." His voice rasped in the darkness. "I'll go in front in case there's anyone at the top." He waited until the sewer widened and then pushed past her. The ladder rattled against the wall as he started to climb.

Daena clasped the pipes. They were so cold, she could feel the burn through her sodden gloves. She pulled herself up, put her foot on the bottom rung, and almost collapsed in agony. Putting weight on her ankle was torture. The cold and the long crawl had stiffened it almost unbearably, and she couldn't help the soft whimper that escaped to echo in the narrow pipe.

"What is it?" Reece demanded from above her.

Surely, he knew? Surely, he'd seen the scars when he took off her shackles? She didn't bother to answer, merely forced herself upward, relying on her arms to pull her and her good leg to push. Letting herself drift on the waves of pain.

"Is there a problem?" he hissed. "Tell me now."

She looked up at him, wishing any of the other Hawks could have been her partner in this awful mission. And then immediately regretted it—they didn't deserve this hell. "No problem," she muttered and then looked away, focusing on pulling herself up one more rung. And another after that.

The clank of the sewer lid opening startled her, and she clung to the ladder as dim gray light filtered down, bringing the dripping moss-covered brickwork around her into view. Reece motioned for her to wait and then pushed himself out in silence. She could hear him stalking around above her as she clung to the ladder, dreaming of the comforts of her cell.

Eventually, he leaned back down to help pull her out. His grip was firm as he hauled her from the pipe into a narrow alley. Someone—Reece, presumably—had blocked the entrance with an ancient, upturned cart, and the few windows that overlooked them had long since been boarded up. They were alone.

Reece gave her disgusting gray dress and the thin cloak she was wearing a brief glance. "Take that off."

She wrapped her arms around herself, chafing at her icy skin. "Wh… what?"

Reece rolled his eyes. "You can't walk around the city in that. You'll freeze, and it stinks. Take everything off and throw it back down before the dogs follow us." He was already stripping off his own clothes as he spoke.

She could have looked away. She *should* have. She'd only just met Reece, and they were definitely not friends. But her eyes caught on the smooth ripple of muscle over his shoulders as he leaned over to drop his tattered shirt into the sewer. Scales flickered along his ribs as he stood, the deep indigo blue of the center of a peacock's feather. She had the

insane urge to run her hand over that warm flesh, to feel the
scales undulating under her hand. But then Reece dropped
his hand to his cotton breeches and tugged them down, and
she spun away, face hot, grappling at the clasp of her dress.

Reece chuckled behind her, and she knew he'd done it
on purpose. Stupid bastard. It wasn't as if his were the first
male buttocks she'd ever seen. Or even the best. Well, no,
that was a lie; still, he didn't need to know that.

She slid her arms out of her destroyed cloak and tugged
off her dress, imagining the best way to tell him how
mediocre his ass was, when a stream of bitterly cold water
crashed into her back.

She screamed and started to turn, remembered that she
was naked, and froze. Only to have a bucketful of water
thrown down her side as well.

She stood gasping and shivering, trying not to cry in
outrage and shock, when Reece pressed a rough cotton
towel into her hands and growled, "Get dry. The water was
full of rosemary, so it should help with the smell. There's a
dress under the cart for you." And then, before she could
tell him what an asshole he was, the bastard left.

She dried herself on the towel, her emotions seething
and churning. Her eyes burned, but her rage was greater.
She muttered death threats as she limped across to the cart.
But the dress was there, where he'd said, and more than
anything else, she wanted to be warm. It was a thick woolen
dress in deep plum with a silk shift beside it. Even a pair of
boots, only faintly scuffed, and a long black cloak.
Everything was her size, and—more importantly—dry. She
pulled it on slowly, her skin prickling, the soft scent of herbs
tickling the back of her throat. He was right, the rosemary
had helped. But it didn't make her like him.

She was tying the cloak at her throat when Reece

returned, now dressed in leathers and covered in a similar black cloak, a sword strapped to his back.

In the distance, she could hear whistles and even a trumpet blaring, but Reece ignored it. He lifted the corner of the cart and dragged it a short distance to open a narrow gap, then gestured toward the street. "Let's go."

Chapter Four

You're being *an ass*.

No. He shook his head. He wasn't. He hadn't said one rude or unkind thing. He hadn't once asked her to defend her actions or suggested that he didn't even begin to trust her. He'd brought her safely through the sewers, as he'd promised.

You haven't said anything kind, either. The beast rumbled. *And she brought herself through the sewers safely, with no help from you.*

Daena sat beside him in the hired carriage, not speaking as she stared out the window. The ferry was behind them. He'd arranged for them to be dropped off at the entrance to a neighboring farm, and they could travel on foot from there.

Gods. The thought sent a wave of unsettled scales flickering up his arms. She'd been limping badly when they came out of the sewer. The cold water and the difficult crawl had clearly tightened her muscles.

He'd seen the injury to her leg and ankle when he'd removed the shackles. Tor had told him that she'd been saved from a fire by Andred, but somehow the stark reality of those wounds was worse than he'd anticipated.

Huh. Maybe she really couldn't run from Andred. Maybe you're the only asshole here, his beast hissed.

Reece sighed, ignoring it as usual, and forced himself to think of something else. Anything else. The collapse of the path into the sewer had gone exactly as he'd planned. Still, those first moments of churning destruction had been horrendous. Not knowing if he'd made a mistake and hurt —or killed—his former squadmates. Gods. When Daena had come around the corner, when he'd realized it had worked, he'd wanted to run to her and haul her into his arms and weep in gratitude that he hadn't killed anyone. It had taken everything he had to force himself to remember exactly who she was.

Bollocks. Now he was thinking of her. Again.

He shook it off, focusing on the explosion. On what he'd achieved. He had always been an excellent engineer—it's what Tristan had recognized all those years ago—but somehow, he'd forgotten how rewarding that challenge was. Pitting himself against rock and stone, forces and structures. Maybe it was time to start remembering who he was.

He'd used some of the coin from Andred—what was left after the explosives and transport—on new clothes for Daena and himself, and he'd spent time shining his boots and cutting his hair. It was good to be clean. Good to be doing something other than sitting in a tavern contemplating his fuckups.

Daena, however, did not look like she felt good. He could only see her profile, but her mouth was thin and tight, lines of tension radiating around her eyes. And she was completely silent. She'd been that way since they emerged from the alley.

At first, he'd been relieved because she wasn't complaining or arguing. But now it was grating on his nerves. Her silence was heavy. Occasionally she would drag her fingers down the burn scars on the side of her face, and he wondered if she even knew she was doing it. He wanted to tell her to stop, but he couldn't find words that didn't sound cruel. And he didn't want to speak to her anyway.

I want to speak to her, his beast muttered. *She's interesting. She's so much stronger than I expected. And she doesn't take your crap.*

"Shut up," Reece grunted, half under his breath. Daena must have heard him, because she turned to glare at him over her shoulder before looking out at the passing fields once more.

He sat, stewing, ignoring his beast and Daena's outrage, until the carriage pulled up outside the opulent, carved gates as Reece had requested. He climbed out and paid the driver before turning back to see Daena had already made her way out and onto the side of the road, where she stood, arms crossed, waiting for him.

The rain had stopped, and the low winter sun had emerged from behind the clouds, bathing her in a pale light that brought out the deep mahogany of her hair. They were close enough that he could see the violet of her eyes and smell the slight scent of rosemary.

Her spine was straight, her gaze intelligent and thoughtful, and for a moment, he almost forgot everything else he knew about her. For a moment, they were the only people in the world.

Gods. She's beautiful.

His beast startled him. Bollocks. He had to focus. He had to remember just how important this mission was, and just how fraught. If Daena betrayed them all—again—it would be a disaster. Sure, she smelled of rosemary, the scent he'd always associated with home, but underneath that was a good whiff of the sewers too.

He turned away from her and watched the carriage until it was out of sight, not speaking. Then, when they were alone in the rapidly fading light, he started to walk, and she followed. Slowly.

Shortening his stride to match her limp made him feel like a bastard. He had made her crawl and walk a long way. But the guilt made him irritable. And the confusion made him wish Andred had never fallen for this idea in the first place. It was easy to dismiss Daena when she was as good as imaginary. Now she was a person.

I like her.

Reece grunted. She was pretty, sure, and she clearly had a deep core of iron. He'd seen warriors crying and screaming when they'd been caught in a cave-in, but she had held herself together and kept moving. But she gave off such a powerful aura of "don't fuck with me" that it was hard to see her as attractive. Not that her appeal was relevant. At all.

It was nearly dark by the time they reached the Wraiths' manor and the watchers on the road had whistled ahead long ago. Reece flicked his fingers at the guards standing beside the gate. Royn was back, along with his usual partner. Neither of them looked at all happy to see him or Daena—who ignored them completely—but they opened the gates anyway.

The front door was open when they got there, and Caius stepped out with Usna behind him.

Reece had thought the silence was heavy before. Now it was leaden. The two large Apollyon looked Daena up and down with the kind of sneering contempt Reece had only ever seen on the battlefield. It was shocking to realize just how little regard they had for her. He'd expected…. Bollocks. He didn't really know what he'd expected. But definitely not this.

You looked at her the same way.

Fuck. He wanted to deny it, but he didn't think he could. And now… now a large part of him wanted to step closer to her, to protect her somehow. But that would be a disaster. They could never be seen as working together. Not if they wanted to live. And she certainly showed no sign of wanting to be closer to him either. If anything, she had sidled further away.

Caius glared pointedly at Daena. "Strip."

Her already pale face tightened, but she didn't budge. "No."

Caius's hand fell to the hilt of his sword. "You freed our prisoners, brought total destruction to our camp, and now you've spent weeks with people who will gladly kill us all. I want proof that you're not coming in here with weapons. Strip."

Daena laughed, a rough, brittle sound. "I've spent weeks living in a cell waiting to be hanged as a traitor for my support of you. I had the option to help Tor or die. Did you think I wanted to run up a mountain gorge with another out-of-control fire closing in behind me?"

Reece bristled, his scales hardening into a sheet of blue over his arms and throat. She was speaking with utter conviction, as if she genuinely believed she would have died if she hadn't helped Tor.

She means she would have died in the camp, his beast rumbled inside his head.

Did she? Or did she mean she'd only helped Tor because she had to? How could he possibly know?

"I honestly don't care. Strip now," Caius ordered.

"I'd rather die," Daena replied, voice ringing with sincerity. Her shoulders were back, her chin lifted, but she was holding her left foot slightly up, with only her toes on the ground, as if she couldn't bear to put any weight on it at all.

Make them stop. Or I will.

Reece growled quietly back at his beast. This was a balance. A very delicate game of power. He couldn't intervene, not yet. If that was even the best play here.

It's not a game. The rumbling of his beast climbed a notch.

"Fine," Caius said, sliding his sword from its scabbard. "You want to die. That, I can arrange."

Gods. That was taking it too far. Even if he had offered exactly the same thing just a few days before.

"Enough," Reece muttered. "This is ridiculous. We crawled through a sewer to escape. I assure you, everything we were wearing is now sitting in a stinking pipe or torn apart by the dogs. She's already had to strip." He took a step closer to Caius, positioning himself between him and Daena. "I did what you wanted; now let us in."

Caius glared at Reece. "I don't trust *you* either."

Reece let out a bark of sardonic laughter. "None of us trusts each other. I told you all—repeatedly—to leave this woman where she was. But Andred wanted his display of power. He wanted to disrupt the trial that was going to make him look like a fool, and get his pet truth seeker back, all while setting an impossible test. A test that I passed. So let us fucking come in."

Reece grabbed Daena's wrist and strode forward, dragging her behind him, trying his best to ignore her stifled whimper, reminding himself that she was a traitor, a liar, and Andred's lover in the first place. "I honestly don't give a flying fuck about what either of you wants," he growled. "This is my chance to get my life in the palace back. Andred was clear that she's my entrance fee, and she's damn well coming with me."

What the hell? His beast snarled.

"Truth," Daena muttered behind him, her voice prickling at his back, but Reece ignored her—and the sudden flare of renewed guilt. He wasn't there to pander to her. She was his ticket into the Wraiths; that was all.

Chapter Five

HE HONESTLY DIDN'T GIVE a fuck. He *honestly* didn't give a fuck. He wanted to get back into the palace, and she was the price he was willing to pay… and it was all the truth. Gods. How could the Hawks have sent her in here with this man?

Well, fuck him. She could do what she had to, without him.

And wasn't that like liberation all on its own? She'd decided to be here. And now she would make it work. By herself. She would find the names of the Wraiths supporters, she would get them back to Lucilla, and then… she didn't know what would happen then. It was difficult to imagine a future when the chance of having one seemed so small. But whatever happened, it wouldn't include Reece. Thank the gods.

The way he'd looked at her at the side of the road, his gray eyes so utterly focused on hers, his beast growling softly, had almost made her feel like he really saw her. Like maybe he regretted his earlier behavior. He'd even walked beside her, not complaining, not hurrying her. It had felt companionable. And then he opened his mouth and reminded her that he was an ass.

Daena took in a deep breath and held it before letting it out slowly. She forced her shoulders down, kept her mouth shut, and let Reece drag her between Caius and Usna—gods, she truly hated them—and into the marble-floored entrance hall.

They made their way through the gleaming reception and stopped briefly outside a luxurious receiving parlor. It had been designed to be intimidating, to inspire awe with its display of riches and victory. Low settees were covered in plush velvets while rare statuettes in jade and black-veined marble lined the polished mantlepiece. The walls were decorated with painted frescoes. Images of the Apollyon landing in Brythoria and the victory of the conquerors over the land played out in faded pigments. To one side, the images showed a hunt, a dragon dying bloodied on the ground, while a warrior held up a dripping set of claws amidst admiring onlookers. Gods and angels, it was hideous. And deeply insulting to anyone of Mabin or Tarasque heritage.

She glanced back at Reece. His jaw was clenched, a muscle ticking. Unlike the Apollyon Wraiths who probably hardly noticed it, he had seen it, and it had hurt him. And even though he didn't care about what she wanted—probably didn't care about her at all—she wished he hadn't had to.

Andred wasn't there, however. Reece pulled her onward, and she followed. The house grew dingier and more tattered the farther in they went, as if everything of value had been piled into that one front room.

They stalked past an open door revealing a library that had been converted into a sleeping area. The long rows of shelves were almost bare, and the walls showed lighter blocks where artwork had been removed. Bedrolls marked spaces on the floor, and satchels sat in neat rows at the foot of each.

They passed a pair of massive doors, carved with twining Apollyon family markings. Behind it, she could hear men shouting and cheering, as if there was some kind of tournament taking place, and she was deeply relieved when Reece ignored it and continued.

Finally, they reached their destination. The room—clearly once a study—was tattered and faded. The wall hangings needed dusting, and a jagged crack in the ceiling showed how the house had warped and moved over the years. A large window let in the final dregs of daylight, but that extra illumination only showed how small and poorly preserved this part of the house was. Here, she could really see just how little effort had been put into maintaining anything outside of the front reception room.

The study had been turned into a war room. The desk was strewn with parchments marked with neat writing in tidy columns. Large maps covered the nearest wall, one of them dotted with pins marking places, or perhaps people, or even resources, of importance. And behind the desk—his handsome, familiar face set into a deep scowl, dark eyes cold and ruthless—sat Andred.

She'd known this moment was coming. She'd known it in the second that Tor looked at her across the breakfast table in Staith and said he had an idea to infiltrate the Wraiths. And now that it was here, she didn't know what to do with herself. Her mouth was dry, and she had to fight the almost overwhelming urge to turn and run.

Reece entered ahead of her. He looked at her for a moment, assessing, and then settled himself into a wooden chair at the front of the desk, his posture loose and arrogant. She ignored the insult and the aching cramps in her leg—none of them offered *her* a seat—and stepped up to stand beside him.

Caius and Usna crowded in behind her, making the small room feel even more oppressive and blocking the exit. Not that there was anywhere she could run to, even if she gave in and tried it.

She stood in silence, watching Reece and Andred eye each other. The Apollyon general with his black tunic embroidered with the silver fighting boars, and the Tarasque warrior in his leathers and serviceable cloak.

Despite their differences, they had a similar aura. The same tension around their firm jaws and high-handed tilt to their chins. Their expressions were equally deadpan, eyes equally cold, equally suspicious.

They were both tall, strong, and handsome. Used to having their own way. Charming when they wanted to be. The man who had used her, lied to her, and held her prisoner. And the man who honestly didn't give a fuck.

"Daena." Andred looked her up and down, his voice as deep and commanding as ever.

"Andred," she replied, desperately trying to keep her voice from shaking.

His eyes narrowed, but she ignored it. He'd told her repeatedly to call him "General" in front of his men, but she never had. It was her one lonely rebellion. She'd seen him naked. She'd let him into her body. And she wasn't his soldier. Not anymore.

"Come here." Andred tilted his head, indicating the space beside him, behind the desk.

She wet her dry lips, knowing she couldn't refuse. Gods. She took a stumbling step closer to the desk, and then another. No one spoke. No one moved. They merely watched her as she made her way around the desk to stand beside Andred.

"Give me your hand."

She couldn't help her quick glance toward Reece, but his expression was completely blank, his eyes fixed on Andred, and she looked away again.

Slowly, her breath catching high in her chest, she held out her hand. But it was her arm that he took hold of, his fingers curled around her wrist, pressing his fingertips onto the veins so close to the surface there.

Reece leaned forward in his chair, resting his elbows on his knees, watching intently, but he didn't say anything.

"Calm yourself," Andred ordered, and she almost laughed at just how arrogant and patronizing he truly was.

Andred tightened his hand on her wrist, and a flicker of blue scales climbed higher up Reece's throat. Somehow, that flash of color helped. She took a slow breath, trying to slow her racing pulse.

"Where have you been?" Andred asked.

Her gaze flew around the room. What was this? He knew exactly where she'd been. "In a cell, in the Constable's Tower."

Andred watched her carefully. "What is your name?"

Gods and angels. What kind of game was he playing? "Daena," she whispered.

"What is your gift, Daena?"

Her mouth was so dry, she almost couldn't get the answer out. "Truth."

Andred nodded slowly. "And did you betray me, Daena, truth seeker?"

Hell. Her pulse ratcheted back up. Andred's grip tightened painfully, and she knew, without doubt, that he'd felt her heart rate spike. Damn him to the abyss—he was reading *her*.

For a moment she stood, locked in his knowing gaze, fear and horror chasing each other through her blood.

Andred knew her intimately. And, despite what had happened afterward, they'd shared pleasure. He knew her reactions. He knew her secrets. And if there was anyone without the benefits of the archangels' gift in the world who would know if she was lying, it was him.

And yet… as she stared into those cold brown eyes, she realized something. She knew him too. Everything he knew about her, she knew about him. And so much more.

She had loved him. She had watched him and laughed with him. Later, when she realized he'd manipulated and used her, she'd spent weeks observing him. Cataloging his expressions, his commands, his arrogant self-belief, and his certainty that he was always right, bred into him from birth. Andred had spent a lifetime in command, and he didn't have to empathize with or understand his staff, soldiers, or servants to tell them what to do. She had to understand *everyone*, or she would die.

Andred had used her, but he had never learned from her. She, however, had learned from him. She'd learned the power of omission. The subtle skill of manipulation. And she had learned to survive.

She let out a huff of breath, feeling her pulse slow as she slowly recognized that she too had power here. "I followed Tor on pain of death," she said softly, repeating what she'd said to Caius earlier. It was the pain of her inevitable death at Andred's hands, of course. Half-truths and misrepresentation were how she would win this game.

"Since then, I have been locked in a cell. I was never questioned by any truth seekers"—she had gladly volunteered everything she knew—"and I was told that my evidence was to be given in public at my trial." Daena let her arm relax in Andred's grip, knowing her pulse was steady. "My trial for treason. The crime I was charged with precisely because I did not betray you." *For far too long*, she added in her head.

Andred nodded slowly, his eyes flicking back toward Caius and Usna, lingering with a brief sneer at Reece.

"And now?" Andred asked. "Are you still loyal?"

Daena let out a rough snort. "I am exactly as loyal as I was, trapped in your camp, reading truth at the tip of a sword. You found me useful enough."

Andred leaned back, dragging her arm with him, fingers digging into her wrist, clearly displeased with her answer. And with her. "Are you here to help us, Daena? Think carefully."

"I'm here," she spat, "because I was dragged here by that man." She pointed her free hand at Reece, imbuing her words with all her pent-up fury.

"Will you be useful?" Andred demanded, ignoring Reece. "Will you help? Or shall we throw you back to the Hawks, to be tried and hanged as a traitor by their useless queen?"

She shuddered without having to force the reaction. Andred would never throw her anywhere. She had seen his base, his men. She knew where he was and how to lead the Hawks right to him. This was yet another manipulation. A question that couldn't taste of anything other than the truth because it wasn't a declaration of any kind of intent. Gods. She had hated him before. But now he revolted her.

She had to force those thoughts away or risk her pulse starting to climb. "Will I have my own room?" she asked.

"And will you enforce the rule that no one touches me? Including you?"

"Yes, and yes." Andred's tanned skin darkened just slightly as his lips thinned. If there was one thing he hated, it was to be questioned.

Her pulse was still thudding against Andred's fingers— but not spiking. Her entire body hurt. She'd fallen through the cave-in. Crawled through the sewers. And dealt with this room full of assholes. She was done.

She dropped into an awkward curtsey. Her ankle was so stiff and painful that it was a miracle she was still standing, and Andred was holding her arm out in front of her, wreaking havoc on her balance. But she managed it. "Then, I am yours to command."

Chapter Six

REECE STOOD at the library window staring out at the grounds behind the manor house. He'd already done enough sit-ups and push-ups to almost make himself sick. A month ago—when he was still living in his single room, working on the docks to pay for ale and brandy—he definitely would have been.

He was getting his strength back, slowly, day by day, and it felt good. It felt like he was coming back into his body, despite the cage he was living in.

And it definitely was a cage. From here, it was clear that the property ended at the back of the small garden. None of the surrounding fields belonged to this house; it was merely designed to look like they did.

The front entrance was formidable and striking with its costly wrought-iron gates, pristine cobbled courtyard, and massive stables. The back of the property, on the other hand, was a rambling, tiered vegetable patch that had been left largely fallow. All that was left of what could once have been a productive garden were a few frost-burned herbs and a riot of weeds, hemmed in by blackthorn and holly.

This is pointless. I don't care about the bloody garden. We need to check on Daena.

Definitely not. That would be the worst thing they could do. If the Wraiths suspected he had any kind of interest in her, they would both suffer.

Reece gripped the windowsill and forced himself to stay where he was and continue his perusal of the bleak back garden. To identify the thinnest patches in the thorny hedge. To consider how he might force a path out to the surrounding fields, if it ever came to that.

That room.... His beast rumbled unhappily. *I hate that she's in there.*

Reece stifled his own urge to growl. He hated it too. Andred had kept his promise of a room, but he hadn't given Daena one of the upstairs rooms—which would at least have held a bed and given her some measure of privacy— he had given her the tiny, dank little room beside the kitchen. In the past it might have been the scullery. In it, there'd been nothing but ancient brackets on the wall where a workbench may once have hung, a pile of old blankets thrown on the floor, and a bucket of water with a block of tallow soap. The room had been musty with long disuse, ancient mold stained the ceiling, there was no window to let in any light, and the only lock was on the outside. Gods.

A flicker of unfamiliar gratitude unfurled inside him: appreciation for his beast. No matter what else he'd lost, no matter how much they'd disagreed, they'd had each other. He'd never been alone. Even after Helaine's betrayal and Dornar's torture, after he'd left the Hawks, his beast had kept guard. And his beast was very aware, even when they were asleep. Lying in the library surrounded by the Wraiths, at least Reece had known he would have some warning if anyone attacked. It grumbled constantly about how they needed their squad to watch their backs—about how tiring it was to never fully rest—but it had never let him down.

Daena didn't have that. She had no possessions. She had no friends. She only had herself, and no way to escape. Gods. What had her life in Andred's mountain camp been like?

He couldn't think like that. He had to stay aware of all the risks. She had chosen to support Andred. And now… who knew?

A ripple of dark blue scales shimmered up the inside of his arms. *I know. She hates the Wraiths.*

Reece scratched his thumb over his short beard. It certainly seemed that way. Which didn't make a lot of sense, given that Daena and Andred were lovers. But then, he'd thought Helaine cared for him, so what did he know?

His beast growled tiredly, not even bothering to argue. They were both exhausted. His first night sleeping among the Wraiths had not been restful. He knew his beast was listening, but he had woken up multiple times anyway, lying in the dark, ears straining, in case of any trouble coming from Daena's room.

Then, when he'd reported for guard duty, he'd been given someone's spare black cavalry tunic and told to wait in the library. Apparently, despite everything he'd done—despite collapsing the entire front path of the biggest Nephilim court in Kaerlud and smoothly plucking Daena out from under the noses of the Hawks—Andred didn't trust him enough to put him on the guard roster.

What did you expect? His beast grumbled. *Our role was always to get Daena in and then watch over her. She's the one he has to trust.*

That was just the thing: Andred did trust Daena. It felt off. Like Reece was missing something important. And he didn't know if he was missing something on Andred's side… or Daena's.

A series of whistles from the direction of the road warned of a visitor, and Reece spun away from the window just as Caius stepped into the library and grunted at him to follow.

"Where are we going?" Reece asked.

Caius glared at him over his shoulder. "Today, you'll be committing to the cause."

Well, fuck. That sounded ominous. "In what way, exactly?"

Caius ignored him. Before Reece could ask anything more, Caius led him into the elegant front receiving room. Gods, he hated this room.

Reece kept his gaze away from the slaughtered drake depicted in the corner and focused on the Wraiths. Andred was already there. He was seated on a large, gilded chair, his back straight, heavily muscled legs arrogantly splayed. His black tunic had been swapped for burgundy trimmed in silver, the pair of fighting boars at his breast embroidered in lustrous metallic thread.

For a moment, Reece almost stalled. Andred looked like a king. He looked rich and arrogant and stately, and far more regal than Ballanor—or Geraint—had ever been. Which was, no doubt, exactly the impression he wanted to give.

Andred waved Reece toward the side wall where the lower-ranked soldiers were standing at rest, legs braced, hands folded behind their backs. He followed to the end of the line, positioning himself as near to Andred as he could.

Daena stepped in a minute later, prodded forward by

Usna. Hell. The black cavalry tunic she'd pulled over her dress was too big, hanging like a sack over her shoulders. She had dark rings under her eyes, her hair was caught back in a tight bun, and she was limping heavily, faint lines of pain tightening around her mouth with each step.

She stiffened even more during the night.

Fuck. His beast was right. But there was nothing Reece could do except watch as Andred gestured her over and Daena shuffled across the floor to stand beside him, Usna immediately behind her. She never once looked over at him, choosing to stare at the ground instead.

His beast huffed. *We're supposed to be a team. Now she doesn't trust you.*

Reece bit back the reply that he didn't trust her either. But his beast growled softly anyway, as if it knew what he was going to say… and disagreed.

Another whistle sounded from the front of the house. He heard the front door open and then boot heels clicking across the marble foyer. No one in the room moved.

Usna opened the door and held it as three of Geraint's former councilors stepped through, followed by the remaining Wraiths, who moved to stand along the back wall, facing Andred.

Reece recognized the councilors immediately: Pellin, Dionys, and Gaheris. They were rich beyond anything Reece could imagine, indulged and privileged since the day they'd entered the world. Their cloaks were lined in fur, and rings glittered on their heavy fingers as they moved, stalking forward with arrogant assurance. Under Geraint's rule, they'd been the three most powerful men in the kingdom.

Pellin was an older copy of Tor, but infinitely colder, his expression blank and calculating. Dionys, clearly once a very handsome man although his face had softened into jowls, was sneering in a way that suggested it was his permanent expression. Gaheris, the youngest of them, closer in age to Ballanor, had been one of Geraint's favorites. There'd even been talk—given Geraint's obvious loathing of Ballanor—that the king might choose Gaheris as his successor.

All three had hated Ballanor, but when Geraint died, they had bowed to the new king nonetheless. Pellin had disowned Tor, his own son, trying to win Ballanor's favor, while rumor on the Kaerlud docks suggested Dionys was even more dedicated to gaining Ballanor's support. He had committed his fortune to the war in the north and had invested heavily in building ships that would transport spoils back from the far Verturian mines, and he'd needed Ballanor to confirm the contract. Of the three, Gaheris had lost the most when Geraint died, but he too had supported the new king, somehow managing to hold on to the authority and influence he had accrued.

But then Ballanor had died and Lucilla took the throne. And the very first thing she did was strip the councilors of their status and have them escorted from the palace. They had lost their status and much of their power. They'd also lost their war and all the money they'd invested in it.

They had been disgusted by Ballanor, but they *loathed* Lucilla.

Pellin had met with Andred before—he'd led Reece to the Wraiths after all—but the other two seemed to be visiting for the first time. Their eyes flicked over the expensive ornaments, they nodded approvingly at the Apollyon victories displayed across the walls, and they looked at Andred with respect. A recognition that he was one of them. Rich. Noble. Entitled. Apollyon.

Andred rose slowly from his seat and dipped his chin. Taller than most Apollyon and pristine in his regal court attire, he looked as if he was bestowing them with an honor. He waved toward a set of three ornately carved chairs set out in the center of the room. "Welcome, gentlemen. Please, make yourselves comfortable."

The three former councilors lowered themselves into their seats while Andred watched, eyes glinting.

A few seconds later, he sank into his own seat, and it became obvious that his chair was taller than theirs, and the councilors would have to spend the meeting tilting their heads up to look at him. For the first time, a slightly disgruntled look crossed their well-groomed faces.

"It's good to see you again, General Andred," Pellin announced with an arrogant twitch to his upper lip. "I have brought my colleagues as promised."

Andred gave him an irritated look. The councilors may have seen him as one of them, but he saw himself as set apart. Set higher. "*Lord* Andred," he stated coldly. "Son of Flavius, son of Otso, cousin to Bar-Aloys, and direct descendent of Aloysius, the first king of Brythoria." Andred leaned back in his chair. "You may call me 'my lord' until we're back in Kaerlud. And then you may call me 'Your Majesty.'"

There was a moment's silence as the three men considered their response. Pellin was first to dip his chin. He replied smoothly, voice dripping with deference. "Of course, my lord." A second later, Dionys and Gaheris followed his lead.

"We were glad to be invited here today, Lord Andred," Pellin continued for all of them, lips twisting up into a smile that never quite reached his eyes. "We would be grateful to learn more of your plans. And, of course, how we might help."

Andred lifted his hand and gestured for Usna to speak. "Please share the updates from Kaerlud."

"The Blues are in disarray," Usna reported smugly. "They spent yesterday sending large numbers of soldiers through the sewers and sweeping the city. Their forces are divided and distracted. They still have squads of cavalry in the north, searching the towns and cities that we left behind weeks ago." His expression became grim. "In addition, however, they've put soldiers onto every house associated with the Wraiths. Including the families of those brothers we lost in Ravenstone. Their widows, even their children are being watched."

The soldiers in the room—too well-trained to complain or even move—grew still. A heavy air of animosity settled over their stiff forms. They had already sacrificed a great deal, and now their families were under surveillance.

"All the former councilors have the queen's guards outside their homes now too. But they're spread thin, and many are fresh and untrained." Usna gestured toward the three Apollyon. "We took these gentlemen through the stables at the back of a tavern. The soldiers watching the front never even noticed."

Reece kept his face blank. Tor had planned to have the youngest and least experienced recruits on guard duty for precisely this reason. The soldiers had to believe in what they were doing. And the Wraiths had to believe the queen's forces were inept and helpless.

"Why aren't *you* being watched?" Dionys asked, leaning back and folding his arms over his chest as he looked at Andred.

Andred's eyes narrowed at the question, and for a moment Reece thought he might not answer. But then he replied coldly. "They'll never look here. This was my father's mistress's home. He kept it entirely secret. Even I only learned of it when I received the keys in his will. Ballanor didn't know of it, and neither do the Hawks."

Scales ran up Reece's torso and over his back as his beast shifted uneasily. This was where Andred's father— Flavius, he recalled vaguely—kept his mistress. He'd stuffed her away in this mockery of a home. And yet… wouldn't it be more comfortable than living on the streets? Wouldn't it be better to be here, with walls and beds, warm fires, and enough food?

Yeah, we could have been somewhere like this. Somewhere without our real papa, the papa who loved us. Where Mama was an embarrassment, and you were hated—if they even let you live. Do you think you would have made it to the Hawks then?

He didn't know. Was his beast right? Would he have been killed, his mama kept a shameful secret? Or would he now be sitting beside Andred, one of his trusted lieutenants, one of the select group of boys who had grown up together, with the best tutors and best equipment, secure in their lifelong friendship and their path to power?

His beast snorted. *Andred is a traitor.*

Yeah. Now he was. But he didn't have to be. Geraint had loved him. He would almost certainly have considered him for the throne alongside Gaheris.

And it wasn't about the power anyway; it was about safety. About living in a house, not on the street. About the opportunities that were stolen from him by a lie.

Don't pretend this is about a house. It's never been about that. You were a child who'd lost his parents. You were angry and sad, and you made yourself believe you still had a father somewhere. It was easier to blame Mama, easier to feed that anger, than to lie on those cold cobbles, hiding under piles of rubbish against some dirty wall, and grieve for everything we'd lost. But now you need to grow the fuck up.

Gods. It was the most his beast had said in months. And the most damning. But somehow, he'd known it was coming. This was what he'd been hiding from all those months when he drank the beast into silence.

Reece gripped into such tight fists behind his back that his nails pierced his palms. It was too much to deal with. Too much to think about in this room filled with Wraiths and former councilors plotting war.

"Lucilla will destroy our kingdom," Andred was saying, voice filled with scorn. "Firstly, she's a woman. It's against the gods' order to have a female on the throne."

That was the stupidest thing Reece had ever heard. Wasn't the Apollyon goddess female? Hadn't she been the one to send them to Brythoria in the first place?

We have the gods of earth and air and fire beside us. They do not care about such things as male and female, only courage and honor, the beast rumbled pointedly.

"Second," Andred continued, "Lucilla is utterly unprepared to rule. Her actions since she took the throne: removing the council, wasting resources, harassing innocent families, even killing her own Lord High Chancellor, clearly show that she has no idea what she's doing."

Fuck. Dornar was the Lord High Chancellor Andred was talking about. Scales hardened over Reece's back, and his left arm throbbed.

Andred folded his arms over his chest, heavy muscles bulging. "Finally, and most damning of all, her consort is Tarasque. Her children"—his nostrils flared—"will have scales."

Reece's beast rumbled low in his belly. Here it was. The unacknowledged—until now—reason Tor was asked to join the Wraiths but Reece never was, despite his long friendship with them. Tor was Apollyon, blessed by the Goddess, and Reece was Tarasque.

The majority of the kingdom had left those outdated prejudices far behind. But not the last remaining bastions of Apollyon nobility. Not these men. If they could, they would drag Brythoria back to the war, back to all the cruelty and hatred Lucilla was fighting to end.

We're descended from fucking dragons, his beast growled; whether at Reece or at the men in front of him, he couldn't tell. *These are the assholes you spent our entire time in Kaerlud palace sucking up to…. And you're giving Daena a hard time.*

"I couldn't help noticing," Dionys said, flicking his hand toward Reece, "that you have one of them here."

"Reece is here to help," Andred said frostily.

"How?" Pellin asked, nostrils flaring, before adding a more respectful, "My lord."

Andred looked the former councilors up and down slowly before answering. "He has proven his commitment by returning our misplaced truth seeker, and we need access to the palace—access that no Wraith can get. He is our key."

"How is he the key?" Gaheris asked, speaking for the first time.

Andred shrugged, not bothering to reply, and Gaheris slowly settled back into his seat, eyes narrowed. Surprisingly, it was Dionys who couldn't seem to let it go.

Dionys twisted in his seat to glare at him. "Who are you, boy? Where are you from?"

Gods. No one had called him "boy" in the eleven years since he'd joined the army, and it was a battle to hold in the biting rejoinder aching to be set free. Reece glanced at Andred, who waved a hand as if to say he should answer.

"Corp—" Bollocks. He wasn't a corporal anymore. "Reece… sir."

Dionys gave him another slow look, rubbing his chin with his fingers. "How old are you?"

What the fuck was this? "Twenty-six, sir."

"And who was your father? Did he serve the king?"

Reece gripped his hands behind his back, ignoring the scales tightening across his skin. Multiple possible responses flitted through his mind in a confusing rush. But everyone was watching him, Andred was getting irritated, Dionys wanted an answer, and he had to say something.

In the end, he said the only thing that felt right. "My father was a sailor. Brennan—he worked the fishing fleets, catching herring and cod in the Asherahn sea."

He tried to resist, but he couldn't help glancing at Daena.

She dipped her chin and whispered, "Truth."

Dionys turned to Daena and narrowed his eyes. "His father was a sailor?"

She nodded firmly. "Yes."

Hell. Reece rocked back on his heels. Daena didn't know about his past. All she knew was what she sensed from him. Was it possible? Did he genuinely believe that Papa was his true father?

His beast growled. *Obviously.*

Dionys waved a ringed hand. "It doesn't matter anyway. He's still Tarasque." He turned to Andred. "I don't accept him here. I've had experience with his kind before… you can't trust them."

His beast growled, long and low. A harsh vibration that, for the first time in months, Reece had no desire to stifle. The recognition that had started to form earlier—that he should be grateful for his beast—came back in a flood. This primal awareness was a gift, and he'd been locking it away.

He'd silenced his beast to fit in with the Wraiths, and it had made him less.

And with that rising gratitude, a piece of his fractured soul quietly fitted back into place. A piece that he'd been missing for most of his life without realizing it.

He let out a slow, shuddering breath, wishing he could have realized all of this somewhere far away from the Wraiths and their war room. But he didn't move. He couldn't, not without betraying himself and the mission he'd been given.

Andred laughed, shaking his head at Dionys. "I'm not getting rid of him. We need him. But you don't need to worry, none of us trust him whatsoever." He sneered. "I trust my brothers. The men who stood beside me on the battlefield and who will stand beside me as we take back our kingdom and return it to glory. No one else."

"Surely you trust us," Pellin muttered.

"Not yet," Andred stated coldly, gesturing toward Daena. "But that is why you're here after all."

Daena stepped forward, and Andred took her wrist between his fingers once more. He ran his eyes over each person in the room, meeting their eyes one at a time. "State your name and your rank. Then say, 'I commit my loyalty unreservedly to Lord Andred and swear to support his cause until he has gained the throne or I have died in the attempt.'"

Gods.

One by one, the soldiers along the back wall repeated the words. Each time, Daena nodded and Andred shifted his gaze to the next man.

The soldiers on Reece's side started swearing their oaths, man after man, as Daena nodded her approval.

Fuck. This was the moment it all came down to. Now was the time when she could betray him utterly.

Daena wouldn't—

Reece hissed under his breath. His newfound gratitude toward his beast only went so far. He couldn't lose focus and take the risk that he was unprepared when the time came. If Daena betrayed him now, she could earn a true place with the man she'd already given everything up for once. What had she said to Andred? "I am yours to command."

Reece's beast grew more agitated. Scales hardened on his forearms like vambraces, and over his heart like a cuirass. The berserker rage was rising in him, and it made thinking clearly almost impossible.

What would she do? Would she betray him, like he'd suspected she would all along? Or would she risk her own life to tell the lie?

Andred's fingers tightened over her pulse. Reece wanted to cut them off. Or maybe that was what his beast wanted? He couldn't tell.

He forced himself to breathe, and to stay standing against the wall and watch Daena. Her face was pale and tight. Her weight leaned heavily on her right leg. She lifted her eyes to his and stared at him, unblinking.

The soldier beside him finished his statement, and all eyes turned to Reece.

He cleared his throat and said the words he had to say. "I commit my loyalty unreservedly to Lord Andred and swear to support his cause until he has gained the throne or I have died in the attempt."

The room was utterly silent as Daena looked from him to Andred and back again.

Chapter Seven

DAENA HAD SPENT the night lying on the hard floor, a cold breeze skittering under the door and slowly freezing her no matter how tightly she curled up under her rough blankets, her skin scrubbed raw from her attempts to get rid of the smell of the sewer, and her entire body aching.

It was bitterly uncomfortable, but she had known pain before—she'd been caught in a burning building, clouds of bitter smoke scorching her lungs, wooden beams collapsing around her and on her, shattering her bones as they burned her skin. She'd lived through the torture of Andred hauling her out from under the pile of heavy timbers, carrying her through the blazing temple, and leaping with her into the icy mountain-fed waters of the small river that wound through the orchard. And she'd survived her time in his camp as her body slowly healed but her heart broke apart. This was nothing compared to all of that.

She could have slept if she'd wanted to. Instead, she'd closed her eyes, ignoring how her exhausted aches stiffened into a rigid mass of cramping muscle and contracted sinews, and concentrated on her pulse.

Andred didn't break tools he was still using, not on purpose, anyway, which made everything simple: she had to convince him she was still useful. But she had to do it in a way that kept Reece safe too.

Andred wasn't immoral or even uncaring. He was deeply loyal to his men: he would die, without question, for his Wraith brothers. He made time for anyone in his squad who wanted to speak with him and always considered their views. He was courageous and formidable on the battlefield. And he truly believed in his right to take the throne. He was utterly convinced that the kingdom needed him and that he was the legitimate heir to the throne. It was how he'd convinced her, after all. When he told her he could save their kingdom, he'd believed it.

But he was also ruthless, strategically brilliant, and completely dedicated to his cause. He would weigh up the costs and benefits of any action and then do exactly what was most effective. If that required sacrificing a game piece, he would.

It had been too late when she'd realized she was only a tool to him. It had suited him to keep her alive to deal with the reivers and deserters he was recruiting into his new army.

He'd been there when the temple had collapsed—in hindsight because he had orchestrated it himself—and he'd come in to get her before everything was destroyed. Unfortunately, he'd been moments too late, and her room was already on fire. But he'd still had use for her, so he saved her. That was all.

She needed him to continue to believe that was true.

Hour after hour, she pressed her fingers into her wrist

and tried to make her pulse rise and fall. She imagined everything that could go wrong, took short breaths, bit her tongue, thought about what her family must have felt when they discovered she'd been alive but in hiding... and succeeded in making her pulse spike.

Bringing it down and keeping it stable was much harder. Eventually, she fell back on the breathing meditations she'd learned at the Nephilim Temple in Eshcol. The techniques she'd learned at Ramiel's side, back in the days when her family hoped she would follow his footsteps into the courts of truth, maybe even all the way to Supreme Justice.

She focused on those long-ago lessons and controlled her pulse as best she could, and by the early hours of the morning, she could hold her heart rate steady.

Now, as each soldier made his promise, as pain spiked up her leg and through her hip, as Reece watched her, his indigo scales settling on the sides of his face, she ignored everything except her breathing.

In for five seconds. Hold for five seconds. Out for five seconds. Hold for five. Start again. The pain faded. The room faded. Andred's grip on her wrist faded. There was only her, and her breath.

The other soldiers finished, and all eyes turned to Reece. It was his turn to speak the oath. He was taller than she'd realized. Now that he was standing beside a row of Apollyon, it was clear how much leaner he was, too, his muscles long and athletic. He was too far away to look into his eyes, but she knew they were gray, and, even across the room, they were fixed on hers.

He didn't flinch. He met her gaze, and as if he was speaking directly to her, made his promise. "I commit my loyalty unreservedly to Lord Andred and swear to support his cause until he has gained the throne or I have died in the attempt."

The extreme bitterness of willow bark flooded her mouth. Gods, it was foul. Saliva pooled, and every instinct drove her to swallow it away or spit it out. Instead, she held it. Held herself.

She glanced back at Andred and then turned her face toward Reece. The space between them seemed to shrink until it was only him and her in the room. His expression never changed. He showed no fear or concern—except for a tiny wrinkle down his forehead and those deep blue scales, the color of the sky at night, slowly creeping up his neck.

Andred was watching her, his fingers tight enough on her wrist to hurt. But she ignored him. She kept her focus on her breath and her eyes on Reece. She ignored the taste in her mouth, the soldiers in the room, even Andred's tight grip on her wrist. And nodded. "Truth."

"Are you certain?" Andred asked, gesturing toward Reece.

She swallowed as delicately as she could. "Yes. Completely." A fresh wave of bitterness washed over her tongue, but she was ready for it, and she didn't react.

Andred stared at her for a long moment while no one moved. She didn't look at him, she stared over the top of his head and concentrated on her breath. Her pulse never spiked; she was certain of it.

"Good," Andred declared, his gaze moving back into the middle of the room. "The Wraiths have proven themselves."

Gods and angels. She wanted to collapse back against the wall and let it take her weight, just for a moment. They'd done it. She'd heard the lie and not reacted. She'd told the biggest lie of her life and got away with it. She'd kept them both safe, as she'd promised.

Many people thought truth seekers couldn't lie. They could, of course—as Andred clearly knew—it was just more difficult to get away with when your whole body rejected it. But she'd done it. The knot that had been tightening in her neck loosened a fraction. She'd faced the true test, and she and Reece had both survived.

Andred looked down at the three former councilors. "My men are loyal. Now *you* prove yourselves to them."

Daena had to force herself not to slump. The nerves that had been holding her up were slowly draining away, leaving her even more acutely aware of her screaming muscles and the long sleepless night. Thank the angels that these last three would be easy.

Pellin leaned back in his chair, folding his arms over his big chest. His voice was clear and firm as he made his oath.

Andred looked at Daena and she nodded. "Truth." One down, two to go, and then, if she could hold on for a few more minutes, hopefully, a chance to escape and collapse somewhere. A chance to rinse out her mouth and rest. To massage the worst of the cramp out of her calf. Maybe even sleep.

Dionys raised his voice, his jowls shuddering with the force of his words as he too made his oath. "Truth," she whispered.

A few more minutes, and then she could have something to eat. She'd been too worried to make herself venture into the Wraith's kitchen to find breakfast earlier. Now she was famished. And cold. Maybe she could boil water and make tea? She'd seen some frost-burned mint hidden beneath the weeds when she'd looked out the kitchen window that morning. That would take the taste—

Gods, the sharpness of sour wine flooded her mouth. Harshly acidic, almost vinegar.

"…gained the throne or I have died in the attempt," Gaheris finished, sending another wave of acid burning over her tongue.

She was tired. And worse—she'd allowed herself to relax. Her lips pursed before she could stop them, her pulse shooting up, and, beside her Andred noticed.

He spun in his seat, his grip tightening once more. Damn it to the abyss. Fear rattled through her, cold sweat sliding down over her ribs. Gaheris was lying.

Did it mean Gaheris supported Lucilla? If so, what the hell was he doing here? Or did it merely indicate he wasn't prepared to die for Andred? Or perhaps he was committed, but not unreservedly? This uncertainty, this helplessness—and the harsh toll of her talent—was exactly why she hated being a truth seeker. Why she had never wanted this role.

Andred twisted in his seat to look at her, his expression utterly merciless. "Did he just lie?" he demanded.

"I don't know. Gods. Please… I…." The words wouldn't come. Her breath that she had worked so hard to control caught in her lungs.

Andred lifted his free hand to beckon Caius, who stepped forward immediately, sliding his sword out to rest the tip against Gaheris's throat.

"Did you lie to me?" Andred hissed, staring at the frozen former councilman.

"No," Gaheris replied instantly.

Hell. Daena's mouth filled with another flood of bitter acid. It was all she could do not to retch it out. She'd thought that the worst of the day was over. But now every man in the room was staring at her, their faces hard, and she knew it was only going to get even more unpleasant.

Andred tilted his head to the side, watching her closely as she swallowed, and then swallowed again. "Daena?"

"Something was a lie, but I don't know which part," she whispered.

She glanced back toward Reece, looking for the connection they'd shared. For some kind of anchor. But he didn't meet her eyes.

Caius pushed his sword deeper into Gaheris's skin until a thin trickle of blood oozed down his throat.

Gaheris raised his hands, beads of sweat breaking out over his forehead. "I'm not lying! Gods. You can't do this. I have a family, children——"

A low growl rattled through the room, and her eyes flew back to Reece. He was motionless against the back wall, but his beast was snarling, and his scales were solidifying over his throat and face.

"My men have families too," Andred spat. His lips had pulled back, baring his teeth. "We have lost too much. We have been betrayed and abandoned by one cowardly nobleman already, and I will not risk everything for a man who doesn't know where his loyalty lies."

Pellin and Dionys shuffled back, away from their pale-faced colleague, neither of them defending or helping him in any way.

Andred stood, dragging Daena's arm up with him as he glared down at Gaheris. "Speak the oath again. Slowly."

Gaheris coughed, the motion jarring the sword against his throat. Another drop of blood slid out from beneath the blade. "I commit my loyalty unreservedly to Lord Andred," he rasped. "And I swear to support his cause." Gaheris took a shaky breath. "Until he has gained the throne or I have died in the attempt."

Damn it to the abyss; it was *all* a lie. Gaheris didn't

commit his loyalty and he didn't support Andred's cause. But Daena still didn't know why or whether she should be trying to defend him. Her gut churned, sending bile rising through the sourness in her mouth. What the hell was she supposed to do?

For the first time, Gaheris looked at her. His eyes were wide, unblinking, his throat moving as he swallowed. He'd lied, and he knew that she knew. Had he not realized that Andred had only called this meeting after he had his truth seeker back? Or had he simply been so arrogant that he'd not considered he might be caught?

Either way, his fate lay in her hands. She shuffled her feet, wincing as a white-hot shaft of pain arrowed up her leg, trying to find a way through this nightmare. There wasn't one. Andred knew she had tasted the lie, if she tried to hide it now, everything would be lost.

"Daena?" Andred prompted, voice colder than snow in the Thabana Mountains.

"Some of it's a lie," she hedged. "I can't tell which parts. Maybe he simply doesn't want to die?"

"It's not enough, my lord," Caius argued. "The last time we let someone live, he stole two valuable prisoners and burned our camp to the ground."

Andred looked at Caius, and Caius glared back, a long silent communication. Eventually, Andred sank back into his chair. "You're right, Caius, my friend. You advised against keeping Tor alive, and I should have listened." Andred waved a hand to the door. "Take Gaheris out to the fields and kill him."

"No! Please!" Gaheris scrabbled away, falling off his chair in his desperation, but Caius grabbed him by the collar and hauled him out of his seat. Two soldiers stepped away from the wall and helped the lieutenant drag the bucking and howling Apollyon out of the receiving room.

She could hear him begging and fighting all the way. A door slammed at the back of the house. Daena stood, frozen, her entire being focused on the direction they'd gone in. There was a muffled scream. And then silence.

Gods. The silence was almost worse. She'd helped to kill a man. She wanted to throw up.

Andred looked at her and dipped his chin. "Thank you, Daena. You did well."

Against the wall, Reece had settled into a stony silence, his condemnation pulsing off him in waves.

Daena pulled away, and this time Andred let her go, turning back to his meeting. She wrapped her arms around her belly, swallowing hard, forcing herself not to be sick. Forcing herself not to cry. She would not show weakness in front of these men. Never again.

Chapter Eight

REECE WATCHED Caius saunter back into the reception room through slitted eyes, forcing himself to stay silent. His scales were climbing over his face, and his forearms ached from clenching his fists behind his back, but he made himself stay still despite the rage thundering through his veins.

Rage at Andred and Caius. At Gaheris too. What the fuck did he think he was doing walking in here? Surely everyone in the city had heard about the truth seeker at the heart of the conspiracy against the queen. But also at Daena.

That is utterly unfair.

No, it wasn't. She could have saved the man's life if she just kept her mouth shut. Instead, she had done the most expedient thing. She had given Andred what he wanted—and earned the general's approval in return. Possibly even earned some greater privileges within the Wraiths.

If she was doing the most expedient thing, she would have sacrificed you.

Maybe that was true. But Gaheris had begged to be

allowed to go back to his children, children who would grow up alone, without a father—maybe even on the streets now they'd lost everything—and it had sent Reece right back to the dark place. The place where rage ruled. Where his fury kept him alive.

It didn't help that he was already overwhelmed. That his beast had spent the entire meeting whining in his ear. That he desperately wanted a sip of the brandy in his flask and couldn't take one. That a huge part of him had been furious with Andred for the way he was treating Daena, never mind the stress and tension of his own potent lie. Everything had accumulated inside him until all he felt was rage.

The rest of the meeting passed in a blur of ignoring his beast and glaring at Daena. Pellin and Dionys, both sweating and pale, were only too glad to cut the discussions short, with promises to return when Andred was ready to discuss further plans with them, and almost falling over themselves with their assurances as they fled the house.

Andred called the meeting to a close, and Usna barked out orders for two men to follow the former councilors and a squad to relieve the sentries who had been on duty.

Finally, Reece and Daena were free to go.

His beast growled, long and low in his belly as he watched Daena duck her head and bolt, weaving through the last remaining soldiers. She was faster than he expected, clearly determined to get away. But she was not fast enough.

Reece stalked after her as she limped into the kitchen and then out the back door.

Yes. We need to find her, speak to her. Gods of fire, that was a disaster.

It was definitely a disaster. Horror and outrage swirled in his gut as he checked behind him. No one followed—Andred,

Caius, and Usna had stayed behind to make plans, and everyone else was either on patrol or going to rest—and Reece took his chance to slip through the kitchen door behind her.

He ran his eye over the garden, confirming that they were alone among the beds of scraggly herbs and weeds, and then shut the door roughly behind him.

Daena startled, spinning back toward him, her eyes wide. "What are you doing?" she hissed, glancing between him and the kitchen door. "You can't be out here."

"What the fuck was that?" Reece snarled.

His beast churned and growled in his belly. *No. No, this is not what I meant.*

Maybe not. But this was what he needed. Reece took a step closer, and then another, expecting her to back away. Didn't she realize how dangerous a Tarasque warrior could be? Didn't she know how close he was to the primal battle rage?

Either she didn't know, or she didn't care. She drew herself up, her hands coming to settle on her hips as bright patches of angry color crept up her throat. "You don't get to question me, Corporal Reece."

She's right. Look at her. For the love of the gods—

He ignored his beast and glared. "I have every right to question you. How can I trust you when you just killed a man?"

Daena gasped. "I did *not*. I did everything I could to save him from his own bloody stupidity. I—"

Reece jabbed his finger out toward her, his fury singing through him—the same righteous outrage that had kept him safe on the streets and then seen him through a war— and which she had more than earned. "You sold Gaheris out to Andred. You chose to betray him in exchange for your own reward." He mimicked Andred as he hissed, "Thank you, Daena. You did well."

Her expression shut down completely, and his beast howled, but he ignored them both. "Children will go to sleep tonight without a father because of *you*."

Somewhere deep inside him, Daena merged with Helaine, taking his request for a safe house and running straight to Ballanor—almost destroying the Hawks in the process. Deeper still, she reminded him of his mother, soft and pretty and smelling of rosemary, telling Reece she loved him and then ripping it all away.

All the revelations about his true love for his papa, even his gratitude toward his beast, meant nothing in this moment. He was a boy left alone in a frightening city. He was the youngest member of the squad, responsible for Tristan's capture and torture, his friends almost being burned alive. He was screaming on the dusty road as Dornar broke his arm again and again.

He knew it was wrong, even as he said it. But all that hurt had overwhelmed him, and the only defense he knew was attack. "Are you happy?" he demanded. "Now that you've killed an innocent man? Now that you're truly one of them?"

"No." She shook her head roughly, the color in her cheeks fading as her face paled. "Children will go to sleep tonight without a father because of Andred and Caius."

Guilt flickered, worming in his gut, but the words were pouring out, and he couldn't stop them. "If you hadn't betrayed Gaheris, he would be on his way home to his family right now. All you had to do was keep your mouth shut."

There was a moment when he thought she might cry. When he thought she might concede. But she didn't. If anything, his words only firmed her resolve. Her eyes grew harder, her spine straighter. "Now you're just showing your ignorance," Daena spat. "If you don't understand truth seekers then you don't get to judge us."

Reece took another step forward until he was looming right over her. Close enough to smell the herbal scent of her skin. Close enough to feel the heat from her body and, for the first time, appreciate the tiny flecks of blue and purple in her eyes. Close enough to realize that her whole body was trembling.

Don't do this, Reece. You're on her side. She's on your side—she fought for us in there. For once in your life—

Reece crossed his arms over his chest. "Enlighten me then."

Daena glared at him. Her breath shuddered slowly in and out, and he could have sworn she was counting under her breath. Eventually, she shook her head. "No. I don't owe you anything."

She moved to step around him, but he grabbed her arm without thinking. "We can never work together if you won't tell the truth!"

Daena laughed, but she was not amused. "You wouldn't believe the truth if it bit you." She glared down at his hand still wrapped around her bicep and sneered. "Now I see how you got so close to the Wraiths. Tor told me all about how popular you were in the palace before the Hawks were betrayed. He thinks it's because you're a naturally friendly person, but he's wrong, isn't he? It's because you're just like them—obsessed with status and your own selfish needs." She tugged at her arm. "I've had enough of arrogant bullies demanding my truth. Now get your fucking hands off me."

Gods. She thought he was like Andred.

You are *like Andred. You're holding her just like he did.*

Reece dropped her arm like it was burning, flinching back. "I'm nothing like them."

"Lie," Daena spat back.

"I am *not* like them!"

"Lie, again." She clasped her hands in front of her belly, mouth pinched. "Have you ever thought, Corporal Reece, that all this anger of yours is just deflection? That maybe the truth is, you're angry with *yourself*."

"I…." Gods. He *had* thought it. His beast had said it multiple times.

He closed his eyes for a long moment. She was right, and he had hurt her. Gods. He was better than this. He had to be.

"Daena, I—"

She limped away, ignoring him. She reached the door and turned back to glare at him over her shoulder. "I left Eshcol precisely so that I would never have to pass judgment on anyone. I never wanted to serve as a justice. I fled that destiny, and look where it got me—imprisoned by Andred, imprisoned by the Hawks, and imprisoned by *you*. I hate reading the truth. I hate knowing you're all liars. And I hate being blamed for the lies other people tell."

You did this. Fix it! Fix it now.

Fuck. His beast was right. He had done this, and it was up to him to fix it. "Daena!" he called, louder, striding after her.

She paused, shoulders slumped. "What now?"

"I didn't mean to—"

Her lip curled, and he swallowed the rest. He had meant to follow her out of the house. He had wanted her to understand exactly what she'd done. He'd let his fear and history influence him. It was only now that he realized it was a terrible mistake.

A million trite comments flowed through his mind. Compliments and flattery had been his best tools for so long. When he wanted something, he charmed someone for it. But Daena would know that none of it was genuine. He couldn't just tell her she had pretty eyes and hope for the best. And, honestly, he didn't know that he could do it anymore, anyway.

"I'm sorry," he admitted.

She stood there, hand on the door, for a long, painful moment. And then she dipped her chin. "Truth."

A long, relieved breath rattled out of him. "I was...." He closed his eyes for a moment, trying to find the words. He owed her an explanation. "My papa died when I was fourteen. Mama died a year later. I was alone in Kaerlud, with very little money and no family, living on the streets. I spent my entire life trying to get away from there. I worked so hard to make a life in the palace...." He left the rest unsaid. They both knew what had happened to that life. "Gaheris being killed, leaving his children alone, it... it took me back there. It's not an excuse, though, and...." He cleared his throat. "Please forgive me."

She blinked slowly, digesting his words, perhaps testing them for truth. But it was all genuine, more genuine than he could ever remember being.

"Okay," she replied softly. "I'm sorry that happened to you."

Thank the gods, his beast whispered.

Reece reached out toward her, but then dropped his hand. He didn't dare touch her, not now. "We're stuck here, together, and we can't fail. Can I... can you tell me how it works, so I know what to expect?"

She leaned heavily on the door, watching him. "Did

Jeremiel ever tell you how he reads the truth, or Rafe ever explain his healing?"

"No. I never asked." He knew the Nephilim never gave up their secrets, and he'd always respected that. Bollocks. He dropped his gaze. She should refuse. He hadn't earned this truth from her.

"I taste it." Her voice was so low, it took him a moment to recognize what he'd heard.

His gaze flew back to hers. "What do you mean?" he asked, leaning closer.

"Lies. They have a taste… for me anyway."

A ripple of scales itched as they fluttered up his arm. "What do they taste like?"

She shrugged. "It depends. Sometimes sour things like lemon rind or raw rhubarb. Sometimes something bitter, or rotten. Curdled milk, or meat that's been too long in the sun. It's hard—for me, anyway—not to react."

Hell. What would he do if his mouth filled with curdled milk every time someone lied? Every time *he* lied. How had he never realized this about his friends, his own squad? "Is that… would Jeremiel…?"

She huffed out a sad laugh. "I doubt it. It's different for everyone. He might get an itch on the back of his hand or see a cloud of smoke. My uncle, Ramiel, hears a buzzing noise when someone lies." She closed her eyes for a moment, resting on the door.

The last time he'd seen anyone look quite so tired and yet still force themselves to stand was after Ravenstone. Something painful flickered in his chest, and he rubbed it away.

"I've often thought that it wouldn't be so bad if I could see something or hear it. Maybe then I could have lived with it," Daena whispered. "I could have been the truth seeker everyone wanted."

Fuck. He had no idea of how to respond to that. "Was it true?" he asked instead, turning the subject. "What Andred said?"

Daena rubbed her thumb slowly over the scar on the side of her face. "Andred said a lot of things."

"That I'm in. That I've proven my commitment."

That you're the key, his beast whispered, but he let that go.

"He believed it," Daena muttered.

Reece opened his mouth to say something, anything. To thank her, perhaps, or maybe ask her more about what she meant when she said that everyone wanted her to be a truth seeker. But she'd already turned away and slipped back into the kitchen, leaving him standing alone in the bleak garden, surrounded by weeds.

Chapter Nine

Daena glared at the door to her room. She was going to step through it. Any moment now.

It would be so easy to hide in her room. As dark, cold, and miserable as the tiny scullery was, it was still better than her tent in the Thabana Mountains. Rain didn't run down the walls, no reivers were strolling around outside, and more than that—far more—she had decided to be there in the first place.

And yet... the walls felt too close, the room stagnant. The howling wind outside made the house shudder and groan until the walls seemed to be falling around her. And sitting there alone really did make it feel like a prison cell.

It was true that she'd been imprisoned by Andred, but it wasn't the whole truth. She'd been complicit. In many ways, she'd imprisoned herself. She'd looked at the steep mountainside and the cold lake and told herself that she couldn't do it.

She didn't tell herself she "couldn't." Not anymore.

Once upon a time, she'd been brave enough to stand up

to her family, to resist generations of expectations and Nephilim pressure, and tell them she wanted to be something different than they'd planned.

Somehow, between trying to give Andred what he wanted, the long, lonely process of recovering from her injuries, and discovering just how wrong she'd been about the man she'd loved, she'd learned to doubt herself. She'd made herself smaller, hiding away, only doing what she was told. But now she was starting to find herself once more. She was slowly remembering that she was strong. And she wasn't going to sit in her room hiding from a man ever again. Not Andred—no matter how much she detested him—and not Reece either.

Gods and angels. Just thinking about Reece was confusing. He reminded her of the Sasanian raspise berries cultivated in the conservatories in Eshcol; dense thickets filled with tiny fuzzy-looking thorns and hidden berries. The thorns looked so mild and soft that it was easy to ignore them until they'd burrowed in, under your skin, burning and stinging. That was when you remembered how vicious the thorns really were. And that their only purpose was to protect the delicate red fruit.

After what Reece had admitted about his childhood, it wasn't surprising that he'd reacted badly to the disaster with Gaheris, and she felt genuine empathy for him. But it didn't mean she was going to grab a handful of thorns, either.

She didn't want another run-in with him. And yet she couldn't hide in her room forever. There had to be a way to face him without getting stung. She sighed softly. Hopefully she'd figure out what it was soon.

She stood, eased out the tension in her leg, and straightened her spine. Then she made herself step out.

Rain was beating heavily against the misty windows

while the wind raged outside. Grunts and thuds echoed from the training room the Wraiths had made in what had once been the formal dining room, followed by catcalls and laughter. The men not on guard duty were blowing off steam.

All except Reece. *He* was sitting at the small table, big hands wrapped around a tankard, taking slow sips as he stared out at the pelting winter shower. Close enough to her little room that if she didn't know better, she might have thought he was guarding her door.

His position gave her a moment to look at him properly. Sitting like this, relaxed, but with an aura of awareness, he was even more attractive than she'd realized before... and she had definitely been aware of how gorgeous he was, even when he was being an ass.

Maybe it was because she was starting to understand him a little, to see the man underneath the armor. For the first time, she could see a hint of the partner the Hawks had promised.

His hands tightened on the mug, and, for a moment, she wondered what it would be like if he put those hands on her. They would be hot and firm, his fingers long and capable. He would drag them over her skin, his intensity utterly focused on her. He would—

He turned to look at her, gaze flickering over her face, his expression blank and unreadable, his armor firmly back in place.

Hell. She let out a slow breath, letting her ridiculous thoughts go too. They'd had a moment out in the garden, but it didn't mean anything. She'd already decided to work alone. And given where this particular mission was most likely to lead, that was probably for the best, anyway.

Daena ignored the ache in her chest as she made her

way into the kitchen. She helped herself to a small mug of ale from the barrel beside the door and then hesitated. She didn't want to take the only other chair; the one next to Reece at the small table.

Instead, she walked to the hearth, careful not to get too close, and sipped her ale. It was watery and slightly sour, but it was refreshing too, and it distracted her from thinking too closely about the flames.

The door to the kitchen opened, and she looked up to see Andred striding inside. He was looking at her with such intense disdain that she couldn't stop her flinch. She immediately fought to hide it, blanking her face and stepping away from the fireplace. The last thing she needed was to be caught between Andred and the flames. But Andred didn't even seem to notice.

Reece, on the other hand…. Hell. He was looking right at her, a furrow deepening down his forehead.

Andred focused on Reece. "I need you to get us more of that black powder, the explosive you used to collapse the path outside the courts."

Reece stood slowly, leaving his tankard on the table as his eyes locked on Andred. She could almost hear the gears turning in his head. He wanted to ask what the powder was for, but they all knew Andred didn't like being questioned. And he would hate it even more coming from Reece.

"What for?" she asked, breaking into the silence so Reece didn't have to.

Andred glared at her over his shoulder. "Nothing you need to know about."

"I can get it for you, General Andred, but not today." Reece gestured toward the window. "The winds are too high. The ferry will be closed."

"Fine," Andred grunted. "Tomorrow, then. You have

four hours to get into Kaerlud and back." And then he strode back out, slamming the door behind him.

Daena watched Andred leave, irritation at his surly dismissal of her question warring with relief that he'd gone. She'd known how difficult it would be to be back with the Wraiths, but she'd spent so much time thinking about the danger that she hadn't really thought about what it would be like to have to see Andred every day. To have to work for him again.

Reece stepped up beside her, his frown even deeper. "I don't understand," he murmured, voice low. "You look at him like you hate him."

"I do hate him," she replied quietly. Although, in all honesty, hate probably wasn't strong enough for what she felt.

Reece looked down at her, his expression genuinely confused. "You chose to support him. You told me you never wanted to be a truth seeker, and yet you were... for him."

Hell. Maybe she should have stayed hidden in her room after all.

She had explained everything to the Hawks. They'd accepted her summary of what had happened without expecting her to explain her feelings. They'd never asked, and she hadn't wanted to relive it ever again.

But now, looking into Reece's sincere gaze, she knew she was going to have to. This was important for him to understand. He had shared the pain of his past; now it was her turn.

"You already know I left Eshcol because I didn't want to be a truth seeker," she started. "I wanted to be a herbalist. I was looking for better treatments for the red plague."

Reece's beast rumbled, the soft noise blending with the

tapping of the rain as a flurry of unsettled scales fluttered at his throat, but he didn't comment, so she continued. "I moved to Staith against my family's wishes." She'd been young and arrogant and so convinced she was right. She was going to save lives. She was going to make a difference. And she was going to show *everyone*.

But it didn't mean she had no doubts; it didn't take away from the loneliness. And that's where Andred caught her. He was handsome, charming, and powerful. He had told her she was beautiful and clever and that she could change the world, and she'd reveled in it. Until everything changed.

"There was a fire," she whispered. "Now I know"—she stroked the scar on the side of her face with her thumb, just for a moment—"Andred set it to destroy the evidence after Ravenstone."

Reece was utterly still, utterly focused on her, but she could hear his beast growling softly in the silence. "He set fire to the building you were in?" he asked, voice strained.

"I don't think he knew…." Her eyes stung. Either way, she'd been an afterthought. "When he realized, he came in and pulled me out. He took me with the Wraiths into the mountains."

"He didn't take you to a healer?" Reece's face gleamed where his scales crept over his hard jaw.

"No." Her voice was a lower than a whisper. "He said it was too dangerous."

And it was… too dangerous for Andred. But she hadn't known that yet. She'd been hurting, lonely, and so very far away from everything she knew. All her hard work was gone —her plants were destroyed—and she was still coming to terms with the scars on her body. She had wanted comfort and reassurance. She'd wanted his love.

She'd thought he'd saved her. That he'd brought her

with him on his mission. And she'd wanted to prove herself to him. In hindsight, she should have known better. Should have seen that only she could recognize her own value. *That* had been a harsh lesson to learn. But back then, she hadn't learned it yet.

Andred—the man she loved—wanted this one thing. This one thing that only she could do. "He said he needed help. He needed... me. Because otherwise, the kingdom would be in danger. People would die."

So, she'd done it. She had become a truth seeker. Catching lies and revealing truths. She had forced herself to stand and listen to the reivers and the mutineers and the deserters, and by the end of every day, she'd been utterly exhausted and filled with revulsion.

Food had begun to taste of ash and acid. Her life was a never-ending stream of foul lies. But she did it because she loved Andred, and because she believed him when he said they were saving Brythoria.

She had forced herself not to think about the family she'd left behind. The family who she'd fought with bitterly, their very last conversation one of irritation and disbelief—on both sides. And she threw herself into the work she'd convinced herself was the right thing to do.

She'd worked hard and ended each day utterly wrung out. But she'd ended it in Andred's arms, and she slept deeply. Andred was the king of their world, and she was his queen.... Until the night she'd woken to the sound of rough voices.

Men were arguing outside the front of the tent she shared with Andred. Not just any men: Caius, Usna, and Andred. Maybe the lieutenants realized she was sleeping just on the other side and wanted her to hear. She never knew.

Caius and Usna had tolerated her when she was living in Staith, but they hated that she was with them in the mountains. She was not a soldier, and she was not Apollyon. She was their weak link. And, even worse, Andred had given her some small amounts of power.

They didn't care if Andred fucked her, but they did care if she was going to take the authority they saw as rightfully theirs. And they cared a great deal about having a Nephilim as their queen.

The three men were arguing about Ballanor. News had come in that the new king had died in combat against Lanval of the Hawks. News that no one had bothered to share with her. Gods. It had been shocking, the horror of realizing she hadn't been told something of such vital importance to what they were doing.

What was the point of the war they were preparing for if Ballanor was already dead?

She had raised herself slowly on the low cot, ears straining. Andred wanted to ride south immediately and take his place on the throne. He wanted to ensure that no northern princess could take his rightful place. Caius and Usna felt they weren't ready. They wanted to recruit more soldiers and spend the winter training them. There was talk of Tristan supporting Alanna—Val was his best friend, after all—and what it might mean if the widowed queen brought in Verturian forces. Caius and Usna were concerned their small untrained force with reivers outnumbering Wraiths three-to-one would quickly lose.

Andred had laughed. "We don't need more soldiers," he'd said. "We can pick up men on the way south. Soldiers are waiting for us in Kaerlud. We have powerful men ready to support us. You know this."

"We won't know if they're loyal—"

"Daena will test them."

"What if she——" Caius started.

"She will do as she's told," Andred had retorted. And although his tone had stung, she'd held her breath and waited.

"Fuck Daena," Caius had replied heatedly. "I still think——"

"I do," Andred had cut him off, amusement threading through his words. Gods, his voice had been so smug. So arrogant. "That's what she's here for, after all. Fucking and playing truth seeker."

Playing truth seeker. And for fucking. Not for anything else. Even remembering it made her throat clench around the rising misery, the burn of shame.

Usna had chuckled then, raising his voice mockingly. "You sure? You've been looking very cozy." His voice hardened. "Are you certain you don't want her on the throne beside you in Kaerlud?"

Andred had snorted. "Fuck, no. I've told you this before. Daena has one job. And while she does it, she might as well do it from my bed. Gods, can you imagine her as queen of anything?" They'd all laughed at that. As if the idea was ludicrous. So utterly contemptible. As if she was nothing at all.

Her belly had spasmed, and she'd leaned over retching, shoving the blanket into her mouth to keep from making a sound. Not only at his words. At the fact that they tasted of nothing at all. They were the truth.

She had become everything she hated. She had abandoned the people she loved to become a truth seeker. Everything she'd thought about his feelings for her had been built in her own head. All for a man who didn't respect her at all. Who didn't love her. Who didn't even like her.

Even now, she could feel the churning agony of understanding. She had become a truth seeker, but she was the worst truth seeker in the world. She hadn't seen the truth in the man she had thought she would spend forever with.

"Everything was a lie. The more I learned, the more I realized…." Her voice trailed away into silence. How could she explain the depth of her horror? Her regret? She shuddered, her legs tiring, and she realized Reece had wrapped his hand around her arm. Not hard. As if he was holding her up.

She tried to make herself smile, but she could feel it pulling at her cheeks uncomfortably.

Something inside her had broken that night. But she had still forced herself to stand and dress. Forced herself to grab her battered old satchel, the only thing she had left from her old life, and walk out into the dark night, surrounded by enemies. And that's what she'd been doing ever since.

"Daena?" The worry in Reece's voice brought her back to the quiet kitchen, the rain still streaming down the windows like silver tears.

"I loved him," she admitted. "I thought he loved me. I wanted to help him. And I believed him when he told me he was going to save us all."

Reece swallowed. His gray eyes had a thin ring of sapphire blue gleaming around the irises. How had she never noticed that before? "But you're a truth seeker."

She bristled, and he tightened his grip, turning her to look right at him. "I'm not… I'm not trying to piss you off," he murmured. "I just want to understand. Please."

The weight of his hand was strangely captivating. Some deep part of her wished he would pull her closer. That he would wrap her in his arms and tell her everything would be okay. But he didn't. He merely watched her, waiting patiently, his beast rattling between them.

"Andred is one of the most intelligent people I've ever met," she admitted. "He lives for strategy. For playing the long game. He's very, very good at only showing the cards he wants to show." She dropped her eyes, unable to bear the intensity of Reece's focus. "And I'm sure it gave him something… extra. I'm sure he loved getting away with manipulating a truth seeker. Again, and again."

"Gods." Reece let out a rough sigh. He dropped his hand, leaving her arm tingling in the cold. But he didn't step away.

"I know how that feels," he admitted roughly. "Being lied to and never suspecting until you learn the truth. The horror of seeing the world ripped apart because you believed the wrong person. Realizing that other people have been hurt because of the mistakes you made. It made me… I mean, I *want* to believe in the Hawks, I should be able to trust my squad, shouldn't I? But even them…." He shook his head roughly. "I pushed them all away."

His jaw clenched, and for a moment she could feel the pain that had driven him away from his friends. From the men she knew still saw him as a brother. The pain that he was hiding beneath his thorny words and prickly mistrust.

Reece grunted. The sapphire faded from his eyes, and he looked slightly appalled, as if he hadn't meant to reveal nearly as much as he had. He dipped his chin and let himself out of the kitchen, clearly fleeing.

The door clicked closed behind him, and she finally let herself sink into the hard wooden chair beside the window. The memories, the things she'd revealed, had left her feeling hollowed out and raw, and she needed a moment.

She moved to shove Reece's abandoned tankard out her way and then paused. That wasn't ale. She stared down into the creamy contents of the pewter mug, not quite understanding what she was looking at. Reece had been drinking milk.

Chapter Ten

REECE STEPPED off the ferry into Kaerlud surrounded by the sound of gulls squabbling. The water of the Tamasa River was gray and dark at the best of times, now it was still churning with the tail end of yesterday's storm.

It hadn't stopped the fishing boats though. This time of year, when the waters were cold and dark, the cod came in closer to the shore, and the true monsters could be caught. It was a vital, lucrative time of year for the fishermen and their families—and for the whole of Kaerlud.

His papa had worked those boats. A rough, heavy man, Tarasque like Reece and his mama, broad and strong with a booming laugh.

I miss him.

Gods. How many years had it been since he'd thought about his papa? Too long. Because the truth was, Reece missed him too.

His beast was right. He'd hated Papa for dying and leaving them alone, and then clung so hard to the idea that his real father was still alive, that if he could just make himself into the right kind of son, he would get that family, that safety back. It was only now that he was starting to realize that Papa had been his true father all along.

Daena gave us that.

Reece grunted. Thinking about Daena unsettled him. Everything she'd revealed, the depth of the vulnerability in her eyes when she'd told her story, had made him want to hunt Andred down and kill him slowly.

He'd had to get away from her, because if he hadn't, he would have taken her in his arms right there in the kitchen, and if any of the Wraiths had seen it… gods.

We have to keep her safe.

And that meant not exposing her to any more pain from Andred. And also meant that he had to make good use of this short reprieve. He needed to get in, update Tor, get the explosives Andred wanted, and get back as quickly as possible. All without being seen.

He turned into a narrow alley, leaned against the wall, and settled in for a cold wait. Andred had given him four hours and most of the first hour was already gone, but he had to be absolutely certain no one had followed him.

By the time the road had filled and cleared twice, he was confident no one was behind him. He lifted the hood of his cloak over his head, took a moment to stoop his shoulders and bend his knees, then staggered from the darkness, bumping into things, mumbling and doing his best to look like he'd spent the better part of the morning drinking.

No one even glanced at him. Perhaps Daena's endorsement had finally convinced the Wraiths to trust him after all.

He reached the dingy pub and pushed his way inside, still muttering loudly about brandy, and sidled along the wall until he could settle into the darkest corner. This had become their usual table, and Tor was already there.

Every time they met, something lifted a little inside Reece. A spark of surprise and relief. It wasn't that he thought Tor would ever break his promise—he'd said that he would be there for an hour every morning in case Reece could get away, and Tor always did what he said he would—it was more that Reece knew how he'd behaved, how rude he'd been to Alanna, to Keely, but also to Tor, Mathos, Tristan… everyone.

Tor grunted his hello and pushed a tankard of ale across the table. Reece didn't need to take a sip to know how vinegary it would be. And, for the first time, he found he didn't want to take that first sip. Didn't need his beast to be half asleep before he could have this conversation. He pushed it to the side as he greeted his friend.

Tor folded his heavy arms over his chest, black and red tattoos visible in the gap where his heavy cloak had fallen open. He gave Reece a long, slow inspection. "How are you?"

Reece shrugged. How was anyone in this situation?

"How is she?" Tor asked.

"She's… complicated."

Tor's eyebrow rose in such a familiar way that Reece almost laughed. It came out as a half snort instead, and Tor's eyebrow rose even higher.

"She's fine," Reece muttered. And then he found himself adding, "She has a… depth to her. I didn't expect…."

You were expecting Helaine.

Gods. Was that true? Maybe it was. He'd definitely expected Daena to be fickle and untrustworthy. And it had been unfair. He'd been an ass when all she'd done was try to help. She'd gone back to the Wraiths for Lucilla when it was clearly a living hell for her.

Daena's brave. And strong. Beautiful—

It was true. The beast had been saying it for days, but now he saw it too. Reece swallowed hard and then choked on nothing. Gods. What had happened to him? He used to be so suave.

His beast huffed out a burst of mocking laughter.

"How are the Hawks?" Reece asked, desperate to change the subject. "Is everyone well?"

Tor watched him silently for a long moment, dark eyes fixed on his, and Reece waited for a brief, impersonal response that didn't mean much, or perhaps a query as to why he wanted to know. But all Tor did was nod slowly. He must have seen something in Reece, some need to feel closer to the people he'd walked away from because instead of answering, "Everyone is fine," and then retreating into his usual silence like Reece expected, Tor started to speak.

"Val and Alanna are still in the north, but they've sent messages," he murmured, too low for anyone else to hear. "They're well, although they're both looking forward to the snow clearing so they can come home. I don't think Alanna likes being in Duneidyn with her mother telling her what to do. Thankfully the treaty is signed."

Thank the gods of fire. Finally.

"Tristan has taken to spending an hour every day training Nim and Lucilla on how to use a sword properly," Tor continued. "Although I don't know how much longer he'll last, now they're starting to do some real damage."

"What about Keely? Couldn't she join them?" Reece asked, indignant on her behalf. She was astonishingly good with a crossbow, and it grated that she hadn't been included.

He still felt deeply ashamed about the things he'd said to her, and this only made it worse.

"Of course, now that her morning sickness is so much better. But she—"

Reece stilled. "Her... what?"

"Her morning sickness," Tor replied quietly.

Gods. Everyone else must have known. Tor had said it so matter-of-factly. But Reece had stayed away for so long. He'd missed so much. And now.... "You're having a baby?"

A slow grin spread over Tor's face. An actual grin. On the most stoic man Reece had ever known.

"Yes," Tor replied. And in that one word, Reece could hear whole poems, volumes even, of Tor's utter, overwhelming delight.

Tor was going to be a father. Tor, who had been disowned. Whose blood family was even now plotting against the queen. He had come back from that... to this. He'd become the man grinning like the sun had risen on everything he ever wanted, despite sitting in the dingiest tavern in Kaerlud, sipping the worst ale in the world.

This is what Mama gave us.

Gods. Mama had given him a family who had truly wanted him. A father who had known the truth... and chose him anyway.

Reece rubbed at the heavy ache in his chest, only half listening as Tor explained that Keely was more experienced using a sword than Nim and Lucilla—and didn't want to join their mock battles, which were getting increasingly violent—so she was focusing on the crossbow until after the baby came.

"Congratulations, Tor," Reece said, his voice thick with emotion. "You'll be a wonderful father."

Tor smiled softly. "That's what Keely said."

Reece cleared his throat. "Please send my congratulations to her. Tell her… tell her I wish you both only the best."

"Thank you, Reece. That will mean a lot to her."

Tor said it with such quiet sincerity, such utter belief, that Reece couldn't help but believe it too. And another fracture in his soul quietly healed.

They sat together for a long moment as Tor sipped his ale and Reece's beast rumbled gently. He would have loved to sit there all day, learning more about what had happened since he left. Feeling as if, even from a distance, he could be a small part of the Hawks family. But he couldn't stay. As much as he wanted to know more, as much as he kicked himself for not asking before, he had to get back to Andred.

And to Daena.

Tor pushed his ale to the side with Reece's abandoned tankard. His frown deepened once more as he turned his focus entirely to Reece and lowered his voice even further. "Have you found anything?"

Reece updated him about the councilors' meeting with Andred. It physically hurt to have to say that Pellin had been there, especially when Tor started cracking his knuckles, his relaxed grin long gone.

By the time Reece had finished explaining what had happened with Gaheris, Tor looked liable to murder someone. "I don't like this," Tor muttered. "Maybe we should pull you both out."

"We need to know who they're working with," Reece replied. "You know as well as I do, if we destroy the Wraiths now, someone else will simply step into the gap. Until we know which of the councilors are supporting this conspiracy, we'll never be able to trust any of them."

"I wish we could just arrest them all and put them in

front of Ramiel," Tor muttered. "The Supreme Justice can sort it out."

Reece grunted. It wasn't as if he hadn't thought the same thing. But they both knew the answer. If Lucilla started her rule by throwing dozens of potentially innocent people into Gatehouse Prison—never mind the upheaval for their families and households—and then dragged them through the courts based on nothing but her own suspicions.... Gods. "Lucilla would be hated. She would be...."

"Ballanor," Tor finished gruffly. "She would be Ballanor." He gave his knuckles one last crack. "I still hate that you're in there. I hate that this was my idea."

"We'll find out who they are and get out," Reece reassured him.

Tor gave him a slow look. Reluctance was written in his dark eyes, but after a moment he dipped his chin in agreement. "The safehouses we chose are set up for you in Kaerlud. We have a squad waiting on the north side of the river and sentries hidden among the farmhouses around the Wraiths, ready to ride in. Do you remember the signal?"

Reece grunted. It was hardly difficult to remember: get a shirt onto the roof. Actually achieving it would be the challenge. The Wraiths had sentries of their own watching the house. They were hardly about to stand around letting him set a signal without immediately responding, and that response would be swift and brutal.

He'd thought of Daena off and on all morning, but now the image of her fleeing the house—running from the Wraiths—rose up in his mind, and his beast growled unhappily.

We should get back.

A surge of concern rose through him. A foreign need to

protect and guard. But he pushed it away. Daena was perfectly fine without him. She was a survivor. Strong and clever. She didn't need him. She—

We need her.

No. That wasn't… that couldn't…. Gods.

"Reece?" Tor prompted gruffly.

Reece focused on his friend, bringing his mind back to the question he'd asked. "Yes. I remember."

"Do you need anything to take back with you?" Tor asked, lifting a heavy satchel onto the table.

"More of the explosive powder, please." Fuck. He'd almost forgotten.

Tor passed him two heavy flasks. "Be careful, Reece. Okay? Promise me."

Chapter Eleven

WAS it possible to hate a room?

Yes. It was. And not just because of what had happened to Gaheris the last time they were in here... but because of the look on Reece's face as he carefully ignored the gory image of the dead dragon on the wall.

Andred had abandoned his small, overcrowded study in favor of bringing a large wooden table into the receiving room. A table currently surrounded by Andred, Usna, Caius, Reece... and her. At least today Andred had given her a stool to sit on.

Part of her wished the Hawks could've simply swooped down on the farmhouse as soon as Reece identified where the Wraiths were hiding, and she'd never had to stand beside the Wraiths pretending to be one of them once more. Part of her wished she could pick up the letter opener lying unused in the middle of the table and stab Andred in the heart, no matter the consequences. But neither of those were options. Andred always had a backup plan for his backup plan. This was their chance to find out exactly who was supporting him, who else would dare to threaten the queen. And the only way to do that was to ride this out. Which meant pasting on a smile, deferring to Andred, and doing her best to look like she actually was at his command. All while Reece watched her.

She had spent the three days since Reece went into Kaerlud harvesting what she could from the kitchen garden, sitting at the small table drinking mint tea, ignoring Caius and Usna… and staying well away from the library.

Reece, on the other hand, had been hanging around the house. He seemed to have made it his mission to watch her. And, when he wasn't sitting with her in the kitchen—which at least included clothes—he was in the library doing push-ups, sit-ups, hundreds of squats, and some kind of abdominal crunch that involved him gripping the doorframe, hands above his head, and then and lifting his legs, grunting with each repetition. Gods, that grunt. It travelled straight down her spine and into her core, every time she heard it.

It was like he'd made it his life's purpose to develop every muscle he had. And he had decided to do it stripped down to only his breeches.

She'd made the mistake of walking past the open door on the first day just as Reece was lowering himself into a one-armed push-up. Sweat had gleamed on his rippling back, his scales an indigo sheen highlighting every defined contour, and her tongue had instantly stuck to the roof of her mouth.

She'd lingered in the doorway, eyes riveted to his movements. The sleek, predatory strength of a powerful Tarasque. Not just any Tarasque—Reece.

Reece, who somehow had come to know more about her than anyone else in the kingdom. Reece, who had shared his secrets first. And who now watched over her like a deadly guardian angel.

She glanced at him while Andred unrolled a set of plans onto the table. His fists were clenched behind his back, his shoulders rigid, a sheen of scales glittering darkly over his biceps. She wanted to stroke her hand over those indigo scales. To taste his skin. To feel those powerful muscles shuddering. Something hot unfurled low in her belly, a feeling she hadn't had for so long, she'd started to believe it was gone forever. She—

Gods and angels. She was sitting at the table beside Andred. She couldn't think like that. Not now. Not when they were surrounded by danger. Maybe not ever.

Reece leaned forward, studying the plans while Andred lounged on her other side. Hell. She was sandwiched between a future she would never have and a past she wished she could forget.

Reece idly scratched his beard with his thumb as he ran his eyes over the hand-drawn schematics. He was still and focused, his gaze thoughtful.

She hadn't thought about how intelligent he was, how much skill it had taken to collapse one tiny piece of road and haul her out from under the noses of the entire city without one person being hurt in the process. But now she did.

Reece swallowed, and the movement of his throat drew her attention. His neck was free of scales, and his throat was tanned. His skin looked warm. Inviting. If she ran her palms over his—

No. Just… no.

"These look accurate to me," Reece said, looking up at Andred. "It shows all the extra fortifications that were added after Ravenstone. Ballanor was a terrible king, but he was as paranoid as fuck." He gestured to the plans. "He added ramparts and battlements with a guarded walkway at the front of the palace and dug through the riverbank to flood the gardens at the back, forming a massive moat circling the grounds. There is only one access point—Court Gate— which is watched by infantry guards day and night."

Andred nodded slowly. "Ballanor was afraid. Rightly."

Hell. Why had she not realized it before? "He was afraid of *you*," Daena whispered.

Caius growled. "If he hadn't double-crossed us, he wouldn't have been afraid. If he'd delivered on his promise, he would still be alive, and we would all be living comfortably in the palace."

Daena almost rolled her eyes. "If he was still alive, you would be at war with Verturia right now."

Caius shook his head. "The Verturians were ready to negotiate. Moireach gave up her daughter without question. A few months of a focused, disciplined siege, and they would have given us the mines too. We would have been back home by now, running the kingdom."

"Home running *what*?" Reece asked, scales gleaming as they slid over his collarbones. "What else did Ballanor promise you?"

"Only what is ours by birthright," Andred replied. "Ballanor appointed me Lord High Chancellor before Ravenstone. He was going to keep the throne warm, and we were going to rule the kingdom."

"No." Reece's scales climbed higher. "Ballanor would never have done that. He was always going to appoint Grendel as his second-in-command. Grendel was his best friend practically from birth."

"Grendel was an idiot with no self-control whatsoever," Andred spat. "Neither of them was fit to rule the kingdom.

They would have spent their days in bed, and I would have made the decisions. Then, when Ballanor inevitably died childless, I would have already been in power. I'd have had control of the Blacks and Blues and the blood of Aloysius in my veins. It would have been a simple thing to take the throne."

"Gods." Reece's face was stark. "You knew about Ballanor. You knew he was never going to manage to…." His voice dropped, threaded through with the rumbling of his beast. "You knew how he treated Alanna."

Caius laughed. "Everyone knew about Ballanor. Bloody hell, Reece, you were at some of those parties."

Reece flinched bodily, the color draining from his face as his scales visibly hardened in a slow midnight-blue wave. "I did *not* know about Ballanor."

His words tasted like air and truth, and his expression was stricken.

Andred shrugged. "Maybe you didn't know. Maybe you didn't *want* to know. I don't care. Either way, we're removing that family from power."

Reece lowered his head, and she could see the battle he was fighting to stay calm. To stop himself from launching himself bodily at Andred. But before she could do something, say *something*, Andred grunted. "Ballanor was a useless child who went back on his word. He put his friend into the position he'd promised me, and then hid behind his hasty fortifications while he stole my future *and* my entire birthright."

"What did he steal?" Daena asked, half hoping she hadn't understood.

"He stole the entire Bar-Otso inheritance. All the lands, the houses, everything. He claimed we had died in Ravenstone. And he took *everything*."

Hell. Andred didn't just hate Ballanor, he utterly detested him.

She almost reached out for Reece, almost took his hand, needing to feel that she wasn't alone in the face of such vicious animosity—needing to let him know that he wasn't alone either—but she stopped herself just in time.

"Our Brythorian people have suffered again and again," Andred spat. "Geraint's line was tainted from birth and entirely unable to rule a kingdom." He smiled, a cold, vicious smile filled with righteous fury. "Which is exactly why we're removing it. All of it."

Daena gripped the rim of her stool and forced herself not to react. Every word Andred said rang with truth and commitment. This was how he'd manipulated her so many times. He utterly believed in everything he'd just said. And he'd left out all the important parts—Ballanor's cruelty, Alanna's suffering, Lucilla's natural aptitude for leadership, her innate strength and the love she had for her people... never mind her birthright to the throne.

"Now," Andred continued, glaring at Reece. "Look at these plans and tell me how to bring down the wall that Ballanor built between the palace and Clock Square."

Reece shook his head. A vibrating growl rumbled from his belly. It was low and lethal, the sound that preceded violence and death. She hadn't thought anyone could hate Andred as much as she did, but Reece was catching up quickly.

Reece jabbed his finger at the plans. "The foundations of the new walls lie beneath the moat. If you bring down the walls, the moat will flood the square in a massive wave, and you'll most likely drown."

Andred stroked his chin, unruffled. "Don't worry about that. Just tell me what you need to bring down."

"You can't bring it down," Reece snapped. "Undermining from within Clock Square is impossible. I heard that Tristan doubled the patrols and added infantry on the roofs. The soldiers on the ramparts will simply shoot anyone who even starts to dig a hole."

Andred glared at Reece. "What would you need, Corporal? Stop giving me excuses." He gestured toward her. "And Daena—I want to know if he's telling the truth. Give me your arm."

Gods, she hated this. Hated his hand on her skin. Hated the way he controlled her. She let out a slow breath and then held out her arm for Andred to grip her wrist. His fingers were painfully tight as her pulse thudded, but she kept her face blank and brought her mind back to her breathing. She wasn't giving him *anything*.

Reece frowned at Andred's fingers pressing into her skin, the thin band of sapphire around his irises flashing. A long, weighted moment passed before he eventually started to speak. "Maybe if you had the flying fire of the Nephilim," he admitted. "If you had one of their cannons, you could take down the wall from a distance."

That sounded horrific—and she could see how much Reece hated suggesting it. How many people would be hurt or lose their livelihoods when the river water flooded out into the city?

Andred shook her arm. "Daena?"

"Truth," she muttered.

"I'll speak to Dionys," Caius said, pleased. "If he doesn't have cannon on his ships already, he'll have contacts who can help. And we already have the remaining black powder."

Remaining? What did that mean? Daena's gaze flew to Reece's, but he looked as horrified as she felt.

Usna ran a finger over the map. "We'll hit both—" he started, but Andred cut him off with a grunted, "Not now." He released her wrist and waved her to the door. "Reece, Daena, you're dismissed."

Reece flashed her an apologetic look, quickly hidden behind his dark frown, before focusing on Andred. "Dismiss Daena." He paused as if he was looking for the right words. "You don't need to involve her in this."

His tone suggested he was undermining her. But the way his hands were bunched behind his back—the way he was standing, angled as if he was about to lunge at Andred— made her think he was trying to help her. Trying to get her away from Andred.

"You are both dismissed." Andred snarled. "That means get the fuck out."

Reece's scowl deepened, but he dipped his head politely and then waited for her to lead him out of the room.

Daena walked slowly into the kitchen with Reece matching her pace one step behind her. She set the kettle onto the fire and then sank into the chair beside the battered old wooden table to wait for it to boil while the tension of the morning slowly drained away.

Reece helped himself to a couple of hard loaves left from the Wraiths' breakfast and a small pot of blackberry jam and set them out on the table before sitting beside her. It was quiet and domestic, a homely activity that somehow —despite the Wraiths all around—felt like safety.

She took a bite, chewing slowly. Gods, she hadn't realized how hungry she was. She'd skipped several meals over the last few days, avoiding spending time with the Wraiths. And, with all the stress, she hadn't been that interested in food anyway. But now, somehow, sitting beside

Reece while his beast rumbled gently, her appetite came back with a vengeance.

They sat together, shoulders almost touching, smearing big dollops of jam onto the bread. The bread was hard, but the jam was sweet with just the right amount of tartness.

"You need to eat more," Reece muttered. He glanced up at her. "I can set something aside for you when the Wraiths eat if that would help."

He sounded so genuinely concerned. And he'd been guarding her, she was sure of it.

It had started to feel as if they'd reached some kind of truce since she'd shared the truth of what happened between her and Andred. But had they really? How could she know for sure?

She finished the last of her bread and licked the jam off the spoon before turning to face him. "I don't understand, Reece. You said you didn't give a flying fuck about what I wanted. You told everyone you don't trust me. Now you're worried about what I eat for breakfast?"

Reece winced. "Sometimes I say stupid shit."

"No, you meant it," she replied. "Truth seeker, remember."

"I meant it at the time," he admitted. "Doesn't mean it wasn't stupid." Reece looked up at her, his face serious. "I used to always know the right thing to say. I was charming, or so I've been told. I made a career of it. Then it all came crashing down, and I couldn't do it anymore. I couldn't say the right thing, so I said all the wrong things instead. And since we've been here"—he dragged his hand tiredly down his face—"I've said several things I would like to take back."

He got up before she could reply, as if he needed to move. He lifted the kettle and poured hot water into a pair of wooden mugs, then added a few of the ancient mint leaves she'd set to dry beside the fire. He settled a mug in front of her, the fragrant steam curling through the air, and then reclaimed his seat.

He looked so alone, his shoulders slightly hunched, his hair in spikes where he'd run his hands through it. He'd been upset and angered by Andred's revelations earlier, but this was something else. He looked… guilty.

"What things?" she asked softly. "What's wrong, Reece?"

He lowered his voice to almost a whisper. "There's something I have to tell you."

Gods and angels. That did not sound good. She wrapped her hands around the wooden mug, letting the steam warm her. "Okay."

"Yesterday, I found out that some of the Wraiths had been following Gaheris long before the little drama Andred orchestrated."

That didn't make any sense. "Why?"

"Gaheris had been gathering support and evidence for his own claim on the throne. Andred heard a rumor from a group of mercenaries he was recruiting and had him followed." Reece watched her carefully. "Daena, Andred knew Gaheris didn't support the Wraiths before he ever questioned him."

Gods. *Gods.* She suddenly understood. "It was a test."

"A test for all of us—you, me, and Gaheris. And a display of strength and power. Pellin and Dionys will have already repeated the story multiple times. The nobles will think very carefully before lying to Andred or trying to cross him now."

"But why would Gaheris…?"

"Same as us, I expect," Reece whispered, almost too softly to hear. "He wanted to learn more about his enemy.

And he probably didn't think through what it meant that you were back with Andred. Or maybe he really was that arrogant."

Daena lifted her mug and took a scorching mouthful. It wasn't just a test, it was a test she'd very nearly failed. A test Gaheris *had* failed—and he'd died as a result.

What kind of hell would Andred have put her through if he thought she'd lied to him? Would she have survived? Or would he have hurt her just enough to make her truly regret it, but kept her alive? Gods.

She wanted to run out the front door and keep on running. She wanted to hide and pretend none of this was real. But she couldn't; she had a job to do, and it wasn't done yet. No matter how frightened she was.

Her eyes burned as her throat tightened around a sob she couldn't allow out. She and Reece were slowly growing to be allies, but it didn't mean she wanted to fall apart in front of him. She had promised herself that she didn't show weakness, not anymore. She swallowed away her tears and lifted her chin.

Reece was still watching her, his face a picture of guilt and remorse, and… respect. Admiration, even. Or was she imagining it? Was she seeing what she wanted to see? Again? Gods. She needed to regroup. Settle herself. She needed a moment.

She stood too abruptly, put pressure on her foot, and nearly crumpled. But then Reece was there. Before she could fling out her arms and catch herself, he was up, hauling her into his chest, his arms just as warm and firm around her as she'd known they would be.

When last had someone held her in their arms? Tor— when he carried her up the gorge? And before that, Andred…. Gods.

Reece's touch was warm and reassuring. He smelled of leather and fresh air, and a rumbling growl from his belly vibrated against her.

She almost nestled into him, almost let herself enjoy the shelter of his firm grip, the rise and fall of his hard chest, the heat of his skin against hers. Almost allowed herself to feel the attraction that had been growing steadily between them for days.

"Gods. Are you okay?" he asked urgently. "Fuck, Daena. You need to be more careful!"

And just like that, he shattered the strange bubble. The very last thing she needed was for Reece to feel sorry for her. She'd been wrong when she thought he admired her; it had been guilt and pity all along. Suddenly his earlier concern felt extraordinarily patronizing. Gods. She was attracted to another man who didn't respect her at all.

She stumbled back, using her hand on the table to stabilize herself so she could find her footing and stalk away.

"I'm fine," she muttered. "And I don't need help from *you*."

Chapter Twelve

REECE WATCHED Daena disappear into her tiny room and slam the door behind her.

Well. You fucked that up.

Gods. He really had. One minute he'd had his arms around a beautiful, compelling woman. A woman who, he was coming to realize, was trying her best to protect Lucilla and the Hawks, despite her fears and the very real danger she was in.

She'd been warm and soft, and she had sighed against his chest. It was such a small, soft noise, but it was the most genuine sound he'd ever heard. Something deeply buried inside him had wanted to hear that sound again. Wanted to be worthy of it.

They'd faced Andred side by side that morning. For the first time, they were true allies, partners even. He'd been grateful to have her there, supporting him, supporting Lucilla, like the keystone of an arch, quietly holding everything together.

And the whole time, he'd known he was going to have to

hurt her again.

He'd seen how devastated she was when he accused her —wrongly—of being responsible for Gaheris's death. He had always been in the wrong, but it was even worse now, knowing how Andred had set her up. Knowing how easily she could have failed.

Her horror had been palpable and a surge of protectiveness had flooded through him, too potent to ignore.

When she'd tripped, he'd started moving before he even thought about it. If she'd fallen, if he'd had to watch her pull herself off the floor with that same devastation on her face, it would have broken something in him.

And then he had fucked it up.

He hadn't meant to. He was just… overwhelmed. The instant he'd wrapped his arms around her, a tidal wave of confusion had swamped him. He was starting to like her and it was deeply unsettling.

He didn't want to be vulnerable to anyone. It was much easier to see her as his enemy, to see *everyone* as his enemy. Realizing he'd got it all wrong was fucking with his head. On top of that, he now had this inexplicable, unrelenting need to protect her—even though she clearly didn't want or need it from him.

He needed her to be safe, damn it. He needed her to take better care. So, of course, he'd opened his mouth and berated her. He'd hurt her feelings and pissed her off. Again. Fuck it all.

He hadn't ever had this problem before. Before Ravenstone, women had loved him. It had always been so easy to say the right thing. To charm and flirt, and then walk away hardly remembering what he'd said and done, entirely unscathed by the experience.

His beast snorted. *I doubt Alanna and Keely would agree. Or Helaine. Or Mathos. Tor. Any of the Hawks, really….*

Yeah. Well. That was *after* Ravenstone. By then he'd lost any kind of ability to charm anyone. And all he'd had left was a bottomless pit of guilt and rage.

And none of those people confused him like Daena did. He certainly had never spent any time wondering what they were doing. Worrying whether they were eating or sleeping. He had never watched the emotions playing across their faces and wished that he could just wipe away the past and start again.

Gods. He hadn't truly understood how much danger she was in. Honestly, he'd expected Andred to take her back with open arms and for her to run straight into them. But the whole situation was far more complex—and far more dangerous for her—than he'd wanted to imagine. And now Andred and his men were sitting around a map of the palace planning their attack.

Reece paced to the window to stare out at the kitchen garden, hardly noticing the low clouds and hazy rain misting over the weeds and brambles as the image of the Wraiths leaning over the schematics played through his mind.

Usna had tapped the map. He had run his finger along the line of the palace wall. But now that Reece thought about it, it wasn't the wall they'd been discussing. Usna had run his finger down the wall on the far side of the palace… the sea wall.

It was definitely a weak point. Hell, they'd rescued Val and Nim through the ancient Water Gate. Since then, Tristan had sealed that tunnel, filling it with stone and adding extra patrols to the battlements. But if a cannon was firing on the front wall, moat water pouring out onto the square, then the guards on the battlements would run to help… leaving the river access poorly defended.

Men on boats could use grappling hooks to haul themselves over the wall and into the palace. Or worse… if they had Mabin with them, their soldiers could simply fly over. Andred would never let a Mabin warrior into the Wraiths, but he would have no problem with using other races when it suited him. Daena was proof of that.

It made perfect sense. A massive diversion and an attack from the rear was exactly Andred's style. But when would he do it? When would the castle be at its most vulnerable?

Tor would know.

Yes, Tor would know. This was how they had always worked—Tor on strategy, Reece on engineering, Mathos tracking and telling jokes, Rafe healing their wounds, and Tristan keeping them all in line. Gods, he missed them. Missed how Jeremiel and Garet always seemed to know what the other was thinking. How Jos took care of them all, and how Val stood at their backs, protective and honorable.

Reece should have told them how important they were before it came to this. Now that he was sober, now that he was working with Daena, he could finally admit that of all the stupid things he'd done, refusing his brothers' support was truly the most foolish.

We need to let them know what we've learned, his beast rumbled.

Reece closed his eyes, considering. He couldn't leave without orders from Andred, not without raising suspicion. If he disappeared and the Wraiths began to wonder whether Daena knew where he'd gone or if she was working with him… fuck. He couldn't risk it.

No, he only had two options: wait until Andred sent him into Kaerlud and update Tor then, or wait until they had enough information to justify running. Then they could run together. But waiting to observe all the nobles Andred was meeting with could take weeks. Weeks they didn't have.

There'll be a list. Once we have the list, we can get out.

"What list?" he muttered under his breath.

A list of all the nobles and councilors working with the Wraiths. You've seen Andred's desk; he has lists for everything.

A list. Gods. His beast was right. Andred would have documented his plan—he needed to keep track of who supported him and exactly what they offered—and he would want to punish those who didn't. But where would he keep it?

It wouldn't be in the study. Anyone could go in there, and Andred was far too relaxed about letting people wander in and out. No, he would want complete control of this information.

Reece's eyes flew up to the ceiling. Damn. Only Andred, Caius, and Usna were allowed upstairs. None of the Wraiths would dream of going into any of those rooms. If Andred was going to leave such a sensitive document anywhere, it would be there. But if Reece was caught in Andred's room, it would all be over. How could he get up there without raising suspicion?

Daena can go up while we keep watch.

Hell no. And also, fuck no. That was a terrible idea. If they caught her, what would they do to her?

His beast growled softly. *Tell her. Ask for her help. Show her you trust her.*

Did he trust her though? He admired her. He liked her. He was attracted to her. He'd shared things with her that he hadn't shared with anyone before. But complete trust? That was a lot.

And yet....

Chapter Thirteen

SHE WAS INSANE. She had to be. It was the only possible explanation.

When Reece had tapped on her door the day after... whatever had happened in the kitchen, she'd been ready to tell him exactly what he could do with his arrogant, patronizing assumptions.

She'd spent many hours planning a perfectly withering speech. And not, in any way, thinking about how hard his chest was. Or how firm his grip was. Or how his skin had smelled of salt and leather. Or how he'd held her as if he couldn't imagine letting go.

She definitely hadn't thought of any of that. Especially when she knew he *would* let her go. Oh, he might want to hold her for a while. They were thrown together here, surrounded by enemies. But then, when all this was over, he would go back to the palace to his parties and his prestige, his beautiful, popular women. And she.... She probably wasn't making it out of this mess. But if she did, she would go back to her seedlings and her quiet solitude.

She was never going to be a palace party girl, and she didn't want to be one, either. If Reece couldn't respect her for who she was, he could fuck right off.

But then, before she had even opened her mouth, he'd apologized. And then he'd asked for help. He'd told her his idea, and he'd said that he needed her. He'd even—gods damn it—said he couldn't do it without her. And he'd looked her in the eye, his words ringing with honesty the entire time.

It was bad enough when he was an attractive asshole. But now he was being reasonable. And vulnerable. Damn him.

Which was why she was creeping up the stairs, desperately trying to avoid any creaking floorboards. Reece had given her one of his daggers, and she'd stuck it in her belt, a reassuring presence at her side. What she would do with it, she had no idea. Dagger fighting wasn't high on the teaching schedule for truth seekers or herbalists. Still, she was glad to have it.

Reece had seen Andred and his lieutenants leaving out the front gate and had confirmed that everyone else was on patrol or sleeping in the library. They had a chance, and they had to take it. And if they could find a list of Andred's supporters…. Reece was right, it was worth the risk.

The stairs groaned quietly with every step, the ancient floorboards warped from long disuse, and the threadbare carpet offered no cushioning either. She felt every squeak like a trumpet blaring, calling out to the Wraiths both inside and outside the house. One of the men in the library might suddenly wake up and wander into the entrance hall to see her sneaking up the stairs. Or perhaps soldiers would come in from patrol, and there she'd be, fully visible from the front door. Gods. She sped up, using her grip on the banister to haul her body up faster.

Reece had promised that he would wait in the hall, standing guard. That he would warn her if someone started up the stairs. But how would that help her? If she was caught in Andred's rooms, no amount of warning would save her.

By the time she reached the landing, she was sweating. Not just from dragging herself up such steep, uneven stairs, but from the constant thrumming fear.

She pressed herself against the wall and looked around. A faded red-and-gold rug ran the length of the short corridor, closed wooden doors marking the rooms that Andred had claimed for himself and his lieutenants.

She hadn't even considered that the doors might be locked. What would she do then?

She wiped her damp palms on her skirt and then tried the handle of the first door on her left. It turned down and the door swung open. A four-poster bed dominated the room. Sun-bleached curtains were tied messily back, blankets and pillows left tangled. The bed looked soft and warm. And they had given her a pile of horse blankets to sleep on. Gods. Just when she thought she couldn't possibly hate the Wraiths any more than she already did, she learned something new.

She looked under the bed, behind the curtains, in the mostly empty wardrobe, but aside from a spare tunic and a bedroll tossed against the wall, there was nothing.

The next room was the same, although far neater. Bed sheets pulled to form sharp angles, a set of shirts neatly folded in the drawers. Usna's room, she suspected. It would fit with his rigid perfectionism. The wardrobe was much bigger—big enough to hold a person—but also almost completely empty. The belongings they'd lost in the fire had obviously never been replaced. Maybe they were waiting for the riches from the palace. Whatever the reason, this room held nothing useful.

How long had she taken? Did Reece have any real idea of when Andred would be back? She bit her lip, listening, but everything was quiet.

She let herself out of Usna's room, crossed the corridor, and tried the opposite door. It didn't budge. Damn it all, this one was locked. From the placement of the doors, it was obviously the biggest of all the rooms—probably Andred's —but it didn't help at all if she couldn't get inside.

She left it and moved down the corridor to the smallest door, right at the end. The handle turned under her hand, and she let out a shaky breath.

Gods and angels, each new room ramped up her fear. Would this be the room she was trapped in? Cold sweat slid down her ribs as she made herself open the door and go inside.

It was a woman's room, dry and dusty with disuse. It was far smaller than the other two—the space being taken by the large adjacent suite—but more feminine. The curtains were a dusky rose, the headboard was carved with stylized flowers, and a small dressing table sat beside the wardrobe, an ancient, abandoned brush still littering its surface.

Hell. There was a mirror.

Daena wandered closer. There hadn't been a mirror in the mountain camp, or her barracks room in Staith, and no one had thought to bring one into her cell. She certainly hadn't reminded them.

Oh, she knew that there was a scar on her face. When the beam landed on her leg, an ember had broken off and fallen on her cheek. She had tried to brush it away, but in the agony and confusion, she'd dragged it over her skin. That line down her cheek had healed into a mix of smooth and rough, the texture so familiar now.

Compared to the damage and pain in her ankle, it was hardly worth thinking about. But there was something especially vulnerable about having those marks on her cheek. Where people could—and often did—stare. Their eyes flickering away from hers to linger for a moment on her face, before darting away once more, embarrassed.

Actually, now that she thought about it, Reece had never done that. He only ever looked her right in the eye. Gods. What a time to realize something like that.

She looked at the mirror, debating. She could leave it. But wouldn't that be the same as hiding in her room? Wasn't it better to know?

She sank onto the threadbare stool and looked at herself for the first time in close to a year. She tilted her head to the side and ran her fingers slowly down the burn. It was a reddish-pink, ridged and swirled, a distinct contrast to the smooth skin on the other side of her face.

She ran her fingers over it as she'd done so many times before, the texture as familiar to her as the image in the mirror was unfamiliar.

Part of her had expected she might grieve, as she had in the long, painful days after her accident. Perhaps feel angry or bitter. Perhaps even wish to have her face returned to what it used to be. But she didn't.

She was thinner, too thin probably, and dark circles bruised beneath her eyes, but she was still *her*. Her eyes were still the same deep violet, her hair the same mahogany, her nose slightly pointed like it always had been.

Her expression was more thoughtful now, more serious.

She'd seen more. Thought more. Survived more.

She felt sad over the loss of her naivety; of course she did. The loss of that blissful time when she'd been so certain of herself and anything had seemed possible. But, with that loss of innocence had come an understanding that she hadn't had before. She'd lost the sense of entitlement she'd grown up with—the daughter of powerful Nephilim, protected and favored—and replaced it with far deeper understanding. Empathy. Wisdom. And slowly, a growing understanding of her own true strength.

Now, sitting here in front of the mirror, she finally let go of the recriminations and self-hatred that she'd spent so much time drowning in. She'd made mistakes, but she was fixing them. This wasn't a show for the Wraiths or Reece. She wasn't hiding her vulnerability. She was genuinely strong.

Without stopping to think about it, she reached out to the mirror and touched its cold surface. She was still here. She was *alive*.

A dog barked somewhere outside, and she startled. She'd taken too long. Spent too much time sitting in front of the mirror.

She pushed herself up and away from the dressing table and quickly searched the room. The wardrobe was empty, as were the drawers. There was nothing under the bed.

There was a curtain in the back corner, and she pulled it back, expecting a painting or perhaps a wardrobe set into the wall. Instead, she found a door with a small, rusted bolt. She slid the bolt to the side, wincing as it grated noisily, and tried to open the door. Nothing happened. She pushed hard against the door and it rattled in its frame, but it still didn't open.

She leaned closer, eyeing the gap between the non-hinged side of the door and the frame. Maybe the door had once fitted neatly, but now the wood had swollen and warped, and there was a narrow opening running down its length. Through the gap, she could see the dark iron of a large latch bar, no doubt used to lock the door from the other side. The door was barred. But she wasn't going to walk away; she had to get into that room.

She leaned her weight against the doorframe, widening the gap as much as she could. Then she pulled out the dagger Reece had given her and slipped the blade under the bar. It stuck for a long moment.

She pressed even harder against the door, forcing the gap as wide as she could make it. Sweat beaded at her temples as she wedged herself in tighter, pushing with all her strength, trying to force the dagger's blade up through the narrow gap. It didn't work.

Leaning on the door opened the gap, but also forced the bar harder into its cradle. Hell. She needed to force the door to the side, slip in the knife, then lean back to raise it. She rearranged her weight and tried again. Finally, with a grinding squeak, the blade shifted. The bar lifted, and the door swung open. She was in.

A glance confirmed her suspicion that it was Andred's room. The bed was covered in rich purple velvet. His burgundy-and-silver tunic hung neatly from a hook on the wall. His spare sword was leaning against the wardrobe, and she recognized the small pile of books on the rolltop desk.

A clock ticked loudly on the mantelpiece, every second beating in her head.

She flew through the room, flicking through the books, pulling out desk drawers, opening the wardrobe, looking under the mattress, beneath the bed, behind the curtains. There was nothing.

She slid the sword out of its scabbard. Searched the tunic for pockets. Crawled on the floor looking behind the wardrobe. Still nothing. Damn it to the Abyss.

Daena stood, panting, in the center of the room. If Andred had a list of names like Reece had suggested, it wasn't here.

Her eyes fell on the beautifully carved rolltop desk. There had to be a multitude of hiding places in there. She went back over it again, checking every drawer, every cubby, and compartment. There was some parchment, dried ink, a few groats covered in dust, nothing more.

She lowered herself gingerly to her knees and looked beneath the desk, tapping the sides, running her hands over the wood. And that was when she felt it—a raised corner on the back panel.

She pressed it and pulled it and tried to force it to open, but nothing moved. She tried scraping at it with the dagger, tried levering it off. Nothing.

She crawled back out from under the desk, ignoring the stab of discomfort. There had to be a way. She felt in the back of all the little compartments looking for a latch of some kind but found nothing.

She pulled all the drawers out and stacked them on the floor. Daena swiped at the sweat dripping down her neck. The ticking of the clock was driving her insane. And now she'd dismantled the whole bloody desk. She'd give herself one more minute.

She ran her hands inside the cavities left by the drawers —and then she found it. A tiny lever, just big enough for her finger. She pulled it and heard the satisfying clunk of the panel falling off under the desk.

She climbed back under the desk to find a pile of musty papers in a shallow hollow. They cracked in her fingers as she pulled them out, aged and fragile. These were not Andred's—they were far too old and dusty—but somebody had thought they were worth hiding.

She was busy stuffing them inside her bodice when a sharp whistle blasted through the house. The shrill noise sent a bolt of fear flooding through her veins. Gods and angels. It could only be Reece, warning her.

She had to get out. But she couldn't leave the room in such disarray. How long did she have? Minutes? Seconds?

She pushed the back panel back into place with shaking fingers and then crawled out from under the desk, heart beating harder than a hammer on an anvil. She shoved the drawers back into the desk, tidied the books into a pile, and frantically checked that the rest of the room was exactly as she'd found it. Any moment now, they'd be on top of her.

She half-limped, half-ran toward the small door at the back of the room. Fuck. How was she going to lock the door behind her? She glared at the forbidding iron for a long moment, wracking her brain.

Reece whistled again, somehow the high-pitched warning was even more terrifying the second time. And then she could hear it. Horses in the courtyard. Men's boots on the cobbles.

She shoved her blade under the bar to lift it, gripped the bolt, and used it to pull the door closed. As soon as it shut, she pulled out the dagger. The latch bar fell into its cradle with a soft click.

Her breath came in rough pants as she ran as silently as she could through the small bedroom. She leaned her ear against the door and listened. Men's voices rose from the hallway. Boots clattered on the stairs. Oh, gods of the earth.

They were coming up, and she had nowhere to hide.

Chapter Fourteen

FUCK. Fuck it all to hell. Reece forced himself to lean nonchalantly against the wall and clean his nails with his small dagger—to look as if the loud whistle that woke everyone up was nothing to do with him—as the disgruntled, half-awake soldier stumbled out of the library and glared at him.

Reece raised an eyebrow. "Can I help you?"

"What the hell is all that noise?" Royn demanded, wiping his face tiredly.

"What noise?"

"The whistling."

"I have no idea what you're talking about." Gods. Couldn't Royn have just slept for five more minutes? Reece needed him gone so that Daena could come down the stairs.

Thank fuck he'd heard the horses' hooves clattering on the cobbles outside and had time to alert her while whoever was out there stabled their mounts.

It couldn't be Andred, could it? He hadn't even been gone for two hours yet. Not nearly enough time to get down to the river, cross the ferry, and then make the return trip, let alone actually achieve anything in Kaerlud. And yet, no one had called the alarm from the street outside. If it was anyone else, there should have been some warning.

The door opened, and Andred stepped inside, closely followed by the two men Reece had once considered friends. All three had the slightly smug expressions of people who had achieved exactly what they wanted.

"What's going on here?" Andred demanded, his air of satisfaction dimming as his eyes landed on Reece.

"Nothing," Reece replied before Royn could say anything. He forced his face into the friendly grin that had always worked for him in the past. It was tight and uncomfortable. "In fact"—he clapped his hand on Royn's shoulder—"we were just going out."

"That's not—" Royn spluttered, gasping as Reece tightened his grip, digging his thumb into the vulnerable area just to the front of Royn's underarm. Not hard enough to drop him, but hard enough to help him shut the hell up.

Andred glared at them both. "What are you doing in the hallway, Reece?"

What he was doing was losing his mind. He'd already been deeply regretting asking Daena to check the bedrooms. He'd thought she'd be safer up there, working on her own, while he kept watch. No one would accept her loitering around in the hallway and the bottom of the stairs, especially after how pointedly she'd avoided the Wraiths. And, if it came to it, he could run interference with the guards in a way she never could. But, if he was being honest, he'd also been certain they had hours before Andred came back.

But now... now it seemed like the height of stupidity to ask her to go up there. Now he was staring in horror at

Andred, wondering why he was back so quickly… and worse, imagining all the awful things Andred might do to Daena if he caught her.

He couldn't say any of that. Obviously. But his fear for Daena was making it impossible to think of what he should say and his beast was growling loud enough that even Andred heard it.

Andred's eyes narrowed. "What the hell are you doing here?"

Reece released Royn and gripped his hands behind his back. "As I said, I was on my way out. I assumed Royn wanted to join me."

Andred took a threatening step forward, hand resting on the hilt of his sword. "Why?"

"You won't let me out on patrol. I was tired of the library. And the kitchen is uncomfortable. I thought I should see to the horses."

It was clearly complete bollocks. He had grown up on the streets; the slightly faded kitchen was like a palace of warmth and comfort compared to living in the dirt at the back of an ancient alleyway. And his beast was snarling constantly; no horse would want him near them. But he needed to say something.

Andred gave him a long, speculative look. And then did exactly what Reece had desperately hoped he wouldn't. He flicked his eyes to the staircase. Fuck.

His scales hardened in a wave over his forearms as he fought to keep his expression mild. "I'll just go out to the stables then, shall I?"

"Not just yet," Andred muttered making his way up the staircase. "Royn, you're dismissed. Corporal Reece, come with me."

Hell. It was getting worse. Much, much worse. Reece

trailed up the stairs behind Andred and his lieutenants, his scales flashing. What was he going to do?

Reece almost didn't dare to look as they reached the landing. He was so certain he would find Daena caught there, locked in place by the warriors stalking up ahead of him. His entire body was tuned toward the shout of discovery and the punishment that was to come, his thoughts racing with plans for how he was going to get her free.

But it was empty.

Trust her.

He did, but…. There were only four doors. Gods. Daena was behind one of them. She couldn't get past, and she couldn't fly. Andred was going to open a door, and there she would be.

Andred would kill her, and it would be Reece's fault.

Andred flung the first door open so hard that it crashed into the wall. There was a moment's silence as he ran his eyes over the room, and then he moved on, leaving the door open to show a messy bed and not much else. There was nowhere to hide.

Reece ground his teeth, forcing himself not to reach for his sword. One room down, three to go. And then it would all be over.

The second door flew open under Andred's hand, revealing an almost identical—but far neater—bedroom. Andred prowled inside and contemplated the huge freestanding wardrobe. Gods.

Reece's beast was a rigid mass of tension. Scales covered his arms and half his neck. Every breath dragged.

Andred flung open the doors to the large wardrobe. It held only a single tunic. Relief blended with the fear churning in his belly.

She's... I think she's close, his beast growled, long and low. *We can't allow this. We have to do something.*

But what could he do? He didn't dare show his hand too early.

They marched back out and across the corridor to the most ornately decorated door of all. Andred tried the handle, but the door didn't budge. He pulled a long silver key out of his pocket and unlocked the door before stepping inside with Caius, Usna, and Reece trailing behind him.

This room was by far the most magnificent; luxurious bedding, piles of velvet cushions scattered over the bed, and a polished dark oak desk. But it was as undisturbed as the others.

Andred ripped through his room, looking beneath the desk, behind the curtains, under the bed, his irritation growing.

By the time he found her—and she could only be in the next room—Andred was going to be livid. He was going to—

She's behind you.

The hair on the back of Reece's neck stood up in a ripple of horror. He didn't dare to turn around and look. A month ago, maybe even a week ago, he might have doubted, but in that moment, he knew his beast was right. Somehow, it knew where she was.

A floorboard squeaked and he coughed to cover it. Gods. She was sneaking out behind them. She was using their focus on Andred's room to slip down the corridor. He almost wanted to laugh. She had bigger balls than most of the soldiers he knew, and he'd been a sapper.

Reece lifted his arm to lean on the doorframe, making himself as big as possible. He pointed toward the small door set into the wall beside the desk. "Where does that go?"

"The last room," Andred growled. "And then we shall see." He lifted the bar and flung open the door, pulled back a dark curtain, and strode into the final room.

Reece waved his hand behind him, desperately hoping Daena would see it and know that this was her chance. He pulled the bedroom door as far closed as he dared, and then marched forward, crowding Caius and Usna, encouraging them into the next room.

It was clearly the mistress's room. About half the size of the master's. Pretty, in a faded kind of way, but far less opulent. Although that wasn't what was bothering him. It was the locks on the door. What kind of couple barricaded the door between them? What kind of life had the woman who lived here led?

Rage flooded him. But for the first time, it wasn't directed at the Verturians he'd been taught to blame for so much, his mama, papa, Helaine, or even himself. No, it was directed at Andred and the men like him who had filled Brythoria with darkness.

He wanted to tear the Wraiths down. Not just to get his place in the palace back, but because it was the right thing to do.

He took long, shuddering breaths, forcing himself to calm. Forcing himself not to do anything that would jeopardize their mission. Jeopardize Daena.

Reece smiled blandly as Andred stalked through the rooms, displeasure pumping off him in violent waves, and counted down the seconds before he could escape. He needed to get far away from Andred. He needed to find Daena. And more than anything else, he needed to see for himself that she was safe.

Chapter Fifteen

DAENA LEANED against the stable wall, gulping in deep breaths of frosty winter air.

The stone was cold against her back, and the pungent reek of horse manure drifted around her, but she was so relieved to be out of the house that she hardly noticed.

She had rushed down the stairs, grateful beyond reason when the front hallway was empty. She hadn't dared to try and navigate the corridor past the soldiers sleeping in the library or holding wrestling tournaments in the dining room. Instead, she'd slipped out the front door, across the courtyard, and back, past the stable block to the enclosed space between the stables and the high stone outer wall. Here, she was hidden.

A few ancient rhododendrons loomed around her, their leaves drooping and curled by the frost, and the soil was dark and soft under her feet. Gods, she missed her greenhouse. Her rows of tiny seedlings. The smell of earth and new growth. The gentle bubbling splash of the stream she'd helped direct to run through the conservatories.

She'd gone to Staith to learn from the renowned herbalist living there. Together, they had planned to cultivate the rare Snow Lotus plants found only on the high slopes of the Thabana Mountains. They'd begged and bribed the Verturian soldiers to bring back a few precious seeds, and they'd nurtured and loved those seedlings like babies. Tiny buds that one day—with love and luck and hard work—they hoped would offer a powerful cure for the red plague.

Those seedlings were long gone, but standing here in the quiet green darkness surrounded by the scents of manure and rich soil, she remembered them. And the memory helped.

Andred had stolen them from her—he'd taken all her hard work, all her hopes—and now he was trying to steal an entire kingdom. She couldn't let that happen. The fear was worth it. The *risk* was worth it. Daena pushed her shoulders back and lifted her chin, her frightened breaths slowing.

The front door banged closed from the other side of the stable block, and then boots thudded across the cobbles. Gods and angels. She leaned quietly against the wall and waited for whoever it was to go the hell away. But the footsteps came closer. And then the rhododendron rustled. She pulled the dagger out of her boot and gripped it hard, preparing herself to fight back.

Reece turned the corner. His scales glistened along his arms and up his cheeks, and a low rumbling growl vibrated from his belly. His nostrils flared when he saw her leaning against the wall, and the rumbling intensified.

"Go away, Reece," Daena muttered. She was too keyed up. Still buzzing with danger and fear, only just starting to get her breath back under control. And the flare of relief that flooded her when she saw who it was flustered her. She needed a moment to get herself together.

His eyes narrowed. "No."

She folded her arms over her chest and glared at him. "How did you even know I was here?"

"I don't.... my beast...." He shook his head. "I don't know."

He took the last few steps across to where she was standing. Heated, churning energy poured off him, and his beast was growling steadily.

"That was too dangerous," Reece growled. "You're never doing anything like that again."

Hell no. He didn't get to ask for her help, and then storm out here and lecture her. He wasn't her captain; she made her own decisions now.

"I'll do whatever I want," she replied, looking Reece right in the eye.

The sapphire rings around his irises flared. "You are under my protection—"

Daena huffed, still high on danger and relief and starting to get properly annoyed. She didn't want, or need, a protector. She wanted a partner who treated her with respect.

She waved her free hand through the air, gesturing toward the path. "Consider yourself released."

"No. I promised Tor I'd keep you safe, and if that means throwing you over my shoulder—"

Promised Tor! Throw her over his shoulder! Gods. Now he'd gone too far. She waved the knife at him. "Go. Away."

His lips twitched into an amused half-smile. "Have you ever used a dagger, Daena?" he asked smoothly. "You're more dangerous to yourself than you are to me."

She breathed in an insulted gasp, but before she could

come up with a suitably stinging response, he clapped out. One of his hands chopped hard on the outside of hers; the other struck her inside wrist. She lost grip instantly, and the knife flew out of her fingers. Before she could even fully appreciate what had happened, Reece twisted his hand around her arm, pushed her palm down, and pulled her into a debilitating wrist lock.

She tried to escape, fighting to get free, but he didn't budge at all. He wasn't hurting her, just holding her, but it made her furious. How dare he? Insulting... maddening.... And now he was grinning, the utter bastard.

The dagger was gone, she had no other weapons, and the only exposed part of him was his corded forearm. She didn't think. She'd been too afraid. Too angry. She'd done exactly what they agreed, and now he was lecturing her, laughing at her.

No more.

She leaned forward and opened her mouth to bite that naked arm, ready to sink her teeth into his heavy muscles, and *make* him let her go. But his scales hardened into heated armor under her mouth, and her tongue merely stroked against his rippling scales.

Gods. Now she could taste him—salt and skin. She could smell him and feel him pressed against her mouth.

She closed her eyes, fighting for control. This was a mistake. She shouldn't have done it. But she couldn't make herself move back, either.

Reece grunted. He released the lock on her wrist and shifted his grip to drag her back up until he was holding her body flush against his. His scales were warm and smooth under her hands, the crook of his neck so close. If she moved, even an inch, her lips would press against his pulse.

She took in a shuddering breath, filling her lungs with

Reece. Reece who enraged her. Challenged her. Shared his secrets with her. Reece who had followed her, determined—in his own infuriating way—to keep her safe. Gods. Why did he have to smell so damn good?

And then he was moving. Walking her back until she was pressed against the stone wall. He lifted her easily and held her there with his body, her face so close to his that she could feel the warmth of his breath, the steady vibrating rumble of his beast.

She frowned, trying desperately to hold on to her anger. "I'm fine," she hissed. "You can tell Tor you did your job."

"You're not a job." He growled, scales flickering. "I didn't come here because of that," he admitted roughly. "I needed to see you. I had to be close to you. And now…."

His voice faded, but she didn't answer. Gods. What was she supposed to say to that?

The air between them thickened. He watched her, eyes bright, and she watched him, his admission hanging in the air between them. Blood pounded in her ears, but she didn't try to escape. She waited, breathless, until his mouth closed over hers and, finally, he kissed her.

It wasn't some sweet delicate wooing or gently questioning kiss. It was rough and hot and demanding. As if he too had been afraid. As if he was also riding the buzz of fear and relief and gratitude. As if he needed to hold her, to feel her, to remind himself that she was alive. That they both were.

She slid her hands up his arm to twine around his neck and wrapped her legs around his hips, pulling him even closer.

Her ankle ached, her muscles strained, and the papers in her bodice crinkled, but she didn't care. She was drowning in the power of his tongue sliding against hers, in the rough scrape of his stubble on her face.

Reece didn't just kiss her, he poured himself into her, and her entire body came to life like mountain flowers in the rain.

His beast growled loudly, tantalizing vibrations settling right against her center, and she panted, whimpering into their kiss. He dragged his lips away, down her throat to suckle on her pulse and she tilted her head back, making space. The steady throb between her legs ratcheted her up, higher and higher, until she was a gasping, aching, bundle of nerves.

A dog barked somewhere down the road, and they both froze, their breaths loud in the small space as they clung to each other, neither of them moving.

The sapphire faded from his eyes, his scales slowly retreating while she watched. She half expected him to lurch back, horrified. But he didn't. He lowered her carefully to the ground, his hand lingering on her hip as she found her footing.

He took a step back, and then another, and they stood, staring at each other. Daena shivered, suddenly cold and very alone.

Reece frowned and opened his mouth as if to say something, but she cut him off. "If you're about to say that was a mistake, you can fuck off."

"I wasn't going to—"

Her lip curled, the hint of curdled milk already seeping onto her tongue, and he caught himself.

His lips twitched. And then his nose wrinkled. And then he laughed. It was a dry sound, apparently as surprising to him as it was to her. She wasn't sure whether to be irritated or amused. Was he laughing at her? Again?

She started to turn, intending to walk away, but he stopped her with a hand on her shoulder. It was a gentle touch. A question, not a demand. "Please don't go. Not like that."

She paused, looking at him over her shoulder. The ring of sapphire was back, gleaming around his irises. It was thicker, brighter than it had been before. It mesmerized her.

"It wasn't a mistake," Reece whispered. "It was a surprise. It was… complicated."

What could she say? She felt the same way. And every word he'd spoken tasted like the truth.

"I like you, Daena," he admitted softly. "And I trust you." He tilted his head to the side for a moment, as if he was listening to something she couldn't hear. "I wasn't laughing at you," he said aloud. "I was… happy?"

Hell. He'd phrased it as a question. As if he couldn't even imagine that he might feel that way. But it was the truth, nonetheless.

"I wanted to kiss you," he murmured. "I… still want to. But we can't be seen together, and we can't stay here. It's not safe." Reece took another step back, widening the distance between them. "Do you want to go ahead? Maybe go around the house and back in through the kitchen?"

She nodded slowly. He was right; they couldn't stay here, and it was definitely complicated. But hearing him say he trusted her. That he wanted her. It meant more to her than she wanted to think about. Especially because she liked him too. And, angels help her, she was starting to trust him.

"I'll go ahead," she agreed, "but first…." She pulled the papers out of her bodice and showed them to Reece. They were crushed and wrinkled, a few had cracked, and a couple of pieces had broken off. "I found a secret compartment in

Andred's desk. I don't think they're his, but maybe his father's?"

"Flavius," Reece murmured, looking over her shoulder.

Daena rifled through them slowly, holding the papers so that he could read them with her. A few of the sheets were too old, too faded to make out. Of those she could read, one was a deed to a property near Brichtelmes, one was some kind of gambling debt, but the last was different from anything else. A thick ivory envelope held only one word, underlined with a heavy hand: Cat.

Daena broke the aged glue with her thumb and opened the envelope, sliding out a bundle of papers so thin they were almost translucent. They were obviously love letters, written in a looping, elegant script entirely different from the heavy block letters on the envelope. "*My Darling Flavius*," it began—

Reece grunted heavily, a sound of horror and utter dismay. Daena lifted her gaze to see that although the sapphire had retreated from his eyes, leaving them the gray of stormy skies, his scales were back, covering his shoulders, his face, forming a hard shield between him and the world.

"What is it?" she whispered.

He shook his head roughly. "Nothing."

Gods. How did they get back here? She turned to face him fully, looked him in his anguished eyes, and whispered, "Lie."

"I don't know...." His beast rumbled loudly between them, but she didn't feel afraid. She was starting to realize that anger wasn't directed at her. Maybe it never really had been.

She reached out with her free hand to clasp his arm. His bicep twitched under her palm, but he didn't try and free himself. Instead, he dropped his forehead to hers. And as he did, the sapphire in his eyes flared back, leaking through his iris toward his pupil.

"My mother's name was Cateline," Reece said, his voice low and rough. "Everyone called her Cat."

Oh. Oh, gods. "And this—" She left the words hanging. She had no idea what any of this meant.

"I don't know," he murmured. The muscles under her hand tightened even further. "But she... she had a lover in the palace."

He closed his eyes as he whispered, telling her the story of his mother's secret. The father he never knew.

It was a level of trust she had never imagined. A depth of faith that humbled her. He was revealing his deepest vulnerability, and she could only honor it by listening to him quietly, holding his arm as tightly as she could, keeping her forehead pressed to his, hoping he would know she was with him.

When he finished, they stood quietly together in the darkness behind the stables. A bird sang in the hedges, a dog barked somewhere down the road. It all seemed a million miles away.

Eventually, he lifted his head and met her eyes once more. "Do you think I could be Andred's brother?"

"No." The word came out, slightly sharper than she'd intended, and she tried again, more gently. "No, I don't. Cat is a common name. And, other than your height, you look nothing like him."

He raised an eyebrow at her, not convinced. He didn't have to say it, but they both knew he must look like his Tarasque mother.

There was so much here she was unsure of. She didn't know whose letters those were. Or whether they should mean anything to Reece. Was she being selfish, determined he couldn't be Andred's brother because of her own history? She didn't think so. More likely it was that she was starting to understand Reece. And to like him. A lot.

She had accused him of being like Andred, and now she regretted it with her whole heart. He wasn't like the Wraiths at all, and she didn't want that future for him.

He looked down at the letters crushed in her hands. "I have to be someone's son."

She folded them and put them back in the envelope, tucking them away. This, at least, she was certain of. This was the truth. "You are." She reached up and cupped his cheek, waiting until he looked at her. "You're Cateline and Brennan's."

Chapter Sixteen

WHAT DID IT MEAN? That name on the envelope?

Reece lay in his bedroll, ignoring the snores of the other soldiers as he stared up at the dark ceiling.

Nothing. It means nothing at all. It's probably someone else. Catherine. Catia. Catriona. Catrice. It could be anyone.

Gods. He had wished to be Andred's brother. He had looked at the confident, handsome leader of the Wraiths and thought, "Maybe we share a father?" Why not? His mother could have fallen for Flavius. If not him, any one of the rich, influential men Reece knew. Perhaps even Geraint. Maybe he was a prince.

It made his stomach clench. They were the dreams of a child without a father. A boy, alone on the streets. *Maybe I'm really a prince.* Except, he hadn't let them go. He'd taken them with him all the way to the palace. He'd let them fuel him.

Ravenstone had finally put an end to that stupidity. His fantasy that some all-powerful father was going to suddenly claim him and give him back his rightful home had died with Geraint. When they'd learned the truth about Ballanor —when Nim had shown it to them—he'd been horrified. When Tristan asked if the Hawks were prepared to become mercenaries to save her, he'd been only too glad to do so. He'd wanted to get away from it all.

Helaine's betrayal had only ramped his need to get away even higher. He'd spent his life getting close to the nobles of Kaerlud, only to discover how rotten they truly were, and he'd wanted as much distance between him and them as possible.

Of course, he'd gone about it all wrong. He hadn't just pushed away the bad... he'd pushed away everything. And everyone. He'd run from his life in the palace, but he'd run from the Hawks, too.

He'd never appreciated the Hawks as he should. He'd had half an eye on the Wraiths, on his future in the palace. Then, when it all came crashing down, he left them to wallow in his own misery. And now, when he finally appreciated what he had—when he no longer wanted any part of the Wraiths or any of the men like them, when he had a chance to make a new life with the Hawks—this was thrust in his face.

Was he like Andred and the Wraiths? The thought churned, acidic in his belly.

No. We're like Mama.

Was he though? He'd resented Mama. Deeply. And now he had to accept that she'd been right all along. She had sacrificed everything to get him out of the palace... and he had spent his entire life trying to get back there.

Daena says we're not alike. And I believe her.

Reece shook his head. Actually, she'd said they were just the same—obsessed with status and their own selfish needs —they only looked different.

His beast huffed. *She said we're not Flavius's. And she kissed us. She kissed us like she meant it.*

Gods. That kiss. Reece clasped his hands under his head and closed his eyes, but it made no difference. He could still see Daena, flushed and bright-eyed, her lips swollen from their kiss.

It was the best kiss of his life. Oh, he'd been kissed before plenty of times. He'd shared warmth and beds. He'd been kissed in passion and kindness. He'd been kissed with practiced seduction, and he'd been kissed with sloppy drunkenness. But he'd never kissed someone who he wanted to strangle and shelter all at the same time. Someone who made him want to do better. Be better.

Everyone he'd ever kissed had been charmed by his compliments and delighted by his flattery. No one had battled him, fought for control, demanded more of him, or kissed him with such intensity. And he had never kissed someone his beast was so captivated by. For the first time, both parts of him had been utterly, completely engaged.

He didn't regret it. How could he regret something that felt like that? But it was fucking complicated. Especially if he was related to... hell.

He pressed his fingers into his eyes, trying to force the world to come into focus. He still hadn't quite recovered from the terror of believing Andred was about to discover Daena lurking upstairs. He couldn't risk her like that again. Not because she wasn't strong enough, but because *he* wasn't. If he had to stand back and watch her get hurt, it would break him.

He sat up in his bedroll and forced himself to concentrate. He had to come up with a plan to get her far away from the Wraiths as soon as fucking possible. But no matter how he tried, he couldn't find a solution. His brain flitted between the horror of realizing Andred was back, that telling name on the envelope, and the kiss. Back and forth, back and forth—

Hang on. Why did Andred and his lieutenants return so early?

He'd been so wrapped up in his fears for Daena that he hadn't stopped to think about *why*. They hadn't gone into Kaerlud, it was impossible. They weren't gone nearly long enough to have caught the ferry, made their way into the city, done their business, and then caught the ferry back again.

He'd watched them ride away in that direction, though. He'd based his plans on the belief that Andred would be gone all morning. So where did they go? They weren't visiting anyone local; the few surrounding manor houses were empty for the winter, maintained by skeleton staff and local estate managers.

They met someone on the river.

Fuck. Hadn't Caius said he would speak to Dionys about cannon? And didn't Dionys have a huge fleet of fishing boats and merchant ships, many of which were already kitted out for war? Some of which might well already be in the harbor, just a few miles downriver from the Wraiths... and from the palace at Kaerlud.

Andred had looked so pleased with himself. Whatever had happened, he'd been delighted. He must have found the cannon he needed to destroy the front wall of the palace and flood the grounds with the moat.

Reece's beast growled roughly as a shiver of scales flickered over his shoulders onto his neck. *Cannon for the front* and *the back.* The scales hardened, forming a solid coat of armor on his arms and chest. But his beast wasn't finished. *Total annihilation.*

Gods. Could that possibly be right? What had Usna started to say... "we'll hit both"?

The Hawks had based their plans on the Andred they knew. The Andred of parties and women, political power, and the arrogance of having been born into riches, status, and authority. That Andred always had a backup plan. Always had a contact. *That* Andred had played the game, but he always had rigid self-control—he wouldn't destroy a palace he could live in and make his own. But that was before Ravenstone.

Ravenstone had changed all of them. What might it have done to the man who killed his king?

Andred was ruthless, but not completely immoral, and he had always been deeply loyal to his men. For him to have even considered taking Ballanor's orders, he would have had to convince himself that he was doing what was best for the kingdom. He would have persuaded himself that Geraint was poison. That regicide was an honorable action.

Then, when Ballanor betrayed him—not only robbing Andred of his promised position and exiling him to the north, but taking the entirety of his family's wealth and heritage for himself—it would have hammered those beliefs into Andred's very fiber. It would have proven to him that the house of Geraint was unfit to rule.

Gods. This was what Daena had said all along: Andred was credible precisely because he believed what he was saying. He believed—with a rabid fervor—that Geraint's entire line should be purged from the kingdom. And all their supporters with them.

The Hawks had expected Andred to raise support among the nobles and then make a bid for the throne. They had assumed he would meet former councilors and gather their support before moving on the palace; that he would plan to remove Lucilla but aim to avoid an all-out war. But maybe that was wrong.

Andred's hatred was driving him. The Wraiths were still meeting with displaced nobles and taking their money, but he didn't need to spend it on a difficult, focused strike on Lucilla. He didn't need to spend weeks finding a secret way into the palace, he didn't need assassins or contacts who could get him access to the queen. He could simply burn it all to the ground and declare himself the king when he was standing on the ashes.

Gods of fire. They had to warn Lucilla and the Hawks. Tristan and Tor needed to know they were basing their thinking on how Andred used to be. But what was the best way to do that?

If he could hang a shirt somewhere visible, the queen's soldiers would sweep in to get them out. That had always been the plan, and it had seemed sensible. If things were starting to unravel, he could set the signal and creep into the fields and wait for help, run if he had to... but he'd only been thinking about himself. Now it was occurring to him just how bad that could get for Daena.

His beast twisted uneasily. Daena was intelligent and perceptive; she had walked in, knowing that her chance of walking back out was extraordinarily small. He'd known she was brave, but now....

She is glorious.

She was. And he had to get her out of there. But the second the signal was set, they were on borrowed time. The Wraiths would see it the moment the sun came up—assuming they didn't catch him on the roof.

They couldn't take the horses; the gate was always guarded. They could set the signal at night and then make a run for it in the dark. That was an option, but not an easy one. The fields were slippery with ice and full of ruts and holes. Perhaps she could go ahead, and he could set the signal once he knew she was away... if she would agree to that.

You have to talk to her. Ask her.

Yes. And soon. Whatever they did, whatever they decided, it had to be quick. Andred was deeply suspicious after finding Reece in the hallway that morning, and Reece had seen him watching Daena during the rest of the day, his gaze filled with distrustful speculation.

How long would it take before Andred realized just how much he'd given away by revealing his maps and his plans for ships and cannon?

The memory of Andred's cold eyes watching Daena as she moved through the kitchen, as she ate a small portion of the evening's rations—the way he'd looked over to Reece and smirked—sent another heated wave of scales climbing over his skin. Andred suspected them. And he might attack the palace at any time.

Reece launched himself up and out of his bedroll. He needed to see her, needed to know she was safe. And he wanted to talk to her, to share his concerns and hear her opinions.

He left his boots and jerkin behind as he slipped quietly between the sleeping soldiers. Someone grumbled, another snored softly, but no one woke.

He snuck through the half-open library door and into the dark hallway. There were patrols outside but none inside the house, and he was able to make his way in silence to the kitchen. The old wooden frame of the house groaned around him as the wind buffeted the walls, and he paused every few steps to make sure he was still alone.

Freezing air blew over his armored skin—it was as cold

in the drafty old manor as it was outside—but he hardly noticed it. Every one of his senses was focused on creeping through the house undetected. He was in his cotton shirt and loose trousers, his weapons left beside his bedroll. If he was discovered, it would be far worse if he was stalking through the dark carrying a sword. He was surrounded by enemies, in a deadly dangerous game, making a move that if he was discovered would almost certainly get him killed. And yet, he couldn't stop himself. He needed to get to Daena.

The kitchen was a little warmer than the icy hallway. The remnants of the fire glowed orange and red in the grate as he made his way to the small door that led to Daena's room. The door squeaked as he opened it, but he didn't dare lurk outside. It was pitch-black inside—so dark even his Tarasque vision couldn't help him—as he crept in and quietly closed the door.

Before it clicked shut, there was a whirl of shifting air and then a cold blade pressed against his side, hard enough that it pierced the cotton of his shirt and spiked into his skin.

"Daena," he whispered roughly, "it's me."

The tip of the blade withdrew slightly. "Reece?"

"Yes." He twisted to look over his shoulder, straining to see her in the darkness. "Is that my dagger?"

He heard a scrape of cloth that he took to be a shrug. "You left it behind," she whispered.

Had he? Gods. He must have been even more distracted than he'd realized.

Our first gift. His beast sounded deeply smug.

Reece ignored it. It wasn't a gift. It was…. He didn't know what it was.

The knife disappeared, clinking gently as she set it

down. Quiet footsteps suggested she'd moved away, taking her warmth and soft scent with her. "What do you want, Reece?"

You. To hold you again, feel your skin sliding against ours, here in the darkness, finding our way by touch. We want—

Reece spluttered out a choked cough. No. Gods. He wasn't here for that. Memories of their kiss rose through him, but he pushed them away. He needed to talk to her. Talk.

"Could we… could you light a candle maybe?" he asked.

Daena huffed out a rough laugh. "What candle?"

Gods. Just when he thought he couldn't possibly hate Andred any more than he already did. Or himself. He should have made sure she had light. And a weapon. Not as gifts, just human decency. He should have believed her, right from the beginning.

"I'm sorry," he whispered in her direction.

"What for?"

"Everything," he muttered. "For all the ways you've been hurt. I—"

A soft step came closer, and then a hand settled on his arm. "It wasn't your fault."

They both stilled. He could hear her breathing. Feel the soft pressure of her hand, the heat of her palm through the thin fabric of his shirt. Gods. How many times had the Hawks said the same thing to him? *It's not your fault.*

Yet he'd ignored them again and again. He hadn't been able to forgive himself, and he hadn't trusted his friends enough to believe them. He hadn't trusted his own beast.

"I'm sorry," he whispered again. Who exactly he was apologizing to? He didn't know.

Daena's warmth came closer, her hand sliding up his

arm to grip his shoulder, her other hand coming to rest on his cheek.

"I forgive you," she murmured.

Forgiveness. Gods. He hadn't earned it, and he probably didn't deserve it, but he wanted it anyway. He was going to accept her absolution.

This is her gift to us. His beast undulated in his belly. Waves of hot scales climbed over his skin as he heaved out a wavering breath, eyes prickling in the darkness.

He dropped his hands to Daena's hips. Holding her like an anchor. A point of stillness among the chaos.

He felt her move, pushing up onto her toes, and then her lips were on his. Her tongue traced his bottom lip, and he groaned, letting her in. She tasted of mint tea, and she smelled like safety. She tilted her head, and they fitted together perfectly. Her body pressed against his, supple and strong. Her mouth moved over his, heated and demanding.

He slid his hands round, gripping her ass and bending himself over her, needing to surround her, needing to feel her against him in every way. Gods. He wanted to haul that rough woolen dress over her head and find the soft shift he knew was underneath. He wanted to see the delicate fabric bunching and sliding as he dragged it up, over her nipples, to reveal Daena in all her truth. He wanted—

Fuck. It wasn't safe. As much as his body howled for her, Daena deserved more than a furtive coupling in an enemy camp. He'd gone to her room to talk, not to put her in even more danger.

He softened his kiss, pulling gently away to press his lips to the side of her mouth and over her eyes, and finally to her forehead. He was still breathing heavily, and he shuddered as her belly pressed against his aching shaft, a delicious, throbbing torture.

He nestled his face into the crook of her neck, murmuring, "Thank you."

She chuckled softly, her breath floating over his cheek. "It was my pleasure."

He couldn't help the smile that tugged at his lips where he pressed them against her skin.

"Why did you come, Reece?" she asked quietly, her arms still wrapped around him.

He didn't think before he answered, he simply told her the most important truth. "I wanted to be with you."

Chapter Seventeen

THEY SAT side by side in the darkness, their backs against the cold wall, as Reece told her his fears about what Andred might do. She'd taken his hand without thinking, and he'd immediately woven their fingers together. His hand was big and calloused, gripping hers tightly as he spoke.

He wanted to be with her. He'd come to her, not because she could do something for him, or offer him anything—there was nothing she could give him—but because he wanted to be near her.

When last had anybody wanted her just for her? When last had anyone come to her just because they wanted to be near her? Maybe never.

And, gods help her, she wanted him too.

She'd been lying in her blankets, reliving their kiss, their words, every interaction they'd ever had—but mostly their kiss—when she'd heard a suspicious noise in the kitchen and quickly risen to hide behind her door.

By the time her door squeaked open, she'd been convinced Caius or Usna had finally come to kill her. The looks Andred had been giving her that afternoon had gone past suspicion and into outright hostility. It wouldn't take much for his lieutenants to convince him she'd been a liability for long enough—hell, they'd tried to do exactly that to Tor, and he'd been much less of a threat to their power than she'd ever been—or to simply take the initiative for themselves.

The relief of hearing Reece's voice had been overwhelming. Then he'd admitted that he'd snuck through the house to see her, that he'd wanted to be with her, and it had created a warmth that even his stark concerns hadn't cooled.

For a moment, there in the darkness, she'd been certain he was going to rip her dress right off her body, and, gods and angels, she wanted that. She wanted to run her hands down his smooth abdomen and grip that hard length she had felt between them. To lose herself in him while he lost himself in her.

He'd pulled away so reluctantly. His heavy breaths, the way his fingers dug into her hips as he pressed heated kisses over her face, told her he was as unwilling to part as she was. And then he'd thanked her. More truth echoing between them.

Now they were sitting together in the pitch-black night, shoulders pressed together, his hand gripping hers as he explained his fears and asked her opinions. And the more he spoke, the more he explained his reasons for believing that Andred planned to utterly destroy the palace at Kaerlud, the more convinced she was that he was right.

"Was it true?" he asked into the darkness. "All their talk about cannon and bringing down the palace walls."

"Yes, I think so." Nothing they'd said had even the slightest tang of a lie. But she couldn't stop herself from shivering. Andred always told the truth—he just didn't tell all of it. "But it wouldn't be the first time I've missed something," she admitted.

"Do you think there's a genuine risk to everyone in the palace?" Reece asked in a rough voice.

She didn't need to wonder. "Yes." Gods.

His hand tightened on hers. "We have to let them know."

He was right. They couldn't take the risk of waiting, not if Andred had ships loaded with cannon ready and waiting.

"I don't know how to signal whoever is watching the house without alerting Andred," Reece muttered. "Or how best to get us both clear."

"Assuming they don't kill us immediately, we'll be caught between the Wraiths and the Blues," Daena agreed.

Reece twisted toward her, his arm brushing against hers. The sapphire in his eyes glittering blue in the darkness. "I've wracked my brain, but I'm not sure of the best solution. I was hoping you might have a suggestion."

Gods. This was what she'd wanted all her life. To be treated with genuine respect. Reece wasn't only asking her for help or asking for her opinion, he was utterly convinced she was coming with him. And she wanted to, she really did.

A year ago, she might have done it. She might have let her wish to spend more time with Reece, and her fear of Andred—her doubts about her ability to face the man who'd cut her self-worth down so ruthlessly—decide for her. She might have agreed that they had to go together. She might have convinced herself that there was no other choice. That she was doing the best she could. But not anymore.

When Tor had asked her whether she would help Lucilla, when she'd sat in her bare barracks room in Staith staring out at the mountains that had been her prison, she'd known no one would decide for her. In that moment, something in her had started to change. She'd started to find herself again.

The Daena who stood up to the Nephilim and chose her own path, who'd followed what she loved, believing in her dreams, had been hidden inside her all along. The fire, her pain, and Andred's betrayal had locked that woman away for a time, but now she was breaking free once more.

She spoke slowly, looking for the right words. "The answer is for you to go. You should leave me here. Set the signal and get out. I'll cover for you as long as I can."

"No. Absolutely not." A low rumble filled the darkness, almost a growl. "I can't leave you here. We need to find a plan that works for both of us."

She turned and faced toward where he was sitting, finding his eyes by the rings of blue, feeling the scales settling over the back of his hand and the tension radiating from his body. "Thank you, Reece. I can't…." She took a breath, forcing herself to continue. "You don't know what your belief means to me. But you need to go back to them. Someone has to explain what we've learned, and it has to be you."

Fabric rustled, and she imagined he was shaking his head. hard.

"You must have thought of this," she said softly. "Strategically, it's by far the most sensible choice. Get out, set the signal, and then get to the Hawks. If I come, I'll hold you back, I'll lower your chances of escaping. But if I stay here, I can help. I can distract Andred and maybe even delay them. In the worst case, I can keep spying on them, learning their plans. This is where I'm strong."

"No, I never...." His voice was threaded through with his beast's rumbling unhappiness. "I can't do that."

"Yes, you can. You must."

Hadn't she always known it would come to this? She had, and it was the right thing to do.

She should have died in the temple fire, but she was given a few more months. A chance to fix what she had broken. A chance to realize she was so much stronger than she'd thought. A chance to kiss Reece and hold him, to come to know the loyal, intelligent, complex man he was, and for him to choose *her*.

This was her chance to do what had to be done, even if it hurt. She could give her life—one life—sacrificed to save many.

She heard him swallow, loud in the darkness, and knew he was going to argue. Knew that he didn't want to accept what he already understood. He didn't want to leave her.

The seed of warmth flickering in her heart unfurled, growing and spreading in her chest. Gods, she wished they'd had more time.

But they didn't. She cut him off before he could start. "Reece, Lucilla needs to know about the cannon. There isn't time to wait. I can't sneak through the fields, not at the speed you can. We both know I'll slow you down. If I'm here, I can help you. You *have* to do this."

His hand let go of hers and swept up her arm instead, coming to grip the back of her neck as he rested his forehead against hers. "How could I live with myself if I… if you…?"

She choked out a half-laugh, half-sob. For a moment, he had needed her. For a moment, he had seen her. And now she had to be strong. "You can go back and find your squad. They'll help you. They'll tell you this was the right choice."

There was a long, heavy silence, Reece's body tense and rigid beside her, his hand gripping her nape so tightly it was almost painful.

"Reece," she whispered, "they love you. They all spoke of you. Every single one of them told me stories of you, of how important you were to them. Go back. Save them. And let them save you in return."

He grunted, a rough, devastated sound, and she knew he was almost convinced.

"I know things went wrong for you, Reece," she continued, "but I believe—I know—that you love them too. Sometimes doing the right thing is hard, terrible even, but I know you can do it. I have faith in you."

He was utterly still, hardly even breathing, and she wondered if maybe she had pushed too hard. If he would throw his guards back up and the Reece of the tunnels would return, mocking and cold and hidden behind his icy defensive walls.

But then he turned his head, sealed his mouth over hers, and kissed her. There was no mocking. No ice. Just heat and desperation. He didn't taste her, he consumed her, his tongue sliding through her mouth, determined and devastating.

"I don't want to leave you," he rasped out between kisses. "I don't…. It's not right."

She leaned back a little, breathing hard. "I know you don't, but it *is* right."

It was right, it was just difficult to accept. And if they were going to accept it, she wanted something first. She wanted something honest and precious and hers before the end.

So, she did what she'd wanted to do ever since their kiss behind the stables. She rose onto her knees and pulled her dress over her head, then leaned forward to kiss him again. He shuddered against her, his hand smoothing the soft cotton over her waist, lingering on the flare of her hips, as if he was soaking up the heat of her body.

He dragged his lips over her jaw to speak against her cheek. "I didn't come here to take from you. I wanted to talk with you. I wanted a solution. I…. Gods, Daena." He gripped her tighter, speaking in rough whispers. "You deserve more than this."

Daena shivered, heat rising through her, raising goose bumps of awareness over her body. "This is what I want. Before you go, give me this. Please."

He stayed there for a long moment, breathing hard against her skin, and then he seemed to reach some kind of decision, some agreement with himself, and he tilted his head to kiss her again.

His hands slid down to grip her waist, and he hauled her over his legs to straddle him. Her shift rode up her thighs, her knees bare against the cold floor, but all she could feel was him. The breathless fever of his kiss, the glide of his tongue against hers, the rough pants of their breaths. She lifted her hands to his face, relishing the scrape of his stubble against her palms.

"Gods. I knew… I knew it would be like this," he whispered. "You're everything real, Daena. Real and good."

His words wrapped around her, a bittersweet truth that tasted of his kisses, and she ground down, needing the pressure of his cock to balance the ache in her heart.

He was so hard against her, his trousers and her shift barriers between them that she wanted gone. She pressed her hips forward, trying to find relief. Reece slid his hands over her hips, up her sides, until his thumbs came to rest against her nipples, abrading them with rough friction through the fine cotton of her shift as his tongue swept deeper.

But it wasn't enough. She needed more, needed to touch him. She leaned back with a shuddering sigh. "Take it off. Please."

He dropped his face into her neck, breathing hard, as he murmured, "Are you sure? I…." He let out a rough chuckle. "Gods. You make me feel like this is all new."

"I'm certain. Take it off."

A low rumble shuddered from his belly as he dragged his hands back down the hem of her shift and then slowly lifted it up and over her head. There was another rustle as he grunted beneath her and stripped off his shirt.

She shivered as the cold air played over her skin, her nipples tightening into hard points, and then his hands were on her once more. One splayed out over her lower back, the other sliding up to thread through her hair as he pulled her even closer and kissed her again.

She looped one hand around the back of his neck, her breasts grazing his chest with every movement, every rough inhale and heavy exhale.

"Daena," he said, voice lower than she'd ever heard it. "You take my breath away. I feel you moving over me, so hot and tight and sweet. Gods, I know I don't deserve it, but I don't think I've ever wanted something as much as this."

She shuddered, needing him as much as he needed her. "You do… gods, Reece. You do deserve to feel this."

His beast vibrated between them as she dropped her other hand to the button on his breeches and opened the placket. He was even bigger than she'd imagined, long and heavy in her hand. His abdomen rippled beneath her, his cock twitching as she dragged her thumb through the slit. His hand joined hers, spreading precome, and they stroked his shaft together, both panting as his hips shuddered forward, driving him even closer.

He pulled his hand away, leaving her to grip him alone, and brought his thumb to her lips. She immediately opened, tasting the salt and musk on her tongue as she sucked it into her mouth, panting.

Reece groaned. "Fuck, yes. That's how you would take my cock, isn't it Daena? Suctioned around me, pulling me in, wrapping me in the strength of your body?"

She nodded, her mouth tight on his thumb, her hand gripping his shaft, her nipples rasping over his chest. That's exactly what she wanted. And every time he said her name, every time he spoke directly to her, his words ringing with need and want and truth, it drove her higher.

"Do it then," Reece murmured as he slid his thumb from her mouth to tangle his fingers through her hair. "Take what you need."

She raised her hips and used her grip around his cock to angle him into her body as she slowly lowered herself. Gods. The rumble of his beast picked up, vibrating through her hand and then over her clit and deep inside her. She whimpered as she ground down, taking him all the way.

They paused, foreheads pressed together, breathing the same heated air. The wind rattled the old house, and it creaked around them, but the noise was distant, overshadowed by the roar of her pulse in her ears. The bright rings of sapphire in his eyes held her pinned, anchored to Reece as surely as their bodies were locked together, while the rest of the world disappeared.

She raised her hips and then lowered herself again, slowly, so very slowly, feeling the whole length of him, reveling in the way his abdomen shuddered and bunched, his rough grunt as she dragged her lips over his face and into his neck, to bite down on the straining muscles.

He stroked his free hand down between them to find her clit with his thumb, adding a searing new level of sensation. "Show me," he murmured. "Show me how you like it."

She put her fingers over his, sliding through the molten slick where they were joined… and showed him. The exact pressure, the glide, and then the circle, and then… then he took over and it was all him. And she was hurtling, faster and faster toward the pinnacle. The radiant, incandescent pleasure, which was so very close.

She writhed in his lap, face pressed against his shoulder as she whimpered, chasing the peak that was just within her grasp.

His hand in her hair cradled the back of her head, holding her, helping her to muffle her shuddering pleas against his skin.

"You're like a dream," he whispered roughly against her sweat-damp temple. "Like a fantasy. Daena, here in the darkness. Gods."

Jolts of pleasure rippled through her as he matched his thrusts to his thumb on her swollen clitoris, harder now, driving up into her in time with the circle, the glide, and then, holy angels, he pinched her clit and she gasped out a shocked half-scream as she flew over the edge. She spasmed around him, dragging in rough gasps of musky air, his scent, hot and masculine.

"Daena, baby…" He grunted. "I need—"

She pushed herself up, off him, her body still trembling with aftershocks, and he shuddered, groaning, before rolling her onto her back and covering her, his face in her neck, his throbbing cock pressed into her belly.

She slid her hand down and gripped him, hard, in her

fist, and he came in rough spurts, his hips punching forward as he whispered her name again and again.

Eventually, they quieted. The rigid spasms of their muscles slowly released. Air returned to their lungs. Reece rolled onto his back, bringing her to lie against his side, under his arm, against the heavy beating of his heart. And, for a moment, they were alone in the world. The dark, creaking room was adrift among the heavens, entirely isolated except for them, together in the quiet of distant space.

"I wanted...." Reece paused, swallowed, and tried again, his eyes glowing almost entirely sapphire. "I wanted to give you more. I wanted you to have cool silk sheets, a pleasant room, and a hot bath." He pressed a kiss to her forehead. "I would bring you delicious food. The dark chocolate of the Sasanians, if you like that, freshly baked bread with butter and honey. We would feed each other and dirty each other and then rest before starting again, all night."

Daena chuckled. It did sound like a dream. And yet.... "It sounds magical, Reece. But I didn't need any of that. All I wanted was you."

He kissed her again, harder this time. "Gods, Daena. How do you do that? How do you say things that break my heart and heal it at the same time?"

She didn't know how to respond, so she kissed his chest instead, a slow press of her lips to the warm flesh over his heart.

"One day we'll have both," Reece whispered. "We'll have this—but warmth and light too. Okay?"

Hell. Heat prickled at her eyes, and she nodded, knowing she couldn't speak.

But he didn't let it go. "Promise me, Daena. Promise me

that, when the time comes, you'll run and hide and be waiting for me when I get back. Promise me that when this is all over, we can share the light together."

She couldn't make that promise. Everything between them had been real, and she wasn't going to change that now with a lie. So, she kept quiet as she kissed him over his heart once more. And then she rolled on top of him, notching his cock between her legs, feeling it harden against her as she lowered her mouth and kissed him.

She kissed him with tears sliding down her cheeks, knowing he would taste the salt. That he understood all the things she hadn't said.

She kissed him in greeting. A first, potent meeting of their souls.

And then he rolled her over, onto her back, and she wrapped her legs around his hips, drawing him into her body, and she kissed him goodbye.

Chapter Eighteen

THE GROUND WAS FROZEN and crusted over with ice, crunching under Reece's feet, as the pale moonlight cast shadows across the fields.

Part of him still couldn't believe he'd left.

It wasn't sneaking into the library to quietly lift his boots, cloak and weapons, leaving his bedroll and everything else behind, that was so difficult to comprehend. Not climbing carefully onto the roof, hiding in the shadows, timing his movements to the creaking of the house as he tied an old shirt to the chimney. Nor even waiting in the silent darkness, counting down the patrols, ready for the moment when the guards rotated, and then taking his chance to force his way through the weak point in the hedge as it scratched and clawed at him.

No, he couldn't believe he'd left Daena.

Their time in the darkness was like a dream. Surreal and almost magical. She had wanted him as much as he had wanted her. There had been no trade; there was nothing he could offer her—in the end, he couldn't even offer her safety —and yet she'd wanted to be with him anyway.

His entire being ached to still be there with her. But she was right, as usual. He had to get away and warn the Hawks. And disrespecting her choice, dishonoring the sacrifice she was willing to make, would have been utterly wrong.

He'd tasted her tears as she whispered her goodbye, but he'd felt the strength in her too. She could survive this. And he would come back for her the instant that he was able to.

Gods.

Daena was fundamentally, deeply honorable. She'd been caught in a terrible situation out of her control. She had been lied to, manipulated, and used, and yet, here she was, trying to fix it. Willing to give her life to make it right.

She's a Hawk.

The truth of his beast's statement distracted him and he stumbled. Ice cracked under his foot as a frozen puddle hidden beneath the winter leaves splintered under his weight, and he paused, listening carefully for sounds of alarm.

He twisted back to look down the hill, the way he'd come, toward the farmhouse. No light shone out. No alarms sounded. The soldiers patrolling the grounds and watching the road were still blissfully unaware that anything had changed. If he squinted, he could imagine that he could see his white shirt against the chimney bricks, still lost in the darkness of the night.

What was Daena doing? Was she lying in her rough blankets? Was she thinking of him? Did she know that she was one of them—a Hawk—or did she think she was alone again?

If anyone had asked him on the day he'd pulled her

from the sewer, he'd have been convinced she would have run to Andred at the first opportunity. And of course, that was still an option for her. If she betrayed him to Andred, she might still buy her own safety. It could make all the difference on whether she survived the day or not. But now… now he knew she would never do such a thing. When Daena made a promise, she kept it.

We trust her, his beast rumbled.

We. Trust. Her.

Gods. Once, when he was very young, he and his mother had gone to meet Brennan's ship as it came into the harbor. Papa was a fisherman, a big, heavily bearded man with cheeks reddened by wind and salt and an even bigger laugh. They had waited for him near the docks, their coats brushed and faces washed, a strange kind of nervous energy buzzing through them. Papa had turned the corner and seen them, and his face had split into a gigantic grin. He'd opened his arms and they'd run into them, laughing and joyful. And Reece had known he was wanted. Known he was safe.

After Papa died, that safety had been lost. One thing after the other, everything had been lost.

Until now. Until last night.

Until Daena. He trusted her, something he never thought he would do again. The knowledge settled into his soul.

For a moment, he almost ran back the way he'd come. Risked the patrols and the soldiers and Andred's fury to get to her, consequences be damned. But he stopped himself. She expected more of him, and he wouldn't let her down.

He let out a rough exhale, sending a plume of frozen breath out in front of him, and then turned back to climb the low hill.

It felt like it took hours, bent over, flitting between small copses of trees, until he finally reached the weeds and sedge grasses that marked the border of the neighboring farm. From here, he had two options: follow the rutted track down to the farmhouse itself and then onto the road, hopefully having already passed Andred's watchers. Or avoid the road entirely and keep going over the fields.

In the end, speed was his priority. It would be an easy jog down the track, past the empty house, and out to the road. It was worth the slight risk of Andred's watchers being this far south—especially when the Wraiths would certainly spot his abandoned shirt at any moment—to find the squad of sentries Tor had posted as quickly as possible.

His beast rumbled unhappily. It wanted to deliver a warning to the Hawks and get back to Daena. Reece lengthened his stride, adding speed now that he was well out of sight and earshot of Andred's patrols.

Cold air burned his lungs, his boots thudding on the dusty track as he pushed himself even harder. A lark chirruped and whistled somewhere nearby as the air lightened. Slowly, misty gray dawn replaced the shadowy moonlight, and the farmhouse rose, dark and almost ominous ahead of him.

The scales on the back of his neck hardened with a shiver. The house was empty, but it felt too still. As if it was watching him. Aware of him, somehow. He'd thought the Wraiths were too overextended to think of putting sentries into the local houses, but they had been collecting funds. Could they have recruited mercenaries and allocated them the outer watches? It was exactly what he would have done.

The track led through a small gate into a far better cared for kitchen garden than the one he'd left. He ignored it as he followed the cobbles at a run, slipping around the side of the house. A narrow path led down past what seemed to be the kitchen door, hemmed in by a series of greenhouses and sheds. As far as he remembered from the recon he'd done, it would lead out to the stables and then to the front courtyard.

It was dark and gloomy in the narrow space, mist rising slowly from the cold ground, and he almost hesitated. His scales were solid over his neck and face, his beast growling steadily.

Reece slowed to a cautious walk, watching the house, the garden, ears straining for any kind of noise. He took a step into the gloomy shadows, only to rear back as a soft scrabbling noise echoed from the roof above him.

He slid his sword out, a reassuring hiss of metal against metal, just as a large shape leaped from the roof to land heavily on the path. Fuck. Andred *had* recruited more men.

He lifted his sword and widened his stance. Hopefully, there was only one sentry. All he had to do was get past this one man.

"Reece?"

He froze. He knew that voice. Or did he? Surely it couldn't possibly be—

"Thank fuck. It *is* you!"

Reece almost dropped his sword. "Gods… Tristan?"

Tristan laughed. Actually laughed. And it was the weirdest sound Reece had ever heard. He'd heard Tristan chuckle. Grunt. Grumble. Swear. But laugh? And then Tristan wrapped him in a back-slapping, bone-crushing embrace, and all Reece could do was embrace him back.

They pulled apart after a moment, Reece's head still reeling. "How? Why? I don't…."

"We haven't heard from you. We've been so worried. And fuck it all—" Tristan grunted and now, finally, he sounded more like himself. "Mathos said you'd come this way, and he's going to be so bloody smug."

"Mathos?" Reece repeated weakly.

"Apparently Tor still owes Mathos twenty groats from their bet about which way Lucilla would run. Now it's forty, and Mathos is going to be utterly unbearable."

Reece blinked. Last he knew, the bet had been ten groats to find Nim. He'd missed out on whatever they'd been betting on since then. But none of that helped him understand why Tristan was here. Tristan—the Supreme Commander of Lucilla's entire military—had been sitting on a roof, watching the fields in the darkness for the gods knew how long, and it didn't make any sense. "But why are *you* here?"

Tristan grunted. "You didn't think we'd let you go in alone, did you?"

No… but also…. They had a system: safe houses, letter drops, and the reassurance of knowing someone would be watching. He'd known there would be people hiding, keeping vigil, ready to pass a message. But he hadn't thought it would be Tristan, not in a million years.

And why not? Tristan is our brother. All he's ever done is look out for us.

Gods. Reece pinched the top of his nose and took a long slow breath. He wasn't going to cry. He wasn't. He hadn't cried since his mother died. He was an adult. A soldier. He was… he was….

"You're a Hawk."

Oh, gods. And now his eyes were burning, and he had to swallow, hard. "Am I?" He hadn't meant to ask the question, or for his voice to sound so uncertain.

But Tristan didn't hesitate. "Always."

Always.

They stood in silence for a moment, neither of them speaking. Tristan liked silence, and Reece couldn't find the words. He'd pushed and pushed. And he'd thought he'd broken their brotherhood for certain. But here was Tristan anyway. Waiting for him. Saying "always" as thought there'd never been any doubt.

They love you. Every single one of them. Daena told us.

"I'm a Hawk," Reece whispered, and for the first time in a very long time, he believed it. And another piece of soul quietly healed.

And that was when all hell broke loose. A horn call split the air, vibrating through the mist like the wailing of the dead shuddering out from the Abyss. It was the war horn of the Wraiths, meant to instill fear and dread. And gods, it did. Sharp whistles followed, soldiers being coordinated down the road, called in from patrol. Fuck. They'd realized he was missing. Or seen the shirt in the growing light.

He spun to Tristan. "We have to warn Lucilla. We— Daena and I—think Andred isn't bothering with a complicated conspiracy. We think he's going to burn it all down."

Tristan didn't question his conclusion or hesitate. "How?"

"Ships and cannon. He'll aim to bring down the walls, front and back: from the square and the river. Dionys has a fleet of ships, almost certainly heavily armed. We think Andred met with them yesterday and now he has everything he needs."

Tristan gave a brief nod, lifted his fingers to his lips, and whistled a sharp series of notes. The hunting cry of the Hawks.

Less than a minute later, something thudded heavily from the direction of the courtyard, and then Jos was there, running down the shadowy path, his wings folded back and battle-ready.

"The signal, Captain! Reece has—" Jos caught sight of Reece standing behind Tristan. "Thank the gods, you're here! When I saw the shirt and the heard the horns, fuck. It was like being back in the north, waiting for the next battle, not knowing who was dead or alive. I thought… I imagined we'd lost…." He shook his head and then grinned, relief and pleasure pouring from him. "But you're here. You're out, thank fuck."

Jos focused on Tristan, wings softening slightly. "I've passed the message on to the corporal at the river. Tor will be here in the next half hour with the primary squad. More troops will follow as planned."

Hell. Reece didn't know what to say. They were all here. Waiting for him. Watching over him. And he hadn't even realized.

Jos started leading them down the dark path out toward the road. "We need to get moving."

No! Gods of fire, please! Please don't do this. His beast roared in his ears as a wave of scales flooded up Reece's neck and onto his face. It was so potent, so desperate, that it almost took him to his knees.

Reece took a slow step back, heart pounding against his ribs. His beast was frantic and, at first, he couldn't understand why. Then he realized… all the times he'd refused to listen, all the times he'd deadened that voice inside him. The beast didn't trust him.

But he was listening now. "I can't go with you."

Tristan grunted. "Of course not."

"I don't…." Jos squinted into the darkness behind Reece, and then back toward him, confusion drawing stark lines down his forehead. "Where's Daena?"

Chapter Nineteen

DAENA WAITED IN THE DARK, counting down the seconds.

How long did it take to creep through the house? To pull on boots? Sneak outside? Was that scratching on the roof Reece, or just the old house creaking in the wind? She counted to a hundred, two hundred, five hundred. Was he through the garden? Through the hedge? Into the fields? Not knowing was driving her insane.

Gods of the earth, please don't let him be caught.

It was a long time since she'd prayed, but as she lay there, heart thudding, she whispered to the gods and the angels, begging them for one more gift, one last blessing, asking them to keep Reece safe.

Slowly the cold seeped into her body and from there into her heart, and she began to shiver. A rolling tremor that shuddered through her, part misery, part terror. Until, eventually, she couldn't sit still any longer. Not with the scent of sex and Reece lingering in the cold air and her fear for him swirling and churning through her mind.

She pulled out Reece's dagger and cut a strip from the rough blanket she'd slept on, and then used it to strap the dagger to her thigh. Then she pushed herself up to standing and lowered her aching shoulders. She pulled on her boots, rolling her ankle to release the tight muscles, wrapped herself in the warm black cloak Reece had given her, and stepped out into the lonely quiet of the kitchen.

She made herself a cup of peppermint tea—the leaves were old and bitter now, but at least the water was hot and fragrant—and sat at the table under the window as a hazy gray light slowly filtered into the room. The temptation to do something wound her muscles tighter and tighter, but she made herself stay still. To maintain her usual routine.

She took another sip of her tea as a lark sang somewhere out over the hedgerow, trilling and twittering as it welcomed the day. It sounded like joy, and it gave her hope. The house was quiet. Reece was away. Somewhere, out there in the rising dawn, he was safe.

"Daena."

She flinched before she could stop herself. Andred's voice, so hard and cold, meant only danger. She spun slowly in her chair to look at him. He was dressed for parade, his heavy woolen cloak fastened at his throat with a jeweled clasp, slightly open over his broad chest to reveal his black tunic with the silver fighting boars. As he moved, the cloak fell back from his arms, highlighting the way his curling black-and-red family tattoos rose over the top of his gleaming, polished vambraces. His sword shone in its ornate scabbard at his side. He was every inch the powerful general, commander of armies, claimant to the throne. He looked ready to go to war.

"He left," Andred said, watching her carefully.

It wasn't a question, but she answered it anyway. "Who left?"

He folded his arms over his chest, face tight and angry. "Don't play stupid with me, Daena."

She placed her mug of cooling tea carefully on the table. "I have no idea what you're talking about."

He stalked forward, looking down at her, the gray light playing over his hair, adding silver to the dark strands. For a moment, she could imagine what he would have looked like had he never betrayed his king. A powerful lord, handsome, virile, and commanding. He could have sat on the council, the lord of his family, a wealthy landowner, honored general, perhaps a husband. He'd had so very much—but he'd wanted more.

"He didn't take you?" Andred stated, a thin thread of amusement coloring his tone. "Reece left you here alone."

No. He hadn't left her. She had chosen to stay. And it made all the difference in the world. Daena shrugged. "Reece is asleep in the library." The words tasted of dandelion root: sharp and astringent, but she kept her face blank.

"No, he's not. But you know where he is, don't you?"

She did her best not to roll her eyes. "How the hell am I supposed to know where he is? Have you ever seen me go anywhere near the library?"

Andred lowered himself into the chair beside her, legs splayed wide and dominant. "Don't lie to me, Daena."

She took another sip of her cooling tea, using the bitterness to clear her palate, and played his game. She held out her arm, offering him her wrist. "I'm not lying. I don't know where he is." Not precisely, anyway. "And I never go into the library."

Andred grunted, not convinced but not bothering to take her offered wrist either.

She shrugged and dropped her hand back to the table. The most important thing was to keep him talking. Keep him distracted. Give Reece every possible chance. "What do you want, Andred?" she asked.

He looked out the window toward the garden, still swathed in dark mists. "Do you know what it takes to be the king of Brythoria?" he asked.

She knew. Courage. Loyalty. Honor. But she didn't say any of those; she didn't think that was what he meant.

"Three things," Andred stated, not bothering to wait for her reply. "The blood of Aloysius. The approval of the council. And, finally, the support of the people. Geraint had two of those, Ballanor only one. *I* will have all three."

Severely diluted blood. The support of a deposed council. And... what? Why was he even telling her this? "I don't understand."

"We always knew Reece was working with the Hawks. Just because he ran off and threw a tantrum didn't mean Tristan would let him go. Tristan's always been like that. Far too sentimental," Andred said with a sneer.

"You're loyal to your brothers," Daena pointed out, annoyance rising.

He dipped his chin, eyes gleaming. It had been like this when they first met. He liked that she challenged him. He liked sparring. She'd thought it was because he was interested in her opinions, but now she understood it better —he only liked it when he knew he would win. When he thought he knew something she didn't.

"True," Andred agreed. "But they're loyal to me in return. A Wraith who wants out is out forever."

There was a point to this line of discussion. Something

she was guaranteed not to like. And she wanted to get to it sooner rather than later. "So why did you let him come here then?" Daena asked.

Andred rested his hands behind his head, interlacing his fingers and letting his elbows flare out. "We wanted his expertise. We wanted to watch him. We wanted him to do exactly what he did. And we wanted you."

Her mouth tasted of bile, but it wasn't because he was lying—he wasn't—it was because every word out of his mouth was like blight creeping over a crop.

"Why?" The question scraped out of her. She didn't want to know… but she needed to.

Andred leaned back, clearly pleased with himself. "He's done exactly what we hoped. He's run back to the Hawks with stories of ships and cannon and threats to the palace."

"That isn't your plan then?" Gods and angels. She'd told Reece it was true. Would he think she'd lied? That she was working with the Wraiths all along?

"Oh, it's true." Andred grunted, a smug, self-satisfied sound. "It's the backup plan. Dionys has several merchant ships equipped to defend against pirates and already inside the harbor, all neatly tied up at the docks. If our first plan fails, we'll be ready to burn Lucilla's palace to the ground." His voice was so fervent, his expression so intense: Andred *wanted* to burn it all; he was just looking for an excuse to do it.

"What's your first plan?" she asked, unable to keep the horror from her voice.

"The love of the people." Andred's eyes brightened as if it was already a given. "Reece will warn the Hawks about the danger on the river, and Lucilla will immediately close the port. Ships will languish on the seas, their catches rotting in their holds, their fresh water running low, sailors kept from their families through the midwinter festivities. The people of Kaerlud will be without food just as the worst of winter hits, while the families of the sailors will rumble with the unfairness of it all."

Hell. That was exactly what would happen. She gripped the mug tightly in her fists, forcing herself not to leap from the chair and run. They'd thought they'd been so clever, picking up on all the tidbits the Wraiths had accidentally dropped. Meanwhile, Andred had been throwing out crumbs on purpose all this time. Gods. She should have known.

"Then," Andred continued, "just when the people of Kaerlud start to feel really hungry, they're going to find out the truth: that Lucilla blockaded the harbor when she declared war on Verturia. She's gone back on her word to her people. They've seen the soldiers sweeping through the city, the squads in the north, the way that nobles' houses have been searched and disrupted. We've already started rumors that she's betrayed them… soon they'll know she's a liar and a traitor. Just like her brother."

Daena couldn't help her horrified gasp. "But none of that is true! Her people love her. They'll never believe—"

"They will when the Supreme Justice of the Nephilim tells them it is." Andred rocked forward, dropping his elbows to lean them on his knees. "There'll be rioting. They've been pushed and pushed for years. Now they're going to fight back, and we're going to be right there helping them do it. We'll give Lucilla the option to surrender, but if she doesn't, people will die. If she hides in her palace, we'll crush it, and if she comes out to face us, we'll lead the people of Kaerlud against her. She's completely overextended, and she's been running behind every step of the way."

This was his plan? This was so much worse than merely destroying the palace with the queen inside it. This would destroy the city. No, it couldn't be possible. And her family... hell. "Ramiel would never—"

Andred cut her off with an irritated snort. "I never knew Ramiel was your uncle. All that time. But now.... Well. What do you think Lord Ramiel, Supreme Justice of Brythoria, would give to prevent your torture? Your slow and agonizing death?"

"You wouldn't." She could taste the lie in her own words. He would, and they both knew it.

"As we speak, he's busy receiving a rather gruesome package. I would apologize for sending him Gaheris's head before breakfast, but frankly, it's better for everyone if he understands me clearly." Andred pulled heavy leather gloves from his cloak pocket and started tugging them onto his hands. "Ramiel will do as he's told."

No. He wouldn't. Ramiel would do what was right. As she was finally doing. But it would hurt him deeply. And it would hurt Haniel, who would have to put him back together. And her family, who might struggle to forgive him.

"Why tell me this?" she asked in a strangled whisper.

"Because I know you, Daena. You'll have convinced yourself that helping the Hawks is the honorable thing to do. It's not. They're not your friends. When it came to it, they sacrificed you without a moment's remorse. The right thing to do now is to throw all that intelligence of yours behind helping us succeed. Be our truth seeker in earnest and help us to win this war."

She let out a bitter laugh. Maybe the Hawks weren't her friends, but they could have been. In a different world, a world without Andred, they would have been.

"Help you to torture me?" she spat. "Help you perpetrate my own slow, agonized death. Are you insane?"

He stood to lean over her, menacing and huge. "Convince Ramiel to support us, and your torture won't be necessary. I'm not a monster, Daena. We shared... intimate things. I don't want to have to hurt you."

Gods. The worst thing was that it didn't even taste like a lie. She tilted her head back and looked him in the eye. "You *are* a monster. I shared my love for you, and all you ever shared with me was your contempt. If you think I'm going to help you, you really are insane."

His hand clenched over the back of her chair, his jaw gritted, but she no longer cared. What would he do to her that he wasn't planning anyway? She couldn't do anything more to help Reece, and now she was done.

She glared at Andred until he straightened, and then she slowly rose from the table. Her hands were shaking—from fury and fear—but she wouldn't let him see. She smoothed her dress, trying to calm herself, trying to decide how she could help Lucilla, how she could warn the Hawks of Andred's true plans.

Her hand brushed over the sharp hilt of the dagger beneath her skirt. It steadied her. Knowing she had a weapon. Knowing she had options. But she couldn't do anything now. Andred was a powerful man who had been a warrior for most of his life. If she pulled the dagger out, they would fight. And Andred would win. Better to keep it secret and use it when she had a chance. Because she was never going to help Andred again, no matter what he thought.

A door crashed open behind her, and she jumped, whirling to face the new threat.

Caius stalked inside and saluted Andred. "Reece is out. Royn followed him to the neighboring farm."

"And the Hawks?" Andred asked.

"Royn saw a Mabin in the air. One squad has been stationed at the river. We expect they'll be here in the next thirty minutes. More troops will follow close behind."

"Good." Andred straightened his tunic, once again the regal commander. "Mobilize the men; we need to go."

"Yes, sir," Caius agreed. He put his fingers to his lips and blasted a series of sharp whistles. Almost instantly, a horn blew from the courtyard. The war horn of the Wraiths. It gave a loud, ghostly wail that sounded like death and destruction.

Andred gripped her arm and dragged her through the house out to the courtyard—too fast to complain or fight back. Too many soldiers surrounded them to even consider the dagger now.

The Wraiths moved with practiced efficiency, one soldier led saddled horses from the stables as the others speedily tied on their packs and mounted up. Andred shoved her toward Usna, who lifted her onto a large chestnut stallion before climbing up behind her, and then they were away.

Andred led them a short gallop down the muddy main road and then wheeled off onto a path through the fields. The horses' hooves thudded on the hard earth, gulls wheeling and crying in the distance, and all she could do was hold on and ignore the miserable ache in her heart.

They crested a rise, the fens spreading out before them, and moments later there was a loud boom.

Flocks of birds rose screaming into the air as she twisted, trying to look back. All she could see was smoke and dust where the house had been. Gods. Andred had razed his own house to the ground. This was why he'd sent Reece for extra explosive powder. To hide the evidence of where they'd been and cover their retreat? Or to kill the Blues as they swooped down? Most likely both.

Then they were moving again, and she had to concentrate with everything she had to keep her seat. The ground was pitted and uneven, and Usna's warhorse was forced to gallop this direction, then that, leaping over ancient roots and avoiding hollows filled with ice. Her body was exhausted, and her heart was broken. And she was so bloody tired of Andred taking everything she had. Thank the gods Reece was back with his friends. At least she'd done one thing she was proud of.

They passed through a small copse of alder and ash trees, and then emerged in single file onto the open marshland of the fens. The heavy smell of salt and peat, rotting vegetation, and ancient bogs rose around them as the horses dropped to a steady walk on the treacherous ground. These ponds were too deep to freeze, and the mud of the path dragged at their hooves.

The Wraiths had obviously prepared this route in advance. Red string tied around clumps of grass or low bushes marked where the path diverged around ponds and past streams—identifying the safest tracks—the rider at the back tasked with removing them as they passed. Mist rose slowly around them, making the thud of the horses' hooves echo strangely.

A low whistle broke the silence, and she turned to see what had happened. A scout gestured up toward the sky, and everyone looked up. Gods. Light reflected hazily, but if she squinted, she could see what the scout had noticed... a Mabin in flight.

A tiny grain of hope unfurled. Whatever secrecy Andred

had hoped to buy them by exploding his house, was lost the moment they'd been seen.

"Shoot him down!" Andred ordered from the front of the column, his face dark with furious rage. Daena craned her head back, watching in horror as two archers immediately lifted their crossbows. She couldn't let them. She screamed a frantic "Look out!" just as they began firing.

Usna hauled her back, wrapping his gloved hand over her mouth so tight she could hardly breathe. "Shut the fuck up!"

The Mabin—Jos?—reared back in the air. The Wraiths launched another volley, and he dropped farther back and then finally out of sight.

Usna gave her another vicious shake as she huddled toward the stallion's neck, but he didn't have time to do worse. He pushed them onward, driving the horse down the narrow, winding paths between the standing pools as flocks of water birds screamed around them. The horses slowed further as the fens gave way to dunes and they finally reached the beach.

It was a wide expanse, the sand gray and littered with broken mussel shells. And waiting for them there was a squad of soldiers with immaculate uniforms and gleaming weapons, dressed in the black tunics of the Wraiths. Behind them on the shore was a fleet of rowing boats.

The Wraiths dismounted, Usna glaring at her as he helped her down as if he was dreaming of all the ways he was going to make her pay, but she didn't care anymore. She curled her lip and glared back.

The squad leader saluted. "My Lord Andred, Lord Pellin sends his greetings."

Andred dipped his chin in acknowledgment. "You know what to do?"

"Yes, Sir."

Andred reached into his saddlebag and pulled out the burgundy-and-silver tunic to hand to the squad leader. "Gods be with you."

The guard—tall and dark-haired like Andred—pulled the tunic over his head and then called a command to his men.

Before she'd completely wrapped her head around what was happening, the force was split. A squad mounted the Wraiths' stallions and—with one last order from Andred to watch the skies and shoot down any Mabin—they pushed the horses into an ambling run back up the beach toward the fens, and the fields beyond them.

As soon as they were moving, the rest of the soldiers began splashing through the icy sea and climbing into the boats.

Gods. This was too well planned: the mounted soldiers now wending through the fens would prevent Reece and the Hawks from following the Wraiths or even knowing which way they'd gone. At worst, they'd descend on the Hawks in battle.

If she thought about it—about Reece fighting for his life in the fens after everything else he'd survived—it would break her. So she locked it all away. If she lived, she would think about it later.

Gods. *If* she lived. She'd thought she'd made peace with the fact that she wouldn't survive the Wraiths. But now that it came to it, she didn't want to die. She wanted to see Reece again. She wanted to work with plants again. She wanted to live. And that meant she couldn't get into a boat with Andred.

She turned and started to run, but the sand with thick and soft, and her weak ankle turned and throbbed. She'd only managed three stumbling steps when Usna caught her and flung her over his shoulder with an irritated grunt, muttering about how he always knew she was far more pain than she was worth. He threw her into the closest boat, letting her thud hard against the side, before climbing in along with Andred and Caius.

She sucked in burning gasps of air, her back aching where she'd hit the wood, and tried to understand what she was seeing. All the other boats turned immediately south, with the soldier dressed like Andred at the helm. And now she could see one of the smaller soldiers had huddled in the back with a dark cowl over his head and face. Was that… her?

Caius and Usna grabbed the oars and paddled them quickly out to sea as Andred settled himself. And then they turned north, away from the rest of the fleet.

"Where are we going?" she demanded, pushing herself to sit as Caius and Usna hauled heavily at the oars, skimming them rapidly over the shallow waves, but no one answered.

"Why are we going this way?" she tried again.

Andred glared at her. "Keep quiet."

Threat dripped through his voice. She'd told him she would never help him, and he'd believed her. Then she'd warned the Mabin in the fens, proving her defiance. He had no reason to manipulate her or to share any more of his plans. They'd finally reached the stage where she was worth more to him broken. Gods.

Lucilla's squads, when they arrived from Kaerlud, would see the boats heading toward the harbor as they expected and follow the Wraiths south, never thinking to look north, and there was absolutely nothing she could do about that.

She was alone. Andred had taken everything, piece by

piece. But he was wrong about one thing: he wouldn't break her.

She slid her hand over the hard shape of the dagger on her thigh, letting its sharp edges reassure her. She settled back and watched the gray ocean swells rolling toward the ocean. She needed to keep her strength. Keep her eyes open. When the time came to act, she had to take it.

Chapter Twenty

MEN WERE DYING. And for a moment Reece was back in Ravenstone. Swords drawn, shields up, huddling over Geraint as they carried him—already too late—from the battle. Here was Tristan, grunting as he slashed out at his opponent, following up with a savage punch to the man's face. Here was Jos fighting on the ground, his face tight with grim horror, a cut on his arm bleeding sluggishly.

A whistle pierced the fog of memory, and he was back in the fight. In *this* fight.

Tristan had had two destriers hidden beside the farm, and they'd ridden hard, pushing their sweating stallions down the road, past the Wraiths' base, Jos in the air above them. They might have stopped to search it, but Jos had already seen the Wraiths making their way out into the fields, carrying Daena with them. And thank the gods they'd ridden past, because only moments later, the entire building had exploded behind them. A trap, left for them by Andred.

Jos guided them down the narrow paths and into the fens until he was driven back by archers. Then he'd fallen back, dropping down to help them find their way among the twisted paths and treacherous channels.

They'd been making good progress. With every mile, his hope had grown that they would catch up to the Wraiths before they reached the boats they would undoubtedly have waiting. But then the Wraiths had returned. A squad, outnumbering him, Tristan, and Jos five to one, had ridden up from the beach and immediately attacked.

Tristan whistled; a loud distress call echoing through the fens, calling the Blues to them.

Reece glanced back at his captain, and the look on Tristan's face—conviction and grim determination— brought back another memory: Tristan sacrificing himself to Grendel to keep them all safe. And following that, an image of Nim standing on a dusty road, face pale and streaked with tears and soot, not even wearing boots, as she looked up at their captain and told him she loved him. Gods. He couldn't let anything happen to Tristan.

Reece flung himself back into the battle, his body armored in heavy scales, his beast growling low and deadly, his unfamiliar destrier dancing and lurching beneath him. He swung his sword in brutal arcs, deeply thankful for the many hours he'd spent training over the past weeks.

He cut and thrust, lunging and stabbing from his saddle, and never let up. The path was narrow, and the Wraiths could only come at them a few at a time. More than that, with every man he wounded, he realized they didn't have the commitment, or, surprisingly, the expertise the Hawks had. They were struggling. Falling under the Hawk's swords. It didn't make sense.

Reece concentrated on the face of the man whose thrust he'd just deflected. He was a stranger. Fuck.

Not the Wraiths.

A whistle blasted from the rear, and the man he was fighting looked over Reece's shoulder, focusing on something behind him. The soldier's eyes widened, just for a moment, before Reece struck him down.

Another took his place, but the new soldier's heart wasn't in it. These weren't battle-hardened warriors. Fighting on horseback seemed to be challenging them. They were off-balance and struggling to manage the angry warhorses they rode. These men had certainly never been in the cavalry. "Not the Wraiths!" Reece bellowed.

A moment later, Garet landed behind their attackers. His wings were drawn back as he stepped up beside Jos, settling his crossbow against his shoulder.

Thank the gods. Garet had always been the best shot of the Hawks, whether with slingshot or stones, having him here would make all the difference. And then there was another sharp whistle. Another wild Hawks' hunting call—this one from behind him.

Whoever was there had brought reinforcements. He could hear hooves thudding and orders being called. And the fight went out of the soldiers attacking them. One after the other, those who still lived dropped their weapons and raised their hands.

Reece turned in his saddle to see Tor leading a squad of eight palace Blues. He lifted his hand toward his friend and gave him a weary nod. "Thank you."

Tor grunted as he gestured to a trio of Blues to lead the defeated men away. As soon as they were gone, he rode up to Reece and clapped him heavily on the shoulder. "You're safe."

Reece chuckled roughly, wiping sweat and dirt out his face. Gods. He'd missed Tor's entirely true and completely obvious comments. And for the first time, he understood the fullness of what his friend meant. Tor was saying he'd been worried. That he had sweated blood to get to them on time. That it meant the world to him that the Hawks were unharmed. Reece leaned closer and smiled at his friend. "I've missed you."

Tor's cheeks flushed, and Reece wondered for a moment if he'd embarrassed his guarded friend past the point of comfort. But then Tor grinned back and squeezed his shoulder. "I've missed you too."

A Mabin dressed in the blue tunic of the elite palace guards landed lightly beside them. "First Lieutenant Tor, I spotted the boats as you expected. They are making speed toward the Tamasa estuary with Andred at their helm."

"Did you see a woman?" Reece asked. "A Nephilim with dark mahogany hair."

The Mabin shook his head. "I couldn't get close enough, but I did see someone huddled at the back, covered in a cowl. Maybe that was her?"

Thank the Gods. She was alive. If they'd taken her in the boats, they still needed her. They would keep her alive. For now, anyway. All he had to do was get her back.

Tor turned to Tristan as he reported. "We've sent the command to close the harbor. They'll find the blockade already in place when they get there, and we'll arrest them when they arrive. We also have squads preparing to board every ship already inside the blockade. We'll seize Dionys's fleet and tow his ships to the docks as soon as we identify them."

Gods. That was good. It was—

Wrong. Something's wrong…. A thick layer of scales flooded over his entire body, even over his hands, down to his fingers, burning painfully.

"Good work, Tor." Tristan turned to the Mabin who'd

spotted the Wraith's boats. "Thank you, Corporal. Take your squad and follow the fleet from the air. Let us know when the Wraiths approach the blockade."

The Mabin flew off as the others began to turn their horses toward Kaerlud. Jos and Garet made plans to fly back to Kaerlud and update Mathos. Tor spoke softly with Tristan. They were all relieved to be alive. To be taking action after so many weeks of waiting and watching. Once Andred was in custody, this would finally all be over.

But Reece couldn't make himself relax.

They had succeeded. They knew where Andred was. The Wraiths were being followed from the air. The blockade was up in time to stop him from reaching the ships. The palace would be safe. Lucilla would be safe. And yet... his beast said something was wrong, and he believed it.

She's not on that boat.

His whole body froze. "What do you mean?"

Daena doesn't cower. She doesn't huddle in a cowl. She'll go down fighting.

She would. That was absolutely true. But after everything she'd been through, she would be exhausted, frightened....

I feel.... His beast rumbled unhappily. *She's going north.*

"Are you sure?" Reece muttered.

Yes.

"Tristan—" Gods. His voice cracked. He couldn't think of what to say. How could he possibly explain this?

Tristan and Tor both immediately stopped and turned to him in concern, Jos and Garet crowding in behind them.

"What is it?" Tristan asked.

"It's not her. On the boat."

Tristan frowned. "What do you mean?"

"She's not going south."

"How do you know?"

Reece looked at the men who had fought beside him for so many years. Who had saved him from war, from the life he'd fled. The men he should have trusted all along. And told them the truth—a truth he couldn't explain or defend but believed anyway. "My beast says she's going north."

Nobody moved. Tristan and Tor faced him in silent concern, their frowns deepening.

Then Tristan grunted. "Show me your hands."

"What? Why?" Reece muttered. But Tristan was his captain, and his hands were already lifting.

And now he could see why they had hurt so badly. He had claws. Long, lethal blades had punched through the tips of his fingers, through his leather gloves. Gods.

Tristan didn't even flinch. "Okay." He turned to Tor. "What's to the north?"

Tor closed his eyes for a moment, frowning in concentration. "The Svart River." He nodded slowly. "It runs inland, almost parallel to the Tamasa, for miles. It would be easy to land somewhere safe, pick up horses, and come into the city from the northwest."

There was a moment of tense silence, and then Tor continued. "It suggests he expected us to close the harbor. Maybe even planned on it."

Tristan nodded. "If he planned it, he wants the blockade."

"He wants Kaerlud hungry and angry," Tor agreed.

Tristan folded his hands behind his back, expression grim. "Aren't Dionys's family lands somewhere near there?"

Tor's face hardened. "Yes, next to my father's."

"Can we get there first?" Tristan demanded.

"I think so. If we're fast. They won't be expecting us, so

they won't feel they need to hurry or hide. There's a bridge on the great north road; it passes over the river. We can watch from there."

Tristan grunted his agreement. He turned to Jos, voice firm. "Get back to the city as fast as you can. Warn Mathos and Lucilla. If Andred planned on a blockade, we should expect him to have people in the city stirring up trouble. Ask for a company of cavalry to meet us at Dionys's country manor. And tell Nim, please, if there's time."

Tristan looked across at the remaining five men Tor had brought with him. "Three of you, follow Jos, make sure he gets to the city safely. You two, you're with us." Then he faced Reece. "We ride north."

"Thank you, Tristan." His voice grated as his beast rattled, but Tristan understood. They all did.

Reece ignored the steady ache in his fingers as he gripped the reins and dug his heels into his destrier, driving him into a gallop. They had to find Daena.

Chapter Twenty-One

Daena sat in the back of the boat, watching the shore slide closer, ignoring the three bastards in front of her. They rowed backward, facing her, but she had no desire to look at them or even acknowledge that they existed.

They reached the river mouth quickly, but their speed dropped noticeably as soon they entered the fast-flowing waterway itself. The Svart river, as Andred named it, was swollen with winter rains, the waters dark and frothy, rich with the runoff from the fens and seething with crosscurrents where the river met the sea.

Caius and Usna battled hard, inching forward until Andred muttered out an annoyed capitulation, opened the jeweled clasp at the throat of his cloak, letting it fall back to free his arms, and joined them. Soon they began making better progress.

The men sweated and swore, battling the waves and the current, but she sat quietly, racking her brain for a solution.

Should she simply step off the back? She might make it to the bank. She'd been a skilled swimmer as a child, and she was far stronger now. All the Wraiths had swum in the icy lake beside Andred's camp—it was the only way to get properly clean—and she had always swum that little bit further out, away from them all. Even if they followed her into the river, she had a better chance than she did stuck in the boat. And if she didn't make it, well, at least then they couldn't use her to hurt Ramiel.

And yet, deep in her heart, she knew it wouldn't be enough. If she survived, she would have to live with the fact that she'd let Andred go.

Reece growled in her memory, pressing her into the side of the stables and demanding she never risk herself again. Insisting that she stay safe. The thought warmed her, feeding the slowly unfurling seed he'd sown in her heart. She'd been so angry at the time. But now she saw it for what it was; him expressing his fear. For her.

Where was he? Had he made it? Was he safe? Gods, please let him be safe. Angels, please let him be with his friends when he learned Andred had been manipulating them all along. Please don't let him blame himself for another betrayal that was not his fault.

She couldn't bear the thought of Reece alone and hurting, pushed back to the dark place he'd finally begun to leave behind. She might still have a chance to remove Andred from the world, and she had an obligation to try. For Lucilla and the kingdom, but also for Reece.

Andred was distracted while he rowed. He was sitting, unable to loom over her in the small boat. When they were on land, he had all the advantages, this was her best opportunity.

She shifted in her seat, twisting until the dagger on her thigh was hidden between her leg and the side of the boat, and slowly started to drag her skirt up.

They finally cleared the river mouth and out of the waves, but the current didn't abate. The fens gave way to cultivated land, lying fallow for the winter as the men hauled against the oars, sweating with exertion.

She could feel the knife-sheath under her fingertips.

Caius glared at her and she froze, breath tight in her lungs. She was so close, so very close. She just needed—

Andred twisted, pulling the cloak that he was sitting on away with an irritated grunt, muttering about how it was too hot and in his way. And then he tossed it into the bottom of the boat. Right at her feet.

Gods. She stared at it, letting her skirt slide back into place. Andred had walked away from the house, now a pile of ashes. He'd left his saddlebags with the soldiers. He'd only kept his cloak. If he had a list of fellow conspirators, that was where it would be.

He'd given her a gift, but she had no idea how to open it. All three men were facing her as they rowed, and if she so much as touched the cloak, they would know.

She forced herself to stare out at the passing riverbanks as she considered and discarded plans. What would Tor do? He was the best strategist she knew. As good, maybe even better, than Andred. When they'd been in the mountains, despite Keely being under threat, he'd…. Keely. That was the answer.

Daena groaned softly, pressing her hands into her belly. She waited a torturous minute, heart thudding. How long did she have? When would Andred decide he'd done enough rowing and want his cloak back? When would they reach their destination? Gods. She couldn't take too long, but she couldn't overplay her hand either.

Finally, she felt enough time had passed and whimpered miserably, leaning her head against the side of the boat.

"What's wrong with you?" Caius muttered, pulling at the oars.

Daena curled her shoulders in, striving to seem entirely pathetic. Aiming to be exactly what they expected. "I don't… don't f-feel well," she stuttered, swallowing heavily.

"Fuck." Usna scowled at her. "Do not get sick in the boat."

Daena hunched further and let out a pitiful moan, counting down another minute before shuddering dramatically and wiping her face with the back of her hand.

"Daena," Andred growled warningly. "Stop it."

"I can't help it. I'm going to—" She flung herself to her knees, facing out the back of the boat, and retched loudly over the side. And, as she did so, she pulled Andred's cloak with her.

She spat into the water and then rested her head against the wooden side, as if exhausted and nauseous, groaning noisily and swallowing air.

"Gods, you're disgusting," Caius muttered. Daena let out a long, loud burp just to torture him, and then retched over the side of the boat once more.

As smoothly as she could, her back to the men as they rowed, she slid her hand into the cloak's pocket. It held silk lining and fluff, but nothing else. It was empty.

She leaned over and retched again, using the motion to disguise her movement as she frantically searched for the second pocket. But the cloak moved, and all she found was smooth wool. She ran her hand more desperately over the fabric, forcing herself to retch loudly at the same time. Where was the other damn pocket? She couldn't find it. Gods. She tried again.

"What are you doing, Daena?" Andred demanded.

She turned her head to glare at him. "I don't feel well."

Her fingers scrabbled… and found it. Finally. She had the other pocket. She slid her fingers inside it and let out a long sigh of genuine misery. Her eyes burned. If she'd been alone, she would have let herself cry. The pocket was empty.

"Give me my cloak," Andred spat. "Immediately."

She turned and held the cloak out toward him. Why not? It made no difference now. But as she did so, it fell open to reveal a secret inner pocket sewn into the lining. Her arm froze, half extended. She needed to look inside that pocket.

Ahead of them, in the distance, a high bridge spanned the river. Three great stone arches divided the water into channels while willow trees crowded the banks. Behind the willows, dark woods spread out, flanking what had to be a significant road. A road that was big enough to justify such an immense bridge. Most importantly, the banks were lower, the current disrupted by the bridge. It could be the chance she needed.

She pulled the cloak back into her chest before he could take it from her, quickly folding it around the inner pocket, sealing it away.

Andred dropped his oars. "Daena, I'm not going to tell you again. Give that to me right now."

Her breath sawed through her lungs, rough and strained as she pushed herself up, gripping the side of the boat. "No. I don't take orders from you."

Andred leaned forward, elbows on his knees, his face growing dark with rage, lips bloodless where they pressed together. Once, not that long ago, she would have been terrified.

He started to stand, the boat wobbling with the motion. "You will do as you're told, or so help me—"

She spat. A quivering glob of phlegm landed on his

cheek and slid slowly down. And gods, it felt good. "Fuck you."

He roared as he lunged for her, sending the boat floundering unsteadily, and Caius and Usna heaved the oars trying to hold them still. But Daena was ready. She kept a tight grip on the cloak and jumped.

The water hit her body like a burning wave of ice. The current caught her and turned her, dragging her down and around. But she kicked hard, breaking the surface with a shuddering gasp. Bitter cold seized her lungs. Her ankle throbbed as the muscles in her leg spasmed. Her dress caught against her legs. Branches and pieces of river flotsam scraped against her. But she forced herself forward.

Behind her, she could hear Andred roaring out his rage. Caius and Usna were shouting and swearing. But their fury was muffled, deadened by the water rushing in her ears.

Swimming with the heavy cloak was hell. It swirled and dragged and slowed her down. But she kept it gripped tight, desperately praying that the oiled wool would protect the contents of the pocket, swimming almost one-handed as she pushed herself forward.

Behind her, Andred was bellowing something she couldn't hear properly and didn't understand. But with every second, he sounded further away.

Her teeth chattered, her body quickly numbing. But the bank was so close. So very close. She risked setting her right foot down, and thank the gods and angels, she touched the muddy riverbed. She pushed herself forward, limping through the mud, fighting the current and her skirts. She was freezing, losing feeling in her feet, and her breath shuddered in labored pants.

She was so alone, and it was so difficult to keep moving. A part of her wanted to just let it all go. To finally let herself rest. To let herself sink into the darkness. Like the darkness in her room. Dark and… safe. Reece was there. Holding her.

We'll have this, Reece whispered in her mind. *Warmth and light too.*

Warmth and light. She was warmer now. If she closed her eyes… No. She forced them open.

Promise me, Daena.

I promise.

She didn't know if she'd said it out loud or only in her head. But he'd asked for her promise and she given it. She couldn't break it.

She put both feet down and nearly collapsed when her full weight rested on her spasming ankle. She staggered a few steps, almost fell, and then stumbled onward. Freezing water poured down her body, her dress dragging through the water, catching on roots and stones. And then, finally, she was on the riverbank.

She risked a glance behind her; the boat was gone. Had they accepted that they couldn't reach her or were they coming back? Were they landing somewhere close, preparing to hunt her even now?

All she wanted to do was sink to the ground and whimper, close her eyes and drift into the darkness. Soon, the pain would be back. Soon, the numbness would give way to roaring agony. But she'd made a promise. One to Lucilla, yes, but also one to Reece.

We'll have warmth and light. She whispered it to herself. *I promise.*

She pulled out Reece's dagger and cut away the bottom half of her soaked skirt, freeing her legs, before slipping it back into its sheath with stiff fingers. She wrung out Andred's cloak as best she could and put it around her own shoulders, leaving hers behind. And then she turned toward the woods, facing the direction she'd seen the bridge.

Above her, a hunting bird called, high and clear, but she didn't look up. Putting one foot in front of the other took everything she had, and she had to keep moving. She kept her head down and pushed herself forward.

Chapter Twenty-Two

THEY WERE TOO SLOW. Reece didn't know how he knew, but he didn't doubt it either. He had to get to Daena. And he had to get to her *now*.

The claws refused to withdraw, his beast growled incessantly, one long enraged rumble after the other, upsetting the horses and unsettling the men, yet they still weren't moving fast enough.

They'd had to pass through a village, navigating the market traffic. Then the road had curved southeast and they had traveled several miles in the wrong direction before it curved back and finally joined the wide, hard-packed earth of the Great North Road.

At least the main road was flat and straight and they were able to pick up speed. They passed miles of farmland at a ground-eating canter before entering a long, wooded stretch.

Beech trees, many still holding onto pale brown leaves, and some ash, spiked and barren, closed in around the dusty road, and for a moment, with his beast going insane and fear thundering through him, he was back with Dornar. Lying broken on a road just like this one as Dornar smashed his ringed fist into Reece's face yet again. As he lifted Reece's arm and….

His left arm throbbed where it had been healed by the Nephilim. And somehow it was that very stab of pain that broke the spiral. He had been healed, first by Rafe, right there on that dusty road, and then by the healers of Eshcol. And his squad—his brothers—had stood by him even as he tried desperately to push them away.

Daena had healed alone. Never again. He was going to find her, and he was going to—

The high hunting call of the Hawks cut through the air. Garet, scouting ahead, had seen something from the air.

They pushed their horses harder, galloping down the open road until they saw Garet landing lightly just before a wide stone bridge.

"Captain!" Garet called, gesturing toward the water on the other side, upstream. "They're here!"

Fuck. The boat was already through. The Hawks had missed their best chance.

"Archers," Tristan called, signaling to the Blues following them. "Prepare to fire!"

The two men immediately slung their crossbows over their shoulders as the thundering horses jostled for space. They reached the top of the bridge and pulled to a halt in a tangle of sweating horses and cursing men.

Ahead of them, the boat was pulling away. The men on board were rowing hard, sweating and cursing as they cleared the range of the bridge. It was definitely Andred, Caius, and Usna. Exactly where Tor had predicted. But Daena wasn't in the boat.

The Blues released a volley, but the bolts plopped

uselessly into the swirling water. "Keely would whip their bloody asses," Tor muttered. "But where—?"

"Fire at will!" Tristan roared to the archers. "Find us a path onto the bank; we'll follow from the side."

The Blues sped away as Tristan turned his focus onto Garet. "Report! Where the fuck is Daena?"

"Sorry, Reece." Garet rubbed the back of his neck, speaking fast. "She went over the side."

Reece's scales hardened as his beast snarled, his claws growing impossibly longer. But he couldn't find it in him to reply. He couldn't find a single word to say.

She's alive. I know she is.

"What does that mean?" Tristan asked Garet.

"She grabbed Andred's cloak and jumped."

Gods. Of course she did. "Which bank did she make for?" he asked, not even questioning whether she was swimming. There was no way she would do anything else.

"South. The current took her… I expect she'll come onto land about a mile from here."

A sharp call rang out as the soldiers found a path off the road on the other side of the bridge. It looked like it followed the riverbank, but not close enough to reach the water. The best they could do would be to follow through the woods heading west and hope to catch up on the other side.

Tristan ran an experienced eye over the banks. "Garet, follow Andred from the air. Tor, you take one man on the north bank; I'll take one and cover the south. They have to come aground eventually." Then he reached out and gripped Reece's shoulder. "Go get her."

Reece nodded his thanks—not for setting him after Daena, that had never been in question, but for Tristan's unequivocal support—and wheeled his horse toward the south bank, heading east.

He found a path leading from the road and followed it. It was overgrown with brambles and littered with autumn leaves as he pushed the unfamiliar stallion onward. The horse danced and shivered, wary of the beast growling steadily in its saddle.

Every moment hurt. The woods were close and dark, and the clouds building above them were low and heavy. Time was counted in breaths and growls. It felt like it took forever before they passed a small tumbledown shack. Perhaps it had been a woodcutter's or a forester's hut. Either way, it had been abandoned long ago. And that was where the path ran out.

They had to drop to a walk, the horse picking its way over branches and roots, frozen mud crackling beneath his hooves. A light rain started to fall, misting down around them, as visibility worsened.

Reece kept the sound of rushing water to his left, his eyes constantly scanning the trees as he searched. Gods. It would be so easy to miss her.

How long could Daena survive out here after being in the water? Had she even made it out the river?

She made it. I know it.

The litany played in his head, a chant, or perhaps a prayer. His beast's voice blending with his until it was impossible to know where one ended and the other began.

Reece pushed on, nerves on fire, startling every time a bird hopped along the ground, rustling the leaves. He must have gone more than a mile. Surely, he should have seen her or heard her by now? But he still hadn't found her. What did that mean?

Call her. Right now.

He didn't question his beast. Not anymore. He simply lifted his head and shouted as loudly as he could, "Daena!"

His voice echoed through the trees. The woods seemed to pause breathlessly for a long moment. "Daena!" he called again.

And then he heard it. A thin returning shout. "Reece?"

Gods. She was behind him. They had passed each other without realizing. He spun back the way he'd come and pushed the stallion into a reluctant trot. "I'm coming!"

Her shouts grew louder, leading him closer, and then, there she was.

Her wet hair was plastered to her head, her dress—hacked off at the knees—was muddy and torn beneath a too-big sopping-wet cloak. Her lips were blue and her face paler than he'd ever seen it. And she was utterly, heart-stoppingly beautiful.

He wasn't even aware of sliding off his horse, but then he was half running, half staggering over the frozen ground. She limped toward him, whispering his name as if she couldn't quite believe he was real. He couldn't quite believe it either, even as he took her in his arms.

She was so cold. Her whole body was shaking as he lifted her and carried her back to the horse. He set her into the saddle, and then climbed up behind her, wrapping her trembling form in his arms.

Daena nestled into him, her icy face pushed into his neck as she muttered something about keeping a promise. He twisted to look down at her, not knowing what she meant, just as she closed her eyes.

Fuck. That was bad. She had pushed herself too hard, through too much fear and danger, and now she was drifting. He had to get her warm, give her a chance to rest.

He directed the horse through the woods, back to the

hut he'd seen earlier. She slumped over as he slid out from behind her, and he only just caught her safely, cradling her as he kicked open the wooden door and stepped inside.

The hut was spartan and covered in dust. A wooden table, two stools, and a couple of shelves served as the cooking and living area, while a low wooden pallet pushed against the log wall was the bedroom. But there was a fireplace, and the walls blocked the wind and kept off the slowly building rain.

He settled her on the stool, swaying and half asleep, and quickly helped her to strip off a dripping man's cloak, her sodden boots, and the shredded plum-colored dress he'd given her when they climbed out the sewer. A lifetime ago.

She had his dagger tied to her thigh with fraying strips of an old blanket, and the sight of it made him want to howl in grief and rage. She'd been so alone.

The knots were soaked and too tight to pick apart, and eventually he had to cut it off. Daena merely shivered, her eyes half-closed. He stripped out of his cloak, pulled his tunic over his head, and wrapped her in it, then bundled her onto the rough pallet. She didn't complain or open her eyes, and it terrified him even more than the gray pallor of her face and the way she was shivering incessantly.

He covered her in his cloak and ran back outside. He had to get her warm. As soon as the horse was safely tied up under the eaves, he was able to hunt for firewood. Dead branches littered the ground, and it didn't take long to gather an armful of sticks and twigs that had been largely protected from the rain. By the time he made it back into the hut, Daena was huddled into a miserable ball, her teeth chattering loud enough to hear from the doorway.

The flint was awkward to hold in his claws, and he

struck it poorly again and again. "Give me my hands back," he muttered at his beast.

It growled back. *I can't. I want…. I need her safe.*

"So do I. Fuck. Just give me a few seconds."

His beast growled even louder, but his claws retracted for long enough to spark a flame before they slid back out again. He blew on it desperately, willing it to catch. A tiny wisp of smoke curled out, and then the kindling caught. Thank the gods, it was enough.

He fed sticks and then bigger branches into the flames, watching them as they popped and cracked, steaming as the water in them burned away, until finally the fire was burning cheerfully and the hut was slowly warming. Then he set their clothes and boots in front of the hearth and curled up behind Daena, wrapping her in his warmth.

She snuggled closer, threading her fingers through his as she whispered a soft, heartbreaking thanks. Her body slowly relaxed, the shudders fading, until she slept.

He breathed her in, felt her chest rising and falling, her soft warmth pressed into him. And then, for the first time since he'd lost his home and moved onto the streets, he let himself be still.

Chapter Twenty-Three

DAENA WOKE to the feeling of warmth and safety, a hard body pressed up against her back, and a low contented hum —almost a purr—engulfing her.

It felt like a dream. Like a continuation of the dream she'd had in the woods. She'd been so cold, so exhausted, and then she'd heard Reece calling for her.

It hadn't made any sense; he was in Kaerlud, helping the Hawks blockade the harbor. But she hadn't been able to stop herself from following his voice. From drawing on his strength when hers was so severely battered.

And now… was this real? She couldn't explain it. If she could choose, this was the dream she would have wanted. But would she dream the spider spinning a complicated web in the corner of the room? Would a dream include the low crackle of the fire and the steady drumming of rain on the roof? Or the mold growing on the far wall?

She twisted to look over her shoulder and found Reece lying on his side, awake and watching her. His gray eyes were surrounded by a bright ring of sapphire, deeper and more vibrant than she'd ever seen it, and she couldn't help the slow smile that spread over her face. "You're here."

He smiled back, the sides of his eyes crinkling as his beast rumbled out a louder, even more satisfied purr.

Daena rolled over, noticing for the first time that she was wearing his tunic. "I thought you'd be in Kaerlud by now," she whispered.

"I...." Reece gave a self-deprecating half chuckle. His hand settled on the back of her neck. Almost as if he wanted to hold her. As if he thought she might run. But he didn't say anything.

She turned onto her side, wanting to face him, but the pallet was narrow, and the movement brought their faces close enough to touch. Close enough that she could hear his breath hitch. "Reece?"

He cleared his throat, a slight flush reddening the skin of his neck. "My beast knew you weren't with Andred, so we came north."

She blinked, trying to understand. Reece's beast had known where she was. He looked strangely uncertain. As if he'd just admitted something momentous. Something that still didn't make sense. "How did your beast know?"

"It thinks...." He cleared his throat again. "It's chosen you."

It had chosen her. What did that mean? She thought.... Could it be? "Chosen me for what?"

The rumble between them grew louder, more insistent, and it filled her with an emotion she hadn't felt for so long: hope. It was half wanting and half fear. Anticipation blended with an overwhelming sense of rightness, as if her soul had recognized the truth and simply whispered, *yes. Here you are, I was looking for you.* But her mind was not as easily convinced.

She cared for him, a lot. He was attracted to her. And he had shown her again and again that he respected her. But they had different lives, different dreams. He wanted to get back to the palace, while she wanted a quiet life with her plants. Would he be able to accept that? Because she couldn't become someone else for a man, not again.

"It's chosen you as its mate," Reece murmured. Slowly, hesitantly, he lifted his hand to show her the lethal claws extending from his fingertips. "It did this when you were in danger. It retracts them when I'm touching you, but as soon as I stop, they come back."

Bright sapphire flared in his eyes before he shut them tightly, breaking their connection. Almost as if he was hiding.

This big, strong soldier. The man who had brought down the road in front of the Nephilim courts with such skill that not one person had been hurt. Who had stormed them into Andred's camp without flinching. Who'd lived through Ravenstone and the long northern campaign, been tortured by the Lord High Chancellor without ever giving up his friends. This powerful man was hiding from her.

She'd known that he'd been hurt. But even when he'd shared his secrets with her, she hadn't realized just how vulnerable he'd been. And now he was waiting for her to reject him.

A primal rush of protectiveness engulfed her. She wanted his smile back. She wanted him to know how strong and capable he was. She wanted him to have the safety and security he needed—and to be the one who gave it to him.

She lifted her hand to cradle his cheek. "Look at me, Reece."

He opened his eyes slowly, not quite meeting her gaze until she moved her face too close for him to avoid.

"I don't know a lot about mates," she whispered. "I didn't think we——"

His whole body stiffened, and somehow she knew she was going to lose him. He wasn't going to wait for the words he thought would cut him. He was going to kiss her forehead and climb off the pallet and walk away, and they would be done. And she couldn't let that happen.

"Please, Reece, don't go." She gripped him tighter, holding him, knowing he would never hurt her by ripping himself away.

She searched for an easy explanation to give him and failed. There was no way to prevaricate. She was going to have to tell him the truth. She was going to have to do the one thing she had never wanted to do again: make herself vulnerable. "I'm… afraid."

Her words had the exact opposite effect of what she intended. He flinched back so hard that the pallet rocked beneath them.

Gods. She had less than seconds to fix this.

"Not of you!" She flung herself forward and wrapped her arms and legs around him, holding him still as his beast rumbled unhappily between them. "I'm not afraid of you, Reece. Not at all."

He shook his head. "I don't understand."

She pressed her face into his neck. "I'm afraid of the future."

His rough exhale teased her hair. "What does that mean?"

"Honestly, I didn't expect to survive this," she admitted. "I didn't think about the future, or if I would even have one. And if I had… I would have expected it to be alone. Now you're talking about mates. And you're so… you're so…."

Reece rolled, pulling her on top of him, looking up at

her through eyes that were almost entirely sapphire. Scales flickered on his face in gleaming waves as if preparing to shield him from her judgment. "I'm so…?"

"You're loyal and honorable," she replied. "You tell me the truth, and when you look at me, you see *me*. And you're…. Gods, you know how much my body wants you." His beast rumbled out a smug growl, but she had to say the rest. "I have it on good authority that you're also charming, that you love parties and palace functions. I know how hard you worked to get there, Reece, and you've told me, more than once, that when this is all over you want that life back. The Hawks have returned to the Blues, you'll be promoted, and you'll have everything you've ever wanted. But that…." She let out a soft sigh and then forced herself to finish. "None of that is me."

His body was still tense beneath hers, his focus entirely concentrated on her. "What *do* you want?"

"I want to work with my seedlings, my precious lotus plants that were destroyed in the fire. I'll have to go back to the Thabana Mountains to try and find more plants, which means long amounts of time in the north. I like people, but honestly, not parties." She gave him a rueful smile. "Too many people, half of them avoiding the truth, the others telling outright lies. It's exhausting. I like to speak to people a few at a time. And then I need silence for a while. I need to go back to my plants and be by myself."

He lifted his hand and cupped her cheek, his thumb dragging along the soft skin under her eye. It was her left cheek, the one with the scar, but he didn't seem to notice. His eyes never left hers. "Do you feel exhausted like that with me?" he asked gently.

"No," she answered honestly. "You tell me the truth, you respect my opinions, and you don't expect me to be anything other than what I am. I like being with you." She pressed a gentle kiss to the side of his mouth. "But I can't make myself into something I'm not, not again. I can't become the palace truth seeker or the popular party girl. Not even for you."

Reece watched her for long moments, his chest rising and falling on a heavy breath. And then he smiled. "Okay."

"Okay?"

"I understand what you're saying." His hands gripped her waist, and she could feel tiny pinpricks scoring into her skin through the tunic he'd given her. "I'll never ask you to change. Your strength, your resilience, your core of goodness, even your preference for plants over people—" He chuckled. "—those are all things I like about you. Can we just… try? Can we wait until the kingdom is safe before we make any decisions?"

"Yes." The word was out before she could even think about it. No matter what happened in the future, she would take as much time with him as she could. "I want that."

His beast rumbled out a pleased purr as his lips twitched into a smile. He was laid out beneath her, wearing nothing except his breeches, and she desperately wanted to taste that smile. So, she lowered her head and kissed him.

It wasn't the fierce clash of their previous kisses, but a slow, languid tasting. His mouth opened beneath hers and his tongue stroked up against hers in a lingering caress.

The rain beat on the wooden roof, a steady thrum that surrounded them, isolating them in the tiny hut. The fire had burned low, the warm orange light forming a glowing sanctuary hidden from the cold, dark storm outside.

A horse neighed softly from beneath the eaves, and she pulled back, breathing hard. "Do we need to go?" she asked.

"We will soon," Reece admitted. "But we can't go in this downpour. I don't know the way, we're more likely to get lost, and the horse will struggle to carry both of us through the mud."

"Are you sure?" she asked, hoping he would say yes.

In answer, he lifted his head and kissed her again. Their kiss grew deeper, heavier. She slanted her mouth, wanting to reach him, to feel him everywhere. He slid his hands up her hips, dragging the soft cotton of the tunic up, until he could settle his hands over her ass and run his calloused hands over her skin, sending tingles dancing up her spine.

His shaft was thick and hard between them, and she let her legs fall to his sides, straddling him. His hands clenched, gripping her ass, kneading the cheeks, and pulling her even closer.

She rocked against him, notching the heavy weight of his cock right where she needed the pressure, and he groaned. "Gods, Daena. You're so beautiful. Touching you…." He opened his eyes and looked right at her. "Thank you for giving me this."

His "thank you" broke her. He deserved so much more than what life had dealt him. She wanted him to have everything. She pushed herself back, sliding between his legs to settle on her knees, and then opened the placket of his breeches.

Reece lifted himself to balance on his elbows, watching her through heavy-lidded eyes as she freed his cock and pressed a slow kiss to the head.

"Fuck, yes." His eyes drifted closed, his muscles bunching as she tasted him. She ran her tongue over his length, one hand cupping his heavy balls as she teased the underside.

She took him deep into her mouth, adding suction, and

his eyes flew open, sapphire bleeding across his irises, surrounding his blown-out pupils. His voice was rough as he muttered a string of low curses, his hand dropping to the back of her head.

Gods. She felt powerful and beautiful, more alive than she'd been in months.

She gripped the base of his cock in her fist as she sucked him, reveling in his smooth hardness, the way he groaned and twitched. Salty precome bathed her tongue as she bobbed her head, pulling back and then taking him down once more.

His hips shuddered forward, and his hands threaded into her hair, his grip firm but not controlling.

She hollowed her cheeks, sucking hard as he thrust upward, and for a moment she thought he was at the edge, almost, over it. And maybe he was, because suddenly he lifted her, pulling her up his body and then rolling her onto her back.

"I need to be inside you. I have to be inside you, please, Daena." His words were rough and fervent, more undone than she had ever heard him.

"Yes," she whispered. "Yes. Now."

He pushed his breeches off and then pressed a hard kiss against her mouth, a kiss of need and want and rising desperation as she bent her knees and dropped her legs open, inviting him into her body. But then he paused, his body over hers, heated and golden in the firelight. "Does this work for you?" he asked roughly.

For a moment she didn't understand, but then she realized he was making sure she was comfortable, asking if she needed support for her ankle. With his pulsing cock notched at her entrance, his muscles quivering and taut with need, he was checking on her. Gods.

She could love him. Just a little more time together, and she would. Not with naivety, falling for a handsome face and sweet words—the angels knew Reece had given her none of those—but with a genuine understanding of who he was.

"Yes," she murmured, "I'm good." And then she wrapped her legs around his hips and dragged him closer. He slid into her body like he was coming home, and for a moment they stayed locked together, neither of them moving, both of them lost in the intensity between them.

Her inner muscles fluttered around his shaft, and he groaned, a deep rumble, half man and half beast. And then he started to move.

His thrusts were slow and smooth, rocking and grinding into her while he watched her with such concentrated focus that she knew he was cataloging every tiny reaction. What made her eyelids flutter closed, which movements made her whimper.

He smelled of salt and healthy male. His skin was hot, indigo scales flickering over his collarbones. And she couldn't resist running her tongue over his neck, tasting him, before he sealed his lips over hers once more.

She arched beneath him, lifting her hips, chasing the rising pleasure. He kissed her again, then dragged his lips down her neck, nibbling at the straining tendons before rising to his haunches. His cock was still throbbing at her entrance as he kneeled between her legs, settling back on his ankles.

From there, he had complete access to her body. He held up his hands, showing her how the claws slowly retracted. Then he dragged one hand over her breasts, teasing and twisting her nipples before sliding the other down her body to her clitoris, to tease and taunt the swollen bundle of nerves.

And then he thrust again. The new angle took him to her front wall, his heavy shaft rocking back and forth in the place that drove her wild, while his thumb tortured her clit and his fingers tweaked hard on a rigid nipple.

She flung her head back, breath coming in rough pants, fingers scrabbling on the hard pallet, needing something to grip. But he didn't stop. Instead, he started whispering. "Daena, baby. Do you know how beautiful you are locked around my cock?"

She whimpered, body buzzing. Her hands found the wall and she pushed back against it, driving herself harder onto him.

"Can you feel what you're doing to me?" He grunted, thrusting harder, voice ragged. "Can you feel what you're doing to my beast?"

Gods. She *could* feel it. His beast was rumbling continuously, his body vibrating against hers. *Inside* hers. His hands were everywhere. There was a furnace rising through her body, shafts of vibrant pleasure exploding through her blood.

"Daena," he murmured, "you're better than any dream I've ever had." He rubbed her harder, circling tighter, just at exactly the right pressure, and then she was flying. She screamed out her ecstasy, thrashing below him as his thrusts deepened, his pace increasing frantically, and she orgasmed again. Or maybe it was the same climax, a continuous flood of rapture as she gasped for air, whimpering and whispering his name.

He pulled out, collapsing over her as he came in shuddering streams, his cock pressed into her hip, his face buried in her neck as they clung together.

Slowly the air returned to her lungs. Slowly he relaxed, his muscles losing their rigid tension. She wrapped her arms around his neck and slung her leg over his hips, holding him close for long, heated moments until he rolled to one side, taking his weight off her, but keeping his arms around her.

He waited until her eyes fluttered open, until she was looking right at him. Then he locked his gaze on hers, and murmured, "We'll make this work, I promise."

Gods. She wanted to believe. She wanted that so very badly.

For now, there was something she could give him. Something important. She smiled up at him and whispered, "Truth."

Chapter Twenty-Four

GODS, she was breathtaking. Beautiful, courageous, and strong. And her whispered "truth" was still floating between them. He wanted to roll on top of her and kiss her again, taste the honesty between them.

But the rain was slowing, Daena was warm and awake, and the Hawks needed their help. As much as he might wish they could stay in their golden bubble and pretend the rest of the world didn't exist, they couldn't. Not yet, anyway.

When he'd thought she didn't want him, it had been devastating... but not surprising. He'd deserved it for all the things he'd said and done over the last months, all the ways he'd let himself down, the ways he'd let her down. But when it turned out that she *did* want him—that she wanted *them*—it had changed everything. He finally felt whole.

His beast wanted to build. And he did too. He wanted to create beauty, not tear it down. Not anymore.

That could be their life. A life where he could build while Daena grew her plants and worked on her cure. He wanted it so badly that he could almost taste it. But before that could ever be a reality, they had to finish this mission.

He'd left his squad—his brothers—when they needed him before, he could never do that again. And he knew Daena would feel the same. The clouds were lifting, and the day was growing brighter. They had to find the Hawks, help them destroy Andred's plans, and then they would be free to do as he'd promised: try.

He tucked a lock of mahogany hair behind Daena's ear. "I wish we could stay here, I really do, but the rain has stopped."

At his words, she pushed herself up and climbed from the pallet. The firelight mingled with the soft daylight coming in through the window to cast her in shades of gold. Her skin was still flushed, and he wished he could drag her back down beside him, but her expression was focused and determined. She stalked across to Andred's cloak, muttering to herself about river water and secrets.

As soon as she was gone, his claws returned, but he ignored the sharp pain as he stood and strode across the cold floor to join her. He settled the palm of his hand on the soft skin at the small of her back, needing to touch her. She leaned back against his touch, just for a moment, and then she slowly opened the cloak to reveal an inner pocket sewn into the lining.

His beast rumbled out a quiet growl as she opened it and slid her trembling fingers inside. Then, like a market magician revealing a groat from behind an ear, she slid out a pack of papers, wrapped in string, shining softly in the low light.

Daena looked up at him, her eyes wide and full of hope. "It's here. And it's waxed. Thank the angels."

"Do you think it could be…?" He hardly dared to breathe.

"I don't know. Maybe?" She pulled off the string and unfolded the pack between them, falling silent as they both cast their eyes down the page.

It was a list. But not just any list. There were names: Pellin was there, and Dionys, Gaheris too, although heavily scratched out. And at least a dozen others. Each one the patriarch of an ancient Apollyon family. Some of the richest, and in the past, most powerful men in the kingdom. And next to each name was a tally of resources. Money. Land. Soldiers. Even ships. Gods.

"It's what we've been looking for," she whispered. And then she grinned. The widest, most beautiful smile he'd ever seen. "We did it."

He wrapped his arms around her and hauled her to his chest, trying to breathe through the emotion clogging his throat. Peace was finally possible. For Brythoria. And for them.

When Tristan arrested these nobles for the queen, it would fundamentally restructure the kingdom. The changes Lucilla had already started—women in the guard, a Tarasque as Supreme Commander of the military, a Mabin consort to the throne, and a closer alliance with the Nephilim than at any time in the past, not forgetting the first genuine treaty with Verturia—would form the foundations for an entirely new way of life.

It was almost overwhelming. This chance… this *hope*. But it still didn't feel real. It was too precarious. Anything could go wrong and rip it all away.

Whatever Daena saw in his face, she reached up and stroked his cheek gently before pressing a gentle kiss over his heart. "It's going to be okay."

He let her go reluctantly, and she pressed another gentle kiss in the middle of his chest before turning to her tattered clothes. "All we have to do," she murmured, "is stop Andred."

All we have to do is stop Andred, his beast agreed. Gods. As if it was so simple.

Reece pulled his tunic on. It smelled of her, and his beast rumbled its approval. "We think he's going to Dionys's country house," he said, wishing they didn't have to have this conversation. "Tristan and Tor are on their way there now. Jos has flown back to Kaerlud to arrange troops to be sent from there as well."

Daena nodded as she pulled on Andred's cloak, the parchment safely hidden back in the secret pocket. "Andred won't stop. He'll pick up horses and move out fast, aiming to join the ships from within the harbor before they can be towed to shore."

Neither of them said anything; they didn't have to. Instead, they sped up even more. Daena strapped the dagger to her thigh with a strip of cotton cut from her tattered dress, while Reece smothered the fire. Then, without even time for a backward glance, they abandoned the warmth of the old hut, untied the stallion, and climbed into the saddle, Daena at his front.

They pushed hard. The mud clung and leeched at the destrier's hooves, and the trees showered them with sprays of icy water as the wind shook their bare branches. They were both hungry, and the short rest was not nearly enough. But at least they were together.

Daena fitted herself into his body, her movements smooth and fluid, and it would have been deeply erotic to have her sliding against him if he wasn't growing increasingly worried about his squad. Tristan, Tor, and

Garet would be riding into Dionys's property with only a couple of Blues to fight beside them. Who knew what they would find?

They crossed over the Great North Road and continued through the forest, doing what they could to track the river. They got turned around once and spent far too long heading away from the river before emerging back into farmland and realizing their mistake.

Eventually, the forest trail rejoined the river and slowly widened, evolving into a true path. The trees that had hemmed them in for so long began to thin, and finally, they emerged into a small village nestled beside the river.

A couple of boys in dirty breeches and faded jerkins were fishing from the bank and Reece trotted over to them, hoping they'd seen the Hawks pass through. The boys were thrilled to share the excitement of having seen armed men thundering down their small main street and only too happy to point Reece and Daena through the village and out toward the biggest manor in the area. Dionys's.

They followed the boys' directions down a muddy lane flanked by hawthorn hedges, spiky branches still clinging to a few last withered berries. They crested a small hill and looked down on a massive estate. Rolling pasture dropped away toward the river while a huge house dominated a series of perfectly maintained formal gardens. The walls of the manor were plastered in red and gray and decorated with twining ironwork in abstract patterns representing the family's personal tattoos.

It was striking and intimidating, exactly as no doubt intended. But otherwise, the grounds were strangely quiet, the fields empty. Nothing like the pitched battle Reece had thought they might find. It should have been a relief, but something felt deeply wrong.

A hawk whistled off to the left; a signal that he knew well, and Reece immediately turned in that direction. A small wooden gate in the hedge led to a path that ran along the top of the rise to a stand of full-grown hawthorn trees, bent and twisted from years of wind.

The first person he saw, half-hidden in the shadows, was Tor. His sword was drawn, eyes locked on the manor farm. Thank the gods, they'd found the others. Reece was about to whistle back in greeting, but then his eyes adjusted to the dim light, and he realized that Tor wasn't just keeping watch, he was defending the men behind him.

Garet was sitting on the ground, face white, his back pressed against a tree, while Tristan knelt beside him, inspecting his bleeding wing. Gods.

Reece slid down from the stallion and helped Daena dismount before striding over toward his friends. "What happened?"

Garet opened his eyes and gave a weak smile. "Got a bit close. Took a bolt in my wing. Ironic, really."

"Are you…? Is he…?" Reece looked at Tristan helplessly, taking in the silvery stains all over his captain's hands.

Tristan grunted, his face drawn into tense lines as he reached for a new strip of cotton. "Wings are the worst."

"Where are the others?" Reece demanded, beast rattling and churning inside him. Where were the Blues? They should be here, protecting his squad.

"I sent them to watch downriver in case Andred tries to slip past us and escape back the way he came," Tristan muttered, struggling to apply pressure to the wide, leathery wing. "The Wraiths can't go any further upstream. Garet saw a series of steep falls about half a mile to the west."

"Here." Daena pushed past him to Garet's side and settled down beside his wing. "I can help."

"Thank you," Tristan murmured to Daena as they worked together to wind the rough bandages. "We need to get the bleeding under control. We can't move from here until we have more help."

Garet's jaw clenched, his face growing even paler as they tightened the bandage. "Sorry," Daena whispered softly.

Reece turned his focus to Tor. "What are we watching for?"

Tor shifted his grip on his sword. "Andred is in there."

"Andred knows we're watching the river and the road," Tristan explained as he tied off the bandage. "We spoke to some of the villagers on our way through. Dionys is in Kaerlud with most of his guards. He left a squad of mercenaries—probably as part of his promises to Andred— but he made them pitch their tents in the fields. He's been charging them for access to the river." Tristan shook his head at such stupidity. "Tor reached them first and paid them to leave."

Thank the gods of fire.

Scales shivered up Reece's back. They were fucking lucky. Dionys could have had the mercenaries in his stables or his guard rooms. They could have been men with their own hatred of the queen, soldiers who'd thrived under Ballanor and wanted the old ways back. The Hawks could have been completely outnumbered by a group who hated them far more than they loved coin. They would have died.

Garet leaned back, sweating, and Tristan gripped him on the shoulder until he settled. "We expect Andred only found a couple of staff here—the few who were left to keep the manor during the winter," Tristan continued. "But none of them are soldiers. He's cut off on all sides now. But only while we're here."

Andred was only trapped because the Hawks were watching the road and the river—and they didn't have enough men to send anyone back for help. Which meant Garet had to stay where he was, no matter how much he bled, no matter how much pain he was in.

"Gods, Tristan. I—"

He stopped. What was he going to say? Was he going to apologize for going back for Daena? He couldn't; it would be a lie. He would go back for her again and again. And worse, she would hear the lie and it would hurt her that he'd said it.

That wasn't him, not anymore. He didn't lie to himself or his beast. And he wasn't going to lie to his captain.

Tristan would never expect us to leave Daena behind.

It was true. Tristan would have done the same thing. The Hawks never left a brother—or sister—behind. They'd never left him behind, despite the mistakes he'd made.

He focused on Garet. "I'm sorry they got you."

Daena looked up at him, her eyes crinkling at the sides as she smiled, and then she mouthed a silent, "Thank you." As if she'd somehow known the battle he'd had—between the man he'd been over the last months, the man who said whatever came into his head no matter who it hurt, and the man he wanted to be—and valued him for it.

He swallowed hard and then walked over to Daena and knelt beside her, ignoring Tristan's grunt and Tor's knowing look as he took her hand in his. "I would go back for you, Daena. Every single time."

Her gaze met his, the violet of her eyes sparkling, and they stayed locked together for long silent moments, before she whispered, "Truth."

We really don't deserve her.

No, they didn't.

But maybe we can.

He opened his mouth to tell Daena what his beast had said when Tor let out a piercing whistle from behind him. It was high and loud, the Hawks signal for immediate attention. He didn't stop to consider, he simply launched himself to his feet, pulling out his sword, ready to defend his people.

Tor chuckled. "Sorry. It wasn't for you." He pointed back down the road to where a troop of cavalry soldiers cantered toward them. They flew the queen's flag—the midnight blue with silver embroidered fighting boars—and Mathos led the charge with Jos and Rafe behind him.

Tristan grunted behind them. "All we need are Val and Jeremiel and we can have a party." The words were sarcastic, but there was a vibrant note of relief in his tone.

Tor let out an amused snort, and Reece couldn't help but join him. Their brothers were joining them; Rafe was coming, and he would heal Garet. They weren't alone anymore.

Daena pushed herself up to stand, and he wrapped his arm around her, wanting her close. Wanting everyone to see that they were together. Wanting her to know he'd meant what he'd said: he would go back for her every time.

Mathos called a command, and the troop split into quads, peeling off to spread out along the perimeter of the farm, enclosing it in a net of men and weapons. Only the Hawks cantered up the hill to join their small group under the trees.

Rafe took one look at Garet and strode across to kneel beside him, while Mathos and Jos joined them in watching the manor.

"Fuck, Mathos," Tristan grumbled, watching the men stream across the fields, banners glittering. "Is it essential to always make a dramatic entrance?"

"That's what she said," Mathos replied with a wide grin.

Reece snorted. Then Daena started to giggle, pressing herself into his side as her body shook. Even Tristan and Tor chuckled. Gods, he'd missed them all so much.

Tristan updated Mathos and Jos while Rafe worked with Garet. Finally, once everyone was fully up to speed and Garet was resting, Reece cleared his throat. "We also have news." Pride in the women beside him gave the words an extra poignancy. "Daena got us the list of Andred's supporters from right under his nose."

She pulled out Andred's list and gave it to Mathos. Her hands trembled a little, whether from remembered fear or relief at finally having completed their mission, he didn't know. But he held her a little closer anyway.

Chapter Twenty-Five

THEY'D DONE IT. They'd delivered the list, and Tristan had carefully passed it on to a squad of trusted Blues and sent them back to the palace to give it to the queen.

Daena had imagined feeling relieved, thrilled, joyful maybe, but she didn't feel any of those things. Mostly, she felt tired. And strangely wary.

She looked down at the mansion in the distance, so quiet and peaceful. And wrong.

Her half-formed fears crystalized with movement at the massive front door. A young boy dressed in a neat uniform stepped out, blinking uncertainly. The Hawks turned to watch him, their attention riveted as Mathos called out an order to the surrounding squads, telling them to hold.

The boy made his way over the cobbled courtyard, past the central fountain, and looked up toward the hill as if he knew exactly where they were. He stepped out the gate and ran along the road before turning onto the farmers' track that led up to the tree. It was clear that he was terrified. His shirt was damp with sweat and sticking to his thin body, and he was breathing in sharp pants.

He stopped a few yards away, hands lifted in surrender, but he couldn't seem to make himself speak. His eyes flashed from man to man, raking over their drawn weapons and lingering on the gleaming scales of the Tarasque. He swallowed audibly and then took a tiny shuffling step back as if he was about to flee. She couldn't let him do that.

Daena stepped out of Reece's arm and lifted her own empty hands. "Hello." She drew the boy's attention to her as she put herself between him and the warriors. She could hear Reece's beast grumbling behind her—it didn't like having her in the path of the threat—but she didn't have time to reassure him. She had to find out what Andred wanted from the boy.

She took another step forward, holding her palms up so he could see she had no weapons, and smiled. "My name's Daena," she said softly. "What's yours?"

"I… ah…," he mumbled. "Felix."

She reached out a hand and settled it gently on his shoulder. "It's nice to meet you, Felix." He shuddered as he looked between her and the men looming behind her.

She twisted him gently until all he could see was her. "Can we help you?"

"I…I…." He stuttered for a moment and then burst into tears. "My sis… sister… is inside."

Gods. She opened her arms and waited until he took a shuddering breath and stepped into her hold. She rubbed his back gently, but he was almost incoherent with fear.

A few seconds later, Rafe joined them, settling his hand over the boy's shoulder. Slowly his tears slowed, and he was able to speak. "Lord Andred asks…" He hiccoughed. "I dunno the word. He wants to parley. Is that right? But he'll only talk to the Hawks. He s-says—" He hiccoughed and wiped his nose on the back of his hand. "—if anyone else comes close, he'll kill her...them, I mean."

"What else did he say?" Daena asked gently. "Can you tell us what he's planning?"

But the boy shook his head desperately. "My sister is inside. A-And the others. All of them."

"If you could tell us more, it'll help your sister," Tristan observed quietly, but the boy wouldn't budge. He just shook his head, tears tracking down his face.

"I think we have to take this chance," Mathos offered. "There are innocent people trapped in the house; we can't leave them there. And we can't risk them in an attack."

"Agreed." Tristan met each of the Hawks' eyes. "Let's go find out what they want."

Daena looked down at the house, brain churning. Parley? What did that even mean? Andred was going to prison—if he was lucky—along with Caius and Usna, no matter what they said. But there was no way to know how many innocent servants could be caught in the crossfire if they stormed the house. They had to take this chance. And yet....

Andred was down to his very last backup plan. But she couldn't see him giving in without a fight. She knew him best. She had to be there to watch him. She gave Felix one last reassuring pat, then took a small step forward. "I want to come. Please."

Reece's beast growled, low and unhappy beside her as he met her eyes. "Are you sure?" he asked quietly.

She made herself nod. She could do this. "Yes."

She could feel his claws pricking through the fabric of her dress, but he turned to Tristan anyway, supporting her without hesitation. "Daena has valuable insight into how

Andred thinks," he said firmly, "and she's a Hawk too. She should come."

"Yes," Tristan agreed, "she is." He looked over at her. "Do you have a weapon?"

Gods. They saw her as a Hawk. Her eyes flew up to Reece's, and she knew he could see just how much that had meant to her. Her voice was thick with emotion as she replied, "I have a dagger."

"Gods. Another bloody dagger." Tristan glared at her. "When this is over, I expect you to learn how to use a sword." He sighed. "But for now, that'll have to do. Rafe will stay here with our patients; you can ride his destrier. Just stay at the back."

She nodded. "Yes, sir." She hadn't intended to sound sarcastic, but Mathos snorted while Tristan grunted something unintelligible.

Within a few minutes, they were mounted and moving. Tristan took the lead, then Mathos, followed by Tor and Reece with Jos in the air, and Daena right behind them.

They trotted down the hill, along the well-maintained road, through the heavy wooden gates, up the cobbled drive, and into an aggressively opulent courtyard. The space was dominated by a massive marble fountain of an Apollyon warrior brandishing his sword, and everything— from the polished silver of the door handles on the massive black-stained oak doors, to the wrought iron curved into sinuous winding art adorning the walls—screamed of wealth and power.

They rounded the fountain and she realized with a shiver of horror that the marble warrior was standing on a felled dragon. A dragon made of iron, rusted to streaks of deep red in the pouring water, as if it was bleeding out for all of time.

Hell. She positioned herself between Reece and the fountain, hoping he would be too focused on the silent house to notice.

The fountain splashed and played over its macabre subject too loudly in the stillness of the courtyard. They stopped in the shade of the mansion, a row of Hawks, with her last in the line beside and slightly behind Reece, facing the wide staircase and the forbidding door. The horses fidgeted, their breath misting in the cold air.

"Come out, Andred!" Tristan called. "We're here as you asked, and there's nowhere for you to go."

A moment later, the door swung open. There was a long, tense pause, and then a young woman stepped out. She was little more than a teenager, wearing the tidy uniform of a housemaid, her dark hair tied in a neat braid. And she had a sword pressed into her neck. She was crying, silent tears streaming down her face as she stepped onto the marble staircase, Usna looming behind her.

The Hawks froze completely, their stillness a counterpart to the frantic thudding of Daena's heart. Gods. She knew that feeling. Usna's blade pressed into her side, drawing blood. She'd been the girl with a blade in her ribs, and the sight of it brought all her furious, helpless rage screaming back to life.

An older man followed—perhaps the estate manager—his wiry gray hair was swept in streaks over his bald head, his hands clasped at his waist, while Caius's dagger drew blood at his throat.

Next, two more young women dressed in flour-stained aprons stumbled out. Their hands were bound with ropes in front of them and they were visibly shaking, their eyes puffy and swollen, faces streaked with dried tears.

Behind them came an older woman. A dignified

Apollyon with a lined face, her hair tied back in a silvery bun, and a heavy bunch of keys clanking at her waist. She looked up and met their eyes with slowly assessing scrutiny, her gaze seeming to linger longest on Reece, her frown deepening, until she was prodded forward once more. And, finally, behind her, came Andred, his sword resting on her shoulder.

Andred's tunic was rumpled and sweat-stained, his dark hair stood in spikes where he'd obviously dragged his fingers through it, and his lips were pinched into a hard line. He was not the regal authority figure who had stepped out of the house that morning, nor the handsome, smiling man who had charmed her so long ago.

He was angrier, wilder. More feral, somehow.

Had he always had that poison inside him, hidden by his charming exterior? Or had it developed over the months of hardship, as his decisions had taken him down darker and darker paths? She didn't know. But she did know something was wrong. Something niggled at her, scratching urgently at her awareness, like a wasp in a closed room.

"Threatening innocents again, Andred, I see," Tor muttered coldly.

Andred chuckled, turning his attention to Tor. "And how is your lovely wife? I believe congratulations are in order. My friends in the palace tell me she's expecting a spring baby."

Gods. Tension rose through the Hawks in an icy wave.

"She's very well. Still the best crossbow shot in the Hawks," Tor replied smoothly, only the tension of his jaw indicating the true depth of his fury. "How many of your men did she kill, two? Three?" His eyes flicked across to Daena. "But I wasn't talking about my wife."

Andred laughed. A sound of genuine amusement that

made her want to scream. "Daena was never innocent. She was a stupid little girl, but she was never innocent."

It almost hurt. Almost took her back to that moment in his tent, feeling so very small and pathetic. But she shoved those feeling ruthlessly away. She'd given him power for far too long and she knew better now. He did not determine her value, only she did.

"Yes, she was innocent—she still is—and the queen knows the truth," Mathos snapped. "In fact, Daena brought us your list of supporters." He grinned maliciously. "When you're lying in your cell tonight, you can think about how she saved the entire kingdom. How she brought you down."

Andred's face darkened. Not only at the loss of his list, although he must have been utterly enraged that she had dared to steal it, but at the mention of the cell.

Gods. She remembered him standing proudly at the front of his men, the arrogant way he'd spread himself over his raised chair, and knew, deep in her soul, that he would never submit to prison. His pride would never allow it. This was no negotiation for leniency. Whatever was happening here, Andred did not think he would end up in prison afterward.

Andred glared at her for a moment before turning back, not toward Tor or Mathos, but to Reece. "You wouldn't think that she was so innocent if you'd seen the real Daena. Let me tell you about how she used to get on her knees and—"

"Shut. Up." Reece's voice was almost entirely growl. His hand rested on the pommel of his sword, fingers twitching... and were his claws even longer? Hell.

Daena rested her hand on his arm and did her best to smile. "Don't. That's what he wants. He wants everyone agitated and defensive."

Andred rolled his eyes. "What I want, Daena, is to be allowed back to our boat."

Tristan grunted. "Never happening."

Andred ignored him. "We'll take all these—" He cleared his throat meaningfully. "—*innocent* people with us and drop them off when we reach safety."

"No." Tristan pulled his sword slowly from its sheath and held it loosely in his hand.

"Yes," Andred retorted. "You're going to let us quietly walk down to the river and climb back into our boat, or all these people are going to die a horrible death. And it will be *you* who killed them." His lip curled as he glared at Tristan. "How will you sleep again? Every time you close your eyes, you'll remember their screams. Remember the looks on their faces as they die. Maids and old people who've never held a sword in their life. Are you going to run them through? Will you watch them bleed as they writhe in pain, knowing you could have saved them? I don't think so."

"Is that what happened to you?" Mathos asked, voice tight and strained. "Do you close your eyes and remember the screams of the men you killed at Ravenstone? Good, loyal men who served beneath you. Men who trusted you."

Caius flinched, but Andred didn't even blink. "Let us go. Or all of these people will die."

Tristan grunted, a wave of green and pewter scales flickering up his face. "Andred, son of Flavius, you're under arrest. We'll escort you from here to Gatehouse Prison and from there to the Nephilim Courts when you're called. Let these people go; their deaths will only add to the heavy debt you already owe."

Andred's eyes narrowed even further at the mention of Gatehouse—the common prison—not the Constable's tower where royal convicts could expect to be sent. The movement was so slight, Daena was certain no one else would have noticed it. But she'd spent so much time so close to him, she knew when he was getting close to the edge. She knew when—

Gods of the earth. He was holding the sword with his left hand.

His right hand was at his side, curled in on itself. As if he held something there…. But what?

What would Andred do when he was out of backup plans? He must have known the odds of Tristan letting him leave were minuscule. He would have already prepared to fight, and he would fight to the death.

If his hostages couldn't be used as leverage to get a boat, they would become a shield. A human barrier to allow him to wreak the greatest havoc, to take as many Hawks lives as he could, before it was over. That would be his aim now. To cause as much devastation as possible before he died. And she couldn't let that happen.

She opened her mouth to warn them all, but Andred beat her to it. "Now!" he roared, pushing the housekeeper forward with a huge shove, sending her crashing into the nearby horses. Usna lifted the young maid into his arms and flung her bodily at Mathos's stallion, which reared back, screaming as Mathos desperately hauled on the reins.

The other destriers danced back, neighing and snorting as the Hawks fought to prevent the hostages from being trampled. Tristan lifted his fingers to his lips and whistled a high piercing call, ordering the quads back from the perimeter to join the fight.

Andred grabbed one of the women in ropes, holding her close against him. She screamed in terror as the Wraiths pushed forward, taking advantage of the chaos to lash out with their swords, stabbing at the horses.

Jos swooped down as the Wraiths moved forward, landing neatly on the stairs to attack them from behind, forcing them to fight front and back. But he was only one man, and the Wraiths were surrounded by hostages.

Mathos settled the young maid on the edge of the fountain and returned to the fight, beating down at Usna with brutal power, his scaled arms gleaming burgundy as if he'd dipped them in blood.

Reece slid down from his horse, physically grabbing screaming hostages and pulling them away from danger, sending them running down the cobbled drive toward the Blues now thundering toward them.

Daena danced her borrowed horse backward, staying out the way as the man Caius had threatened suddenly dropped to his knees and crawled frantically away.

With a powerful sweeping arc, Tor cut Caius down. The Wraith dropped to his knees, his scream fading to a low groan and then falling silent as he crumpled. And gods, she had hated him, but watching him die still hurt.

She looked away and saw the moment Andred realized he'd lost one of his closest friends. The brother who had stood by him for so long. It tipped him over the edge.

He looked up and met her eyes for a second, his mouth forming one word: "You." Blaming her for everything he'd lost.

It was a surreal vindication. A triumph. Andred blamed her for his failure. And he *had* failed, and she *had* made it possible. She had taken away all the advantages she should never have given him, and they both knew it.

He stared at her, hatred churning between them for a long moment. But then he looked away… and settled his icy gaze on Reece. Gods. Andred had to know what was between them, or at least he suspected it.

If he really wanted to wound her, he wouldn't kill her. No, he'd kill Reece. And leave her behind to live with it.

Andred pulled back his arm, the dagger in his right fist glinting in the weak sunlight, but Reece didn't see it. His was half-turned where he stood, helping the last of the hostages escape back to where Jos was guiding them to safety. The blade would hit him right in the back.

Daena didn't hesitate. She kicked the destrier hard in his flank, roaring out her fear and rage, releasing every moment of helplessness, of horror that she'd felt at Andred's hands, and forced the massive warhorse into a lunging leap forward.

The dagger took the warhorse in his shoulder, and he screamed, a bellow of shock and pain that reverberated through her as he dropped hard to his knees.

The sudden lurch threw her out of the saddle to smash into the cobbles at Andred's feet. She landed brutally on her shoulder, her collarbone breaking with a sharp crack. Vicious pain flooded through her in excruciating waves, and for a moment, all she could do was lie, curled up on the cold cobbles, whimpering and trying not to be sick.

She tried to push herself back up, but her arm folded in agony, and she let out a tortured moan as she collapsed back down.

Gods and angels. She couldn't stay there. She had to get back up. But, before she could even attempt it again, Andred wrapped his thick arm around her throat and hauled her upright.

Her shoulder slumped, her arm hanging useless at her side, helpless tears of agony and rage sliding down her cheeks as the fighting staggered to a halt around her.

Caius lay dead on the cobbles, a dark pool of blood slowly spreading out beneath him. Usna was kneeling,

Tristan's sword at his throat. Jos had gathered the freed hostages into a shivering, frozen huddle. Only Reece moved. His beast howled and raged, scales sliding up his face as Tor held him back. And they all stared at her and Andred.

Andred coughed and turned his head to spit blood on the cobbles, his arm never moving from her neck. "Not so quick to sacrifice the hostage now, are we?" he muttered.

He pulled her with him as he stepped sideways, always keeping his back to the wall, jostling her broken collarbone, and sending shafts of white-hot torture stabbing through her as he slowly rounded the courtyard.

The water splashed softly. Her breath grated in harsh pants, and she whimpered with every jostling step. But no one else moved. The Hawks watched her, horror written over their faces.

She knew them well enough now to know what they were thinking. And she had forgiven herself enough to believe the truth of it. They were thinking that she was one of them. That it would kill them to go through her to get to Andred. But that they couldn't let him go, either.

Andred dragged her another few steps. Gods. He was taking her to the stables. If he made it inside, he would get to the horses. Was there a back entrance? The stables in Eshcol opened on both sides, and it made sense to give the horses easy access to the fields. To the river. It might give him a chance to escape. One man alone, swimming hard then fleeing through the woods on the far side… it was possible.

She looked up at Reece, at the man she could have loved, and tried to smile. "Do it." Her words were a dry whisper and she doubted anyone had heard them. She swallowed the dust from her throat and tried again. "Do it."

"No. Fuck. Tristan, please!" Reece lurched forward but

stopped when Andred growled, tightening his grip on her throat with his elbow and bringing his sword around to rest against her belly.

Gods and angels. She let out a long shaking breath, finding the strength she needed to look into those sapphire eyes one last time. "Reece," she whispered. "We always knew it would come to this." She blinked away a slow trickle of tears. "I just didn't realize how much I'd wish it could have ended differently."

"I don't accept this. I won't." His face was entirely covered by indigo scales, his eyes so bright, she could see their glow across the courtyard.

"Thank you for wanting me. Thank you for believing in me. Thank you for the time—" She swallowed hard, the arm around her throat and her freely falling tears choking her. "You're a good man, Reece. All along, you've always been good. Remember what I said. Remember how much they love you." She held his gaze and whispered her last words. "Goodbye, Reece."

Chapter Twenty-Six

GODS. Oh, Gods. He couldn't do it. He couldn't watch her die. He couldn't stand there and let it happen.

His beast was roaring in his belly, his claws so long now that he could hardly hold his sword. It was chanting in his head; *Remind her. Remind her. Remind her.*

"Of what?" Gods. He could barely hear his own words over the howling.

She can *do this. Only her.*

Only she.... Of course. "Daena." His voice rumbled, more beast than man. "I asked you to promise me something, baby, do you remember? That night in your room."

Her reply was too soft to hear, but he could have sworn she whispered, "Warmth and light."

But then she hung her head on Andred's arm, watching him through pain-clouded eyes, and he knew she was steeling herself for the end. "At least we had that," she said, her lips lifting in a pained smile.

Gods. She was going to break his heart. Maybe she already had.

"No, Daena. Not that. I... I asked you to run and hide... but I was wrong. I was wrong because that's not you. You don't run and hide."

She blinked, half-dazed, and he could only imagine how exhausted she was—disoriented with pain and shock—how far through fear she'd traveled, and out, into numb acceptance.

Gods, he'd been there. And he'd thought he'd come out fighting, but he'd only been fighting himself all along. Daena had never made that mistake. She had been fighting for the truth since the beginning.

"That's not you, because you *fight*. You've been fighting all this time. To find a cure for the red plague. To make a good place for yourself in the world. To save Brythoria." His voice dropped to a deeper rumble. "You fought for me."

He took a small step forward and then stopped when Andred shifted his grip on his sword.

"One foot closer, and I will put us all out of our misery," Andred threatened.

Reece held up his hands, sword dangling loosely from his fingers. As if he wasn't one second away from snapping. As if his beast wasn't demanding blood and retribution and calling for its mate. But he didn't bother to look at Andred.... He was looking at Daena. "I've only ever given you one gift. Do you remember?"

She blinked. And then she blinked again.

"I'll give you better gifts, one day," he promised. "But I need you to remember the first one. I didn't even know I'd given it to you until later."

"Shut the fuck up, Reece," Andred hissed, dragging Daena another cruel step closer to the stables. And for a moment, he was terrified that she was too stunned to know what he was talking about. But then her hand dropped to her side, to the cut-off hem of her skirt, sliding it slowly upward. The movement was shaky but determined. Thank the gods.

He wanted to howl his relief while his beast roared to the sky. There was still hope. But now he had to get Andred to focus somewhere else.

Reece dropped his sword, letting it clatter to the cobbles, drawing Andred's scowling attention. And then he took a threatening step forward. "I can't believe how badly I wanted to be you," he spat at the leader of the Wraiths. "I would have given anything. You were so comfortable in your riches and power. Wanted by everyone. But it wasn't enough for you, was it? And now you've lost it all."

"Fuck you, Reece," Andred rumbled, taking another long step to the side, inching ever closer to the entrance to the stables and his chance at freedom.

"Fuck yourself. Oh wait, you already have. Look around you, asshole—it's all gone."

Andred let out a long, muttered string of curses, but it didn't stop him from dragging Daena another step. Her hand was moving at her thigh, but Reece didn't dare look. Didn't dare give anything away. "You swore to protect Geraint," he continued. "If you'd just done that, you'd be in the palace right now."

Andred growled, low and vicious, but he didn't reply. Instead, his eyes flickered to Caius and Usna as he slowly distanced himself from his fallen brothers.

Reece forced himself to laugh, infusing his amusement with as much mockery as possible. "Hell. If you'd told Geraint about Ballanor's plan, Ballanor would be sitting in the Constable's Tower right now, and you'd have been richly rewarded by Geraint. Fuck, you'd probably be married to Lucilla."

Reece's beast shuddered as he spoke, hardening his scales into an armored mask that covered him from his face to his boots. And somehow, he knew his words were true. Tristan and Mathos grunted roughly beside him, as if perhaps their beasts had felt that same cold shiver. A ghost of what could so easily have been.

They'd cursed it and hated it. Each of them had railed against the horror and the bitter grief of Ravenstone. But, in the end, it could have been so much worse.

And maybe Andred heard the truth in his words too, because his face darkened dangerously. A vein throbbed furiously over his left eye as he paused his slow escape and screamed, "Shut up! Who the fuck are you anyway? You're nothing to anyone. The Hawks only ever kept you around to dig their holes. Expendable when the walls came down." He snarled. "No one wants you. Not even Daena. And I should know… I broke her months ago."

He shouldn't have said that. His beast spread itself, enveloping his entire body in an armor of solid indigo scales while his claws curled into long, lethal talons. He almost felt that with the smallest nudge, he would be able to shift, like the dragons of old, and truly rain terror and death down on Andred.

"He shouldn't have said that," Reece agreed with his beast. Not only because threatening and insulting Daena had pushed his beast to the primal, berserker violence where soon it wouldn't care whether they survived attacking Andred. But because Daena had used the distraction to slide the dagger out from under her dress and slowly flip it in her palm until the blade was facing back toward Andred.

She twisted her head to look up at Andred through the

corner of her eye. And gods, that movement must have cost her. The scar on her cheek stood out, red against the ash-pale of her face, and her lips drew into a tight grimace of pain as she watched him.

"What?" Andred demanded as she stared at him.

She shook her head, a tiny movement, before licking her dry lips. And then she whispered, "I don't forgive you."

The words were nothing more than a croak, only just audible above the splashing of the fountain. And then she drove her fist backward, plunging the dagger into Andred's upper thigh.

Andred screamed, a sound of agony and rage. His arm loosened from Daena's neck, and she fell forward with a cry.

She had hurt him badly, maybe even mortally, but not enough. He still had his sword. She was still too close. Vulnerable and exposed, collapsed on the cobbles in front of a man who had nothing left except his fear and hatred.

Almost in slow motion, Andred lifted his sword high in the air, about to bring it down on her unprotected neck.

Reece was too far away. There was nothing he could do. He leaped forward anyway, desperately trying—

"Drop!" Tristan's roar of command spoke straight to the center of his soul, and he didn't question it. Didn't second-guess or stop to think. He dropped.

A bolt flew through the air over his head, straight into Andred's throat. The Wraith fell back against the stone wall of the stables, gurgling, his sword clattering uselessly to the cobbles. His hands scrabbled weakly, plucking at the thick shaft before he groaned a last bubbling curse and then slid slowly down and closed his eyes.

Men were shouting. Tristan was calling orders. Someone called out to Garet. Mathos and Tor ran toward where Andred had fallen. It was all distant. Fuzzy. It could have been happening on the moon, for how little it meant to him while Daena was lying unmoving on the cobbles in front of him.

He stumbled down to scoop her up into his arms, his beast roaring so loudly that all he could hear was its anguish.

She was unconscious, her body limp, her face tear-streaked and white as bone as he held her against his chest. He had to... gods. He didn't know. What could he do? He tore things down, that was all he knew. He needed.... He needed—

"Let me take her."

Hands tried to lift her from his arms, but he couldn't. He wouldn't. He opened his mouth and roared, almost entirely beast.

"Okay." Tristan's voice broke through the fear. "Tor, Mathos, flank him. Rafe, we need you."

And then there were hands on his shoulders. Men beside him. Not just any men—his brothers, holding him up, supporting him while he held Daena.

He took a slow, shuddering breath, in and out, while his beast howled.

"She's breathing." Rafe ran his fingers over her throat, then rested them against her pulse. "Shock and pain, I think," he muttered to himself. "Broken clavicle. No internal bleeding."

Rafe settled his hand over her collarbone and closed his eyes. Around them, Tristan called orders. Usna was taken into custody. Caius and Andred's bodies were removed. Garet passed a crossbow back to one of the Blues, leaning heavily against the wall. Jos led the hostages inside the house. Reece ignored it all. He held on to the woman in his arms and watched her breathe while Rafe eased her pain. That was all he could do.

Slowly, the swollen redness around Daena's collarbone reduced, while a tinge of color came back into her cheeks. She took a deep breath and let it out on a soft groan, her eyelashes fluttering open. "Reece?"

His beast roared, and his voice was more growl than words, but he managed to whisper, "I have you. I promise."

Chapter Twenty-Seven

DAENA WOKE SLOWLY. The low rumbling behind her told her that Reece was still in bed. In her bed. Their bed?

For a moment, she almost imagined they were back in the old forest hut, but then she shifted her weight and a wave of dull pain spread out over her chest and shoulder and she remembered.

She opened her eyes to golden morning light spilling in around the sides of a pair of dark blue velvet curtains. They were in a suite of some kind. There were tapestries on the wall, a plush rug on the stone floor, a set of comfortable-looking sofas beneath a high window, and a screen at the back that suggested a small bathing area. It was the most beautiful room she'd been in since she left Eshcol.

She vaguely recalled the constant rumbling of Reece's beast. The way he'd held her as he rode, cradling her in his arms, whispering to her that they were going to Kaerlud. That everything was going to be well.

They'd arrived in the dark, and he'd carried her through the palace to settle her in this gorgeous room, but she'd been too tired to pay it any attention. There'd been a bowl of hot water on a stand and a clean shift lying on the bed, and that was all she'd cared about. That, and making sure Reece would stay with her.

He had stripped out of his breeches and jerkin, laid his weapons on the table under the window, and climbed in behind her, his arms coming around to hold her close, his claws prickling softly where they brushed against her skin. And then she'd slept.

Judging by how high the winter sun had climbed, she'd been asleep for hours. But now she was awake. Widely, fully awake. She opened her eyes, gently moving her shoulder, testing it. There was still a blue-green bruise over her chest, but it looked far better than she could have imagined.

"How does it feel?" Reece asked, his voice low and sleepy.

She rolled onto her back, turning her head to look at him. "It twinges, but otherwise it's fine."

His beast rumbled as he propped himself up on his elbow to look down at her, circles of sapphire glowing bright around his irises. "I was worried."

It was the truth, but the lines bracketing his mouth, the dark rings beneath his eyes, told her how much of an understatement it was.

She lifted her hand and cupped his cheek, dragging her thumb over the rough stubble. "Thank you. For worrying over me." She lifted her head and pressed a kiss to the side of his mouth. "For staying with me."

A flurry of indigo scales rippled over his throat as he frowned. "Did you think I would leave you? You seemed concerned about it, last night."

"No, I—" She paused for a moment, trying to find the right words. "I guess I thought you might get called away.

That you would have responsibilities, now you're back in the palace, even if you wanted to stay."

The scales cleared, leaving smooth, tanned flesh as Reece gave her a soft smile. "I'll always stay with you, if you need me."

"But?" she prompted, sensing there was more.

Reece pressed a kiss to her forehead. "Tristan asked to meet with me this morning... but only if you're feeling well enough. If you're not ready, I'll stay with you. Gods know, after yesterday...." He didn't say the rest. He didn't need to.

She wanted him to stay. To have this time with him. She wanted to linger in this warm, safe bubble with Reece, and the temptation to lie and tell him she wasn't ready was almost overwhelming.

But she knew that if she did that, he would stay. And she would have done him a disservice. Reece was finally back with his brothers, finally back in the palace, and he needed to keep moving forward, not hiding away with her. She was bruised and tired, but otherwise well, and she understood that there was work to do. Debriefs to hold. A kingdom to save.

Soldiers weren't given days off to lie in bed because they'd had a tough week. And soon, she would also have to start making decisions about what she was going to do, about where she was going to live and work.

She forced herself to smile back. "You should definitely go and see Tristan. I'm feeling much better."

Reece frowned down at her, his beast grumbling gently. "Are you sure?"

"Yes." She was. Reece needed this, and she wanted him to have it.

He tilted his head to the side, watching her carefully,

sapphire flaring in his eyes. "My beast has suggested that we ask for proof that you really are well enough."

"Proof?" This time her smile was genuine. "What kind of proof did you have in mind?"

"Probably an inspection… to start with," Reece murmured. He dropped his hand to the hem of her shift, dragging it slowly up her body, a whisper of soft cotton and—

"Do you still have claws?" she asked, surprised.

Reece growled softly. "Apparently." His eyes darkened. "Is that okay?"

She kissed him again, letting her lips wander over his mouth, across his stubbled cheek until she could murmur in his ear, "I like you—and your beast—exactly as you are."

His eyes flashed, his beast rumbling loudly, and then he dropped his mouth onto hers. His kiss was almost violent in its intensity, his face slanted so that he could taste her again and again, nipping and sucking. But his hand was achingly slow as he dragged his fingers up her inner thigh, his claws etching long, searing lines along her skin.

He lifted her shift over her hip, allowing cool air to flow over her, a whisper against the growing heat. Reece bent over her to press a long, slow kiss to the peak of her hip bone, scoring it gently with his teeth and then soothing it with his tongue as he dragged his claws back down again. She let her legs fall open, breathing hard, and gripped the hem of her shift, sliding it up to her neck.

He let out a soft groan and skimmed his mouth over her breasts, dragging his tongue roughly over her nipples, then leaving them to pucker in the air as he nuzzled into her belly. He kissed her from her naval to the delicate skin where her thigh met her groin, then pulled in a deep breath of her arousal as he moved to kneel between her legs. Every nerve in her body was tuned to him, vibrating with him.

He settled himself on his belly, face so very close to where she needed him as his eyes traced over her body. They traveled back the way his lips had passed: over her throbbing core, passing the tight curls of auburn hair, to her navel, the rise and fall of her breasts, and then he lifted his gaze to hers.

She could feel his breath, feel his heated skin, his low growl buzzing between her thighs, but he still wasn't touching her.

She lifted her hips, encouraging him, but he didn't lose his focus on her eyes. "You haven't agreed to an inspection," he growled. "I'm going to need to hear you say it."

If this wasn't an inspection, she didn't know what was. She tugged her shift, arching her back and lifting her head so that she could pull it over her head. Each movement pushing her closer to Reece.

"Gods, you're beautiful." He smoothed his hand over her belly and then stroked the underside of her breast with a single claw as she shivered, panting. He dragged his finger up to her nipple, circling it until it throbbed, and then rested the tip of his claw on the tightened bud.

A rough growl shuddered through Reece as he prowled over her. "I didn't realize how much I was going to love having claws." He palmed her other breast, testing its weight, his callouses scraping, and then he leaned down and took it into his mouth, laving with his tongue as he tugged gently on the other side, claws scraping with tiny stabs of jolting pleasure.

Daena bent her knees, lifting her hips, searching for more, but he held his body over hers, dedicated to tormenting her breasts, alternating between long pulls of his mouth and sharp twists between his fingers, the light scratches of his claws, driving her insane.

"You should know how much I love this," he murmured, licking a long line between her breasts and onto her throat. "I could do this all day."

Daena whimpered, sliding her hand down his hard body, looking for the heavy cock she could feel brushing against her leg, but he slid away and down, leaving his hands to torture her breasts as he swirled his tongue into her navel. It was like it connected directly to her core.

He stopped over her mound, breathing hard, and looked up at her. "Daena, baby, you still haven't said what kind of inspection you want. Do you need me to come back up there and start this all again?"

Gods. She wasn't shy about her body, especially not now that she had so much more of an appreciation for its strength and resilience. But she wasn't used to speaking during sex, not like this. But Reece was already starting to move back up to her breasts, to her taut nipples where they still gleamed from his saliva, and she knew he would do exactly what he'd said; he would torture her all day.

She licked her dry lips, and he watched the movement like a predator watching its prey. "I need you to inspect me with your tongue," she whispered.

He grunted, a wave of scales flickering over his chest, and then he dropped down to press a slow kiss to her clit. His tongue flicked out to taste her, running a small circle around the throbbing nerves as she shuddered. But then he lifted his head to meet her eyes once more.

"Where do you want my tongue?" Reece asked. "I want to give you what you need, Daena; tell me what it is."

His words tasted only of truth, and his sapphire gaze was locked on her. There was nothing here except honesty and need, and it was everything she'd ever wanted. "I want you to open me with your fingers; I want to feel your claws. I want you to taste me, Reece, run your tongue through my slit, please. Gods—" She ended on a low moan as he pushed his tongue inside her, his fingers sliding through her folds to hold her open.

He licked her again and again, from inside to the pulsing bundle of nerves where her clitoris throbbed and back again. His beast rumbled, on and on, a constant deep vibration that added another exquisite layer to the overload of sensation rising through her.

She dropped her hands to her breasts, tugging and rolling her nipples in time with his tongue, and he let out a long, pleased growl of approval. Her hips pushed forward, up into his mouth, every muscle tensing as she writhed helplessly, climbing closer and closer to her peak. But she wanted more. She ached for him. She needed—

"Reece." Her voice was rough, desperate. "I want you inside me."

He crawled up her body to collapse on his side, pulling her over to face him and then slinging her leg over his hip. Even in her frantic need, she could feel how carefully he positioned them, avoiding her bruised collarbone, wrapping her stronger leg behind his ass, taking care of her.

He buried his face in her neck, his breath hot on her skin, his hand sliding up to gently collar her throat, his fingers curling over her jaw. And then he slid into her. He shuddered, his groaning half growl rough and broken. As if it was as intense for him as it was for her, this joining.

Her breasts pushed into his chest. She wrapped her hand around his arm, needing to hold him, and his muscles rippled where she gripped him. They were too close, too locked together for long thrusts; instead, he pumped into her in grinding circles, every pulsing, throbbing motion dragging him over the nerves he'd already woken. While their heated breaths filled the almost nonexistent space between them.

This was *not* goodbye. It was *not* some relieved coupling as they celebrated their survival. This was something else, something infinitely more. And they both felt it.

His mouth found her pulse and he sucked her skin into his mouth as her body clenched around his. It was everything she'd needed. His body joined to hers, every movement taking her higher. Gods. She was almost there.

The rising pleasure was a throbbing pulse now. And she *needed*. "Harder, Reece. Now."

He dropped his hand to her ass, holding her steady as he picked up his pace, driving deeper, his beast growled steadily, sending rolling vibrations through their bodies. His scales gleamed with sweat as he whispered against her skin, "Thank you, Daena. Thank you for bringing me home."

It pushed her over the edge. She came, screaming his name as he shuddered, holding her pinned on his body as she spasmed around him, her climax rolling through her in a wave of ecstasy. Then he pulled himself free and took his cock into his hand, jerking it twice before he roared, spilling all over her belly.

He collapsed, pulling her into his arms as they both shuddered, gasping for air. Her body tingled, pulsing as they slowly caught their breaths. She was sweaty and sticky and utterly satiated.

Reece pulled a blanket over them both, wrapping her in a musty cocoon, nestling with her, and then, as if there was nothing else in the world but them, he closed his eyes and drifted back to sleep.

His arm was heavy over her waist. His heart beat

steadily beneath her ear where her cheek pressed against his chest. She had never felt so connected to anyone. Never felt so seen or so appreciated. Ever.

They had survived. They'd made it this far. Andred was dead, and his conspirators had been revealed. But, despite the pleasure she and Reece had shared, despite the beauty of their connection, she couldn't get to sleep.

They were back in the palace. Back in his home. He was so close to fulfilling his dreams. But what about hers?

Chapter Twenty-Eight

IT WAS the same imposing palace. The same cold stone walls. The same high windows in the same places. But everything else was different.

The halls were decorated with boughs of holly, heavy with berries, while wreaths of ivy decorated with pinecones supported thick wax candles. The dark paintings and heavy drapes were gone, as were all the ceremonial weapons. In their place were bright tapestries and crackling fires. The royal standard stood proudly, the two fighting boars no longer facing each other snarling, but standing side by side, fierce and strong as they watched the world together.

Reece walked slowly down from the wing where he and Daena had been given a small suite beside the other Hawks, saluted the guards at the bottom of the stairs and the pair at the entrance to the administrative wing, and made his way onto the corridor where the most senior marshals and stewards did their work.

His beast growled with each step, scales flickering, and he had to resist the urge to rub the back of his neck. Gods.

He was fucking terrified. Why did it feel like his whole life was in the balance?

Because it is?

Reece snorted and whispered back, "Thanks. That's reassuring."

His beast rattled in amusement.

He found the Supreme Commander's door and knocked. Tristan immediately called for him to enter, and Reece swung open the door, only to come to a complete stop when he saw who was in the office.

Tristan was sitting at his desk, back straight, fine lines of tiredness spreading out around his eyes. Queen Lucilla sat opposite him, obviously in the middle of some discussion.

Bollocks. He really hadn't intended to interrupt his queen on his first day back in the palace. He bowed his head politely. "Sorry to disturb you, Your Majesty."

Lucilla looked up at him and smiled. "Not at all, Corporal Reece; you're right on time."

He'd never met her before, only seen her from a distance, but he could immediately see the similarities to her brother—and the differences.

Lucilla was as strikingly good-looking as Ballanor had been, with dark hair and eyes, the royal spiked red-and-black tattoos swirling over her arms drawing attention to her smooth olive skin. The look she gave him was as intelligent and determined as her brother's had been, more so even. But where Ballanor had been sullen and entitled, highly egotistical, and always—even before Reece knew the truth—slightly chilling, Lucilla had the warm, direct gaze of a person who had grown into their strengths. A woman who knew how to work hard, who would speak the truth and live with integrity.

I like her.

He did. And he could immediately tell that it would be a privilege to serve under her. If that was possible.

He bowed lower. "It's an honor to meet you, Your Majesty. Thank you for giving us a room here in the palace. And for... everything."

Lucilla stood and took his hand to shake firmly. "The thanks go to you, Reece. I owe you—both you and Daena—a great debt." Lucilla glanced at Tristan, her smile widening as she lowered her voice as if she was sharing a secret. "And despite all you've given, we have another request to make of you. One I sincerely hope you will consider."

He couldn't even begin to imagine what she might ask of him. But if he could give it, he would.

Lucilla nodded toward Tristan before making her way to the door. "And now I shall leave you to talk to our Supreme Commander. Lovely to meet you, Corporal Reece."

Reece watched her leave and then lowered himself into the chair she'd been sitting in feeling slightly dazed.

Mathos had told him once that Lucilla had an incredible heart. That she would want him back among the Hawks, wearing the Blue. But he hadn't believed it. Bollocks. Mathos was right all along.

Tristan leaned back in his chair, watching him. "What's that look for?"

Reece huffed a laugh. "I just realized Mathos was right about something."

"Gods." Tristan dragged his hand down his face. "Don't tell him, whatever you do."

They both laughed. And it felt good. It felt *right*.

Reece rested his hands on the desk, ignoring the claws that still hadn't retracted. He'd asked his beast about it plenty of times, but his beast had just rumbled and pushed him closer to Daena. It was prepared to retract them when he was touching her—sometimes—but the rest of the time, he was learning to live with them.

He looked up at Tristan, the man who'd saved him on the battlefield, made him a Hawk, and had come for him when he'd needed it most. "You asked to see me."

Tristan grunted. "Yes. We—Queen Lucilla and I—have been working on the new barracks." He reached behind his desk to a tube filled with rolls of plans and grabbed the biggest. He spread it over his desk, pinning it down with a dagger on one end and a whetstone on the other.

Reece ran his eye over the detailed drawings. "These look like…." He frowned. "Is this Eshcol?"

Tristan looked up at him, eyes bright emerald. "Yes and no. These are plans for Kaerlud, but they're heavily based on the barracks at the temple complex." Tristan grunted. "We've cleaned house, and we want to attract the right kind of guards. We're going to have both men and women working here, side by side, possibly married couples eventually. We need a much bigger, better-equipped armory, a new tournament ground, and better stables.

"Tor will be taking charge of the new training program, which will be far more rigorous than anything before it. We're renaming the divisions. No more Blues, Blacks, and Greens; we're all Boars going forward."

"Are we preparing for war?" Reece asked slowly, trying to take in the scale of the changes Tristan was describing.

"No." Tristan leaned back in his chair. He looked tired but content. "We're preparing for peace. Fear has ruled Brythoria for far too long. Magistrats have wielded their power without reference to the courts, powerful families have believed they can do whatever they want. That all ends now."

Tristan steepled his hands together. "The Nephilim are

joining us in this. Starting in Kaerlud, we're clamping down on corruption and any abuse of power. We need a well-trained force to do that. We need Mabin, Tarasque, and Apollyon all working together. And they need to have a home they're proud of defending."

Reece's beast rumbled in agreement. Gods. This was what he had needed all along. He'd been searching for a house filled with material comforts when what he'd needed was a home he could be proud of.

And Daena.

Yes. And Daena.

Reece ran his finger over the plans, digesting it all. "You're going to drain Ballanor's moat."

Tristan nodded. "We need the space. We aim to reclaim the gardens and the fields beside the river, but keep a smaller, narrower moat as protection. We'll leave the walls and the new battlements as they are."

"It's a big job." Gods. No wonder Tristan looked so tired if he was managing this as well as the kingdom's military.

"It is." Tristan chuckled. "That's why I'm giving it to you."

Reece tore his gaze up from the plans to meet Tristan's eyes. "What?"

"Lucilla has agreed. We're promoting you to sergeant major and putting you in charge of the build, reporting directly to the queen."

Reece blinked, emotion and confusion clogging his throat and his thoughts. "I don't... I'm not...."

Tristan leaned over the table to grip Reece's shoulder. "You've delivered everything I've ever asked. You can do this."

It was more than he had dreamed could be possible. It was everything he'd wanted. Back in the palace. A responsible position, using his engineering skills to make a real difference. Building something good. Creating a home he could be proud of. And yet….

He looked up at the man he respected more than any other. "Thank you. I really want this." It came out almost as a whisper.

"But?"

"I don't know how Daena will feel. And I"—he looked down at his clawed hands—"I don't want her to go."

"I understand," Tristan said gravely. "I know Queen Lucilla would be delighted if she joined Jeremiel and—"

Reece's beast growled, scales flashing up to his neck.

"Or… not?" Tristan raised an eyebrow, watching him carefully.

Reece stared down at the plans, tracing the outline of the new buildings. "She would hate to be a truth seeker," he said quietly, as much to himself as to Tristan. "But maybe… maybe she doesn't have to be."

Tristan nodded slowly. For a moment, it almost looked to Reece as if he was going to add something, something serious, but instead he grunted. "You're a Hawk and so is Daena. Whatever you do, wherever you go, that won't change."

Chapter Twenty-Nine

DAENA STOOD AT THE WINDOW, looking down at the kitchen garden. She was free. She was alive. And yet here she was, sitting in her room. A much nicer room, admittedly, but still, she had to get out of it.

She turned away, moving to sit on the sofa under the window, her eyes roaming over the elegant suite. The bed was still unmade, sheets wrinkled. When Reece had woken again, she'd been wrapped around him, holding him tightly, and he'd seemed to sense her uncertainty.

When he sank into her body, it had been so much more slowly than before. He had interlaced his fingers with hers, gripping her hand, his sapphire eyes staring into hers, and for a moment the world had felt right.

But then he'd had to leave for his meeting with Tristan. He'd dressed, watching her with concerned eyes, and she'd promised him—again—that she was well.

A proclamation had been sent out while they were sleeping, explaining that she and Reece had uncovered a conspiracy, that they had helped to save the kingdom.

Somehow, she'd gone from being hated and mistrusted to being a hero. Even the palace maid who'd brought them a tray of breakfast had been thrilled to meet her, murmuring about a real-life heroine.

Reece was excited to be in the palace, back with his brothers, and she was glad for him. Deeply, powerfully, glad. But, as easy as it would be to sit in her room and let him carry them forward, she needed more.

This wasn't her home. It couldn't be the place she stayed just because Reece was there. And although she trusted him, although she knew he meant everything he'd said, it didn't change that they wanted different things.

She needed to find her place. And that meant pulling herself together and taking that first step out of their room, back into the world, and figuring it out.

She walked over to the bed to put the sheets and blankets neatly into order. She plumped the cushions and was spreading a throw over the neatly made bed when someone knocked at the door.

She pulled it open, half expecting Reece to have come back early. Or perhaps Ramiel coming to visit. But it wasn't either of them. Instead, Nim stood in the open door, her wings curled back behind her, her arms full of… clothes?

"Oh good, you're here!" Nim grinned as Daena stepped back, welcoming her inside. "Keely will be here soon. She has crossbow practice with Tor this morning, and we all know how that ends." Nim winked, and Daena couldn't help chuckling. She'd seen Tor and Keely together enough to have a pretty good idea of how that would end. "Lucilla and I would love for you to come to sword practice with us," Nim continued. "Lucilla wanted to come this morning too, but she's meeting with Mathos and the Master of the Treasury."

"Tristan said something about learning to use a sword. Is that what you mean?" Daena asked.

Nim chuckled as she dropped the clothes on the bed. "Yep, we're learning sword fighting—mostly using wooden staffs at the moment. Tristan is teaching us, although I suspect he's going to pass us to one of the other Hawks soon. He spends half the time telling us to put more power behind our strikes, and the other half cringing when we hit each other." Nim shook her head, eyes glinting with amusement. "And we can't train with Mathos either. The one time we tried, he spent the entire time talking about heavy thrusts and the best way to grip the hilt. Then he spent a good ten minutes going on about caring for your weapon. It was hilarious until Lucilla said she had sweet almond oil in her room if he needed to polish his sword, and we didn't see them for the rest of the morning."

Nim snorted, and Daena laughed with her, her heart lifting. This was so much more than sword practice. It was an offer of friendship from a group of women Daena admired and liked a great deal. Not just the temporary care they'd given her as a prisoner soon to be sent on a dangerous mission, but an offer to include her in their lives.

"I would love that," she answered honestly. She resisted the temptation to look down at her ankle. "I'm probably a little behind you and Lucilla. But I can learn, I'm sure."

Nim reached out and took her hand, her voice ringing with honesty. "Daena, I have never doubted that you can do anything you put your mind to. And the Hawks are great at finding what you're good at and enhancing it." Her eyes sparkled. "Perhaps daggers are more your style, anyway."

Daena half choked, unprepared to have the way she'd stabbed Andred become a joke quite so quickly, but Nim just laughed, the sound bright and joyful.

Slowly their laughter faded, and Nim's face grew serious, her wings furling more tightly behind her back. And Daena knew there was more. Something that Nim felt less confident about sharing.

"Is everything okay?" Daena asked slowly.

Nim nodded, but she squeezed Daena's hand before letting her go, as if she wanted to reassure her. "Yes. Everything is fine. But there is something I'd like to talk to you about if that's alright?"

"Of course." Daena led her to the sofa under the window and they sat together, knees turned to face each other.

Nim clasped her hands together loosely in her lap, her face serious. "When I told Tristan I was coming to see you this morning, he asked if I could speak to you about something."

Gods, that sounded ominous. What could Tristan possibly want to talk to her about? Was she going to be prosecuted for killing Andred? No, surely not. Maybe there'd been a problem with the list she found? Or…. Gods. "Is Reece okay?" Daena moved to stand back up. If he was hurt or—

"Reece is fine." Nim laid a friendly hand on her arm, and she stilled. "I would have said something straight away, I promise. But"—Nim looked strangely uncertain—"this *is* about him."

Daena wiped her hands down her dress. Her palms were suddenly damp, her fingers trembling. Reece was so happy. He had everything he'd needed for so long. She couldn't bear for that to be taken from him. More than that, she *wouldn't* bear it. She would fight to help him keep his life here, if that's what he needed.

"You can tell me," she said, trying to keep her voice even and her breathing calm.

"Dionys's housekeeper—her name's Tullia—recognized him," Nim said quietly. "Or rather, she thinks she knew his mother. She's asked to see him."

Gods and angels. "Have you told him?" Daena's voice came out close to a whisper.

"No." Nim pressed her lips together for a moment. "What happened with Helaine… it hurt him badly. Tristan thinks it's something to do with his mother."

Her throat tightened painfully. "Tristan doesn't know?"

Nim shook her head. "He has some idea, but not all, no. Mathos might know more, but they would never discuss it. That's just not the Hawks. I mean, don't get me wrong, they gossip like old men over a garden fence, but they don't share secrets. And they don't leave a brother behind."

Daena let out a slow breath. Gods. Reece had told *her*. She'd known at the time that he was revealing something deeply personal, but she hadn't realized just how much of an honor he'd given her.

"We've all been so worried about him, but now he's finally back home," Nim continued. "I only knew him for a couple of days before Helaine betrayed us all—and they were not easy days—but even then, he had this kind of charm. It was so vibrant and distracting. I don't think anyone ever realized how unhappy he was. Then, after… well, when the charm was gone, all that was left was his misery. And his anger."

Daena's eyes stung. Reece had been so alone for so long. Always hiding his real feelings and never realizing how much the Hawks cared.

"But now," Nim said, leaning forward, her silver-flecked blue eyes holding Daena's, "he's at peace. He's more settled than Tristan remembers him ever being. And the Hawks don't want to risk it."

Everything Nim was saying was true. Daena didn't need to taste it to know. She gripped her hands tightly in her lap, resisting the urge to drag her thumb down her scar. "What do you want me to do?"

"Tristan was hoping you could talk to Reece. Ask him what he wants to do," Nim replied. "Reece obviously cares about you. We hope it'll be easier for him if it comes from you."

Daena swallowed against the tension in her throat. Reece had spent his entire life wanting to know who his father was. This housekeeper might be able to give him that. And more. Knowing who his father was might give him a family, heritage, and financial security. It might give him the place in Brythoria he'd dreamed of.

It might, in the end, also take him away.

But he had to be able to make that choice. She knew what it was like to be trapped, and she never wanted Reece to feel that way. She wanted him to have this opportunity. She dipped her chin, recognizing why Nim had come to her. "I'll speak to him today."

"Thank you." Nim smiled, her wings softening gracefully at her sides.

They sat together in silence for long moments, both lost in their thoughts. Until, eventually, Nim seemed to shake off the heaviness that had surrounded them and strode across to the pile of clothes on the bed.

"Come on, let's take a look at these." Nim rifled through the various garments, laying them out more neatly. "We thought you'd most likely fit best into Alanna's old clothes. She won't mind if you borrow some of these until we can get a new wardrobe made for you."

Daena pushed herself up to stand, grateful for the distraction and Nim's support. She joined the other woman at the bed, forcing her mind away from Reece and the conversation they had to have, to look over what Nim had brought.

There was a gorgeous selection of silk and velvet dresses, some that looked hardly worn, all of them delicately embroidered and absolutely beautiful. But none of the court dresses drew her eye, not like the leather breeches and jerkins and the set of cotton shirts in plum, pale green, and cream.

"We thought those would look beautiful with your coloring," Nim said. "But I've only ever seen you in a dress, so I wasn't sure if you'd like them."

Daena lifted the green shirt, running her fingers over the fine cloth as she admitted, "When I woke up in the camp, Andred gave me two gray dresses. That's all I had. I wore them because I had no other choice."

Nim nodded slowly. "I understand."

Daena looked across at Nim. They'd traveled different paths, but they'd both lost—and gained—so much. They'd both had to face not only cruelty and danger, but themselves. And here they were. Wiser, more understanding, more compassionate. Aware of their own strengths.

"I guess the question, then," Nim said, never looking away, "is what *you* choose, now that you're here."

That was the heart of everything. Could she stay here, in the palace, living the life she'd fought so hard to get away from? Or if she refused to stay, if she left Kaerlud and went north, leaving Reece behind, what kind of life would that be? Would she spend her days alone in the mountains, regretting walking away from the future they could have had, wishing she had given them a real chance?

She looked out toward the window and the winter sky beyond, settling into a new kind of certainty. Reece needed her. And, honestly, she needed him too.

It was time she started to create the life she wanted. She would never hide her truth behind—or from—a man again. But she could stand beside one, as a partner.

She could choose to make a life here in the palace. Not as a truth seeker or a glamourous companion, but in her own way. There was always a need for herbalists. Perhaps Nim or Rafe could help her find a place. Perhaps Lucilla would need someone with her skills in her gardens or the infirmary. She picked up the breeches and the cotton shirt.

She would be here for Reece, and if, in the end, he chose a new family and a different life, she would know that she had given everything she could. She would know she had fought for him. For *them*. And she would have made herself a home, either way.

"Those suit you," Nim said softly, her voice warm and kind, as if she understood exactly what they meant. And then she murmured, "Whatever happens, I hope you know that Reece will always have a family here among the Hawks." Daena nodded. She did know. But Nim wasn't finished. "And so will you, Daena. You're one of us now."

You're one of us. Gods and angels. It meant more to her than she could begin to say.

The word stuck in her mouth unsaid, but somehow Nim must have understood anyway, because she wrapped Daena in a friendly hug and whispered for her, "Truth."

Chapter Thirty

REECE OPENED the door into their suite. He was covered in building dust. He'd skipped lunch and worked on through the afternoon, and now it was late enough that the first lamps had been lit. He desperately needed a wash. But he needed to see Daena first. He had a plan, a proper plan, and he couldn't wait to share it with her.

She was sitting at the small desk, writing, but she looked up at him, her face relaxing into a soft smile as soon as she saw him. Gods. The palace was a strange combination of familiar and unfamiliar. Opening their door and seeing Daena, that was when he came home.

She stood and walked toward him, the lamplight highlighting the strands of deep red and rich brown in her hair. She was wearing breeches that molded around her legs, and a pale mint-green cotton shirt that highlighted the violet of her eyes.

So beautiful. Mine.

Reece grinned at his beast. Yes, she was. Wherever she

went, whatever she did, she was part of him forever. Now they had to make sure *he* was *hers*.

He strode across the room, needing to touch her, needing his lips on hers, her taste in his mouth. He tried to keep a distance between their bodies as his mouth covered hers, to keep from smothering her in dust, but she wrapped herself around him, holding him pressed against her, as if she needed to feel him as much as he needed to feel her.

Her grip tightened, and she whimpered softly, climbing his body, almost desperate in the way that she was kissing him. Something about it, about the tension in her neck, the rough grip of her fingers, was wrong. When he'd left her this morning, she'd been pensive and uncertain, but now she was afraid.

He pulled away gently, disentangling himself enough that he could look down at her, his fingers throbbing where his claws extended further. "What happened?" He looked around the room, hunting the danger, the source of her fear, but found nothing to fight. Nothing to protect her from.

"I'm well. Safe." She shook her head ruefully, but she didn't let him go. "I'm sorry… I meant to ask you how you were. To give you a moment. I wanted…." She blinked up at him, and he knew she was looking for the right words.

The urge to say something to fill the silence was almost overwhelming. A small part of him wanted to charm her, dazzle her, and show her that she needed him. But that wasn't him anymore. Instead, he forced himself to stay silent. To give her time. She had a smear of dust on her cheek, and he lifted his shirt to gently wipe it off.

Daena took his hand and led him to the small sofa, encouraging him to sit. She looked at him for a moment, but then, rather than sitting beside him as he expected, she climbed onto his lap, straddling him, and wrapped her arms around his neck. "I meant to do this so differently."

If it was meant to soothe him, it had the complete opposite effect. Was she leaving? Had she secured a place in the north? Had she decided that the palace could never be her home? Gods. Had someone said something to her about her time with the Wraiths? He would kill them.

"Just tell me, please," he grated out.

"Nim came to see me today," Daena replied softly, settling her hands on his cheeks and rubbing her thumbs slowly over his cheekbones.

"Nim," he repeated blankly. That was the last thing he'd expected Daena to say. Surely Nim wouldn't—

"Do you remember Tullia, Dionys's housekeeper?" Daena asked, confusing him even more.

"The older woman. Andred threatened her." He shrugged, trying to imagine what Tullia could possibly have done to upset Daena while his beast writhed unhappily.

"Yes." She leaned her forehead against his. Her legs were over his, her hands on her face. And she looked…. Gods. The last time he'd seen this look on her face, they'd been in the Wraiths' farmhouse and she'd told him he had to go. She'd been so determined to do the right thing no matter how difficult it was. And she'd wanted to touch him one last time before he left.

What the fuck was happening?

"Reece," Daena murmured. "I want you to know that whatever you decide, I'll support you. Whatever you want, I'll do my best to give it to you. Okay? I'll be here with you —" She cleared her throat. "—for as long as you want me."

Scales settled over his skin; his claws were long enough that he had to shift his grip to make sure he wasn't stabbing into her. What did Tullia want? Was she loyal to Dionys, even after everything? Had she accused Daena of something? Perhaps making trouble for her because she'd stabbed Andred? Whatever it was, they could fight it. He let out a shuddering breath and forced himself to speak. "Okay."

There was a long pause, only their breath shuddering between them. Then Daena whispered, "Tullia recognized you, Reece. She knew your mother."

What?

"She... what?" It was the last thing he'd imagined. He'd been so focused on protecting Daena, it hadn't even occurred to him.

"She knew your mother," Daena repeated. "Apparently you look just like her. They were friends when they worked together in the palace, years ago. There's a chance that she knows...."

"Who my father is," Reece finished for her. His scales slid away, his claws retracted back to their usual shorter length, and he let out a rough bark of laughter. "Thank the gods."

Daena tilted her head to the side, frowning in confusion, and he wrapped his arms tighter around her, dragging her closer. Close enough that her entire body was pressed into his, her head tucked into his shoulder.

He pressed a kiss to her hair, no longer caring how dirty he got her. "I thought that you were leaving. I thought she'd tried to hurt you somehow. Fuck."

"But...." Daena pushed herself back until she could look at him properly, a frown lining her forehead as she settled her hands on his shoulders. "I thought you'd be upset that she'd been there all this time. Angry that you've missed out this time. Anxious to meet your family." She pressed a gentle kiss to his mouth. "This must raise complicated feelings for you."

His beast rumbled, low and dark. It didn't have complicated feelings at all. And for the first time, neither did he.

"I don't want to see her," he admitted quietly, as much to himself as to Daena. "Whatever she might say, whatever she might know, I don't need it anymore."

"Don't you?" Her frown deepened. "But this is your chance. You could be the heir to a fortune. You could have a powerful, noble family—"

"And if I did this? If I discovered that I have some noble father: Dionys or Flavius or Geraint even. What then?" he asked, voice rougher than he intended.

She didn't hesitate at all. She didn't look away. If anything, her grip on him tightened. "Then I'll support you. Whatever you need. Even if you need… to spend time with your new family. Or, whatever…." Her voice faded for a moment, but then she took a breath and continued more firmly. "Tullia's staying in the guest wing overnight. She spent the day with the other hostages, being cared for by Rafe and the healers. Nim said she would be in the library for a couple of hours this evening. I think we should go and see her. Otherwise, you'll always wonder."

His beast muttered unhappily as waves of scales hardened over his shoulders. *I don't want this.*

Gods. A new thought occurred to him. Maybe there was more here he didn't understand. Maybe this was something else, something far worse.

He swallowed against the dryness in his throat. "Daena, is this…. Do you want me to see her because you're planning to leave?"

Her reply was instant, her gaze clear and open. "No. I've decided to stay."

"Stay? Here?" he repeated raggedly.

"Yes. Whatever you decided to do, I'm going to be here. I want to give this—us—a chance."

"Really?" he whispered.

"I promise."

"Okay." He closed his eyes for a long moment, soaking in the feeling of her body on his. Her forehead against his. The promise she'd made. His beast settled back, not entirely, but enough that he could think over the steady rumbling.

"Will you come with me?" he asked eventually.

"Of course. I never expected you to go alone."

He blinked at the prickling in his eyes. Gods. She would stand beside him without question. His hands tightened on her waist as his beast sent a shiver of scales up his arms. *I'd rather just stay here.*

Reece grunted. He also wanted to stay in their room and forget all about Tullia and whatever she might know. But what if Daena was right? What if he started to wonder? Maybe the best thing was to find out the truth; then he could leave it forever.

"Okay," he murmured. "I think we should go." If he was going to do this, he wanted it over. He lifted Daena off his lap, and they stared at each other in silence for a long, heavy, moment before she stepped back.

Her lips were pinched, eyes gleaming a little too brightly as she wiped her hands down her new breeches. But she didn't back down. She took his hand in hers and followed him slowly through the palace to the library.

Lamps shed a warm, golden light on the heavy floor-to-ceiling bookcases and their myriad of valuable books. Clusters of comfortable-looking sofas created separate areas where palace residents could read or meet. And standing beside the window, talking to Nim, Tristan, and a handful of the Hawks, was Tullia.

As soon as Tristan saw Reece and Daena, he led the others away to the far side of the opulent room. Out of hearing, but still in sight. He lifted his hand in a small salute, directed at Reece, silently offering his backing. Reece saluted back, gratitude and uncertainty warring inside him.

They settled awkwardly into a small set of velvet-covered couches, no one speaking. The silence stretched as his beast rumbled unhappily, but Reece honestly had no clue what to say.

Daena laced her fingers through his and gripped them tightly, seeming unaware of the claws that had extended to prick into the skin at the back of her hands. "We understand you knew Reece's mother?" she said to Tullia.

"Yes." Tullia nodded. "At least, I think so." She faced Reece squarely, her eyes traveling over his face. "You're Cateline's son?"

He tried to nod. Tried to find some of the charm that had protected him all his life. But he couldn't find any of it. He looked at Daena helplessly.

She slid even closer on the couch, pressing her thigh against his, as if to hold him up. "Reece is Cateline's son."

"I thought so," Tullia murmured. "You look just like her."

"How well did you know Cateline?" Daena asked gently.

"Very well." Tullia's eyes wrinkled as she smiled. "We started working at the palace at the same time. You can imagine, we were young, independent, earning our own money… they were good years."

"She was happy?" Reece asked, his voice rough and rumbling with his beast's ambivalence.

"Oh yes," Tullia agreed. "Your mother was always the center of every party, the life of every event. She had the charm, you know? Everyone adored her."

Everyone adored her. Such a casual, easy phrase. And yet, it hung in the air, none of them quite knowing what to say next.

Daena shuffled even closer, close enough that he could smell the soft herbal scent of her hair. "Can you tell us about the man she fell in love with? What happened?" Daena asked.

Tullia nodded slowly. "Cateline was so beautiful, so vivacious. It wasn't surprising that she would catch a noble's eye."

His beast growled; none of this was what it wanted to know.

"Did he love her in return, this man?" Reece asked.

"Yes," Tullia said slowly. "I think so."

"Did she work for him?" The question forced its way out of Reece. How much power had this nobleman had over his mother?

"No, never. We were in King Geraint's household. Cateline's lover was one of the king's friends. A widower who came back to the palace when his wife died."

Gods. He really was powerful. But at least he'd never been her master. Or her king.

"So he could have married her?" Daena pressed.

Tullia looked away for a moment before facing them once more, her mouth pulling down in a way that deepened the lines around her eyes, making her look tireder and older. "That was very unlikely. He was one of the highest-ranking councilors—promoted young—but the rest of Geraint's council would never have approved. He would have been expected to resign. And his family was obsessed with the purity of their blood. They counted their forefathers all the way back to the first raiders. They would never have accepted a Tarasque wife. Especially not a former maid from the palace." Tullia tilted her head sadly toward Reece. "And they would never have allowed a Tarasque child. If they'd known about you…." She shrugged. She didn't need to say anymore.

"So Cateline decided to run," Daena whispered.

"Yes," Tullia agreed. "She left without telling him, simply sent back word that she had the red plague, and later, arranged for a note to say that she'd died." She twisted her hands in her lap. "He went a little mad, then. It was clear that he was grieving, heartbroken. He was certain it was a lie, certain she'd left him. He discovered that she'd sold some of the gifts he'd given her, and it made him even more convinced she'd betrayed him. But he couldn't track her down. He couldn't go looking for her—or send anyone after her—without revealing the truth. Without showing the world that he wanted her. Oh, he could have had her hunted down, had her kidnapped and stashed somewhere, but Cateline would never have survived that. And he genuinely cared for her."

Tullia looked over, focusing on Reece. "He hadn't hated the Tarasque before, but after that… he was never the same. He started to believe the poison his family fed him. When his only son died on the northern border, he threw everything he had into building a fleet of ships and supporting the war. Hatred was all he had left. He spent all his money, all his time, dedicated to destroying the people he blamed for taking the last person he loved from the world."

Gods. With that one comment, he knew. They all knew.

A powerful man who hated the Tarasque. Who'd lost his son in the north. Who was dedicated to war with Verturia. Who'd built a fleet—

It doesn't matter. None of this matters.

Daena had gone absolutely stiff beside him, and he knew, before she even opened her mouth, what she was about to say. But he didn't want to hear it. Didn't want to have the words out in the world.

"The man," Daena whispered, "it was—"

He had his hand over her mouth before she could finish. "Don't say it. Please."

Daena looked at him with wide eyes, her lips slowly closing beneath his fingers. His beast was rumbling steadily, a loud droning almost-growl as he shook his head and murmured, "I don't want this."

Daena's head dipped in a small nod. She understood him. She knew that so long as the word remained unsaid, it could remain distant. Something unacknowledged and never quite real.

She kissed his palm gently before lifting his hand from her mouth and holding it tightly, and she didn't say anything at all.

He turned to Tullia. "She was happy, you said. And he loved her?"

"Yes, she was happy and loved."

And then she made a new life, where she was happy and loved.

"There are no other heirs," Tullia started. "I thought you should know. The estates—"

Reece cut her off with a shake of his head and her voice faded.

"I just have one more question. Flavius… do you know whether his mistress was also called Cat?"

The housekeeper shook her head slowly. "I don't think I

ever knew of his mistress. If he even had one, she was never at court. But his wife's name was Catricia."

Gods. That was all he needed to know.

He looked down at Daena. Her body was angled as if she was shielding him, positioned between him and Tullia. She didn't say anything, she simply sat quietly with him. Supporting him. Giving him what he needed.

A lightness surged up through him. Recognition of just how very lucky he was. Gods. He, too, was happy.

And loved.

He looked up at Tullia. "That's all I needed to know."

She dipped her chin, then smiled. "You remind me so much of her."

"Thank you," he said softly. Then he put out his hand, and Daena took it without question as he murmured their goodbyes.

Chapter Thirty-One

Daena followed Reece through the corridors, past the administrative wing, past the kitchens, down a narrow corridor, and out to a massive courtyard. He moved fast, his beast rumbling in his belly, but never too fast; always at a manageable speed. He seemed to need space. An escape. And she wanted him to have what he needed.

They walked down a set of stone stairs and out to a building site. The night was dark, the sky heavy with clouds promising more winter rain, perhaps snow, and torches flickered around the courtyard lighting their way. The wavering light highlighted the string lines carefully pegged out beside the old barracks, showing where the foundations for the new living quarters would be dug. Dirty cobbles were strewn with piles of wood and sand, waiting for the builders to return in the morning.

Reece led her over the courtyard, past the stables with their scent of manure and hay heavy in the icy air, and then up a narrow staircase, lit only by lamps, onto the battlements.

They passed soldiers on their rounds as they followed the walkway, eventually stepping off the new ramparts built by Ballanor and onto the older battlements.

They passed the Old Tower with a wave to the sentries before eventually pausing side by side in the middle of the long walkway. The dark waters of the Tamasa lapped with a slow shushing against the walls as Reece looked out toward the river.

"I would have liked to bring you here in the daylight," he murmured, but then he chuckled softly. "Although, honestly, it looks about the same."

Daena leaned against the cold stones. A fine mist had settled over the water, making the world seem hazy and dreamlike. Isolating them in a cocoon where the only real thing was Reece. The brilliant sapphire of his eyes. The heat of his skin. The firm pressure of his hand where he'd rested it on her hip.

"Are you okay?" she asked gently, wrapping her hand around his bicep, using the connection like an anchor in this strangely disconnected moment. "You stopped Tullia before she could—" Make it real, she'd almost said, but in a way, that would have made it real too.

Reece cupped her cheek with his free hand, his skin so hot against hers. "I didn't need the name." He bent to kiss her tenderly on her forehead, then beside her eye, on her cheekbone, her mouth; a gentle touch of his lips to hers. "I don't need power or fortune, or the recognition of a family who never wanted me," he said quietly beside her ear. "I just want to be with you, building a future for us both."

She understood that. And she wanted it with a fierce ache. But she also wanted him to have everything he was owed. "But—"

He stopped her with another firm kiss on her lips. "Tell

me you know it's true, Daena, when I say I don't want the power or the fortune or the noble family. Tell me what I taste like."

Gods. It *was* the truth. She sighed against his mouth, melting against him.

"You taste of warmth and light," she whispered. "But you would still taste of those. I would still stand with you if you wanted to make this claim."

He ran his cheek along hers, the rough stubble scratching over her skin as he pressed a soft kiss on her bruised collarbone. Then he lifted his face once more. His eyes glowed in the darkness as he murmured, "I don't want a heritage built on dragon blood and hatred. I want to make my own future. With you. I am Reece, son of Cateline and Brennan, and I choose my own family now."

His words curled through the misty air—another part of himself that he was giving her. Honoring her with. And she could give him nothing less in return. "Truth," she whispered.

His grip tightened on her hip, his expression utterly serious. "If you want to go north, I'll come with you. I've spoken to Tristan and Lucilla already. There'll be a place for me in Staith if that's what you want."

She stilled, her hands gripping tight around his biceps as they tensed beneath her fingers. "You would do that?"

"Yes." His answer was unequivocal.

Gods. This man. He was good and loyal and true. And he was hers.

She smiled up at him, letting her joy and relief bubble between them. "Lucilla must think we're losing our minds."

"Why?" he asked, rumbling softly.

"I went to see the queen this afternoon," Daena admitted.

"Probably within hours of you asking for a position in Staith."
She chuckled softly. "I asked for a position here in the castle.
Perhaps working with Nim and Rafe. I feel like there's a lot—"

He snorted softly, eyes crinkling up in amusement.

"What?"

In answer, he reached into his back pocket and pulled
out a folded parchment.

Daena squinted at the vague lines. "It's too dark," she
muttered. "What am I looking at?"

"Plans," he replied, his voice low and deep, echoes of
his beast winding through it. "I had a long meeting with
Tristan today, and then we both went to see Lucilla. They
gave me leave to relocate to Staith if that's what we decide."
Scales glittered on his neck in the lamplight. "But they also
approved my idea to build a conservatory here." He
gestured out across the dark waters. "We're going to redirect
the moat to restore the gardens and claim back the space. I
want to reverse the destruction Ballanor wrought. To build
something beautiful instead: a conservatory, like they have in
Eshcol."

"A conservatory?" she repeated, hardly even daring to
imagine it.

Reece grinned, and she felt his enthusiasm flowing from
him, a wild, rich energy that filled her heart and made her
want to laugh.

"It will be a massive glass greenhouse with access to the
river. Overflowing with plants and herbs and growing
things. We'll fill the conservatory with scholars, healers,
apothecaries, and herbalists—like you—all working together
to help the people of Brythoria."

Gods and angels. It was like picturing a dream.

"We can send a message to Val and Alanna," Reece

added quietly. "Ask them to collect your seeds when they come through the Thabana Mountains—"

Daena couldn't help the laugh that finally bubbled over. "You're going to ask the Princess of Verturia, former Queen-in-waiting of Brythoria, to climb all over the mountains and collect seeds?"

Reece laughed with her. "No, I'm going to ask one of my oldest friends and one of the kindest women I know to climb all over the mountains for us."

Gods. This was real. His enthusiasm was real. *He* was real. She could leap, knowing he would catch her. This was warmth and light... and love.

She took the plans from his hands and carefully folded them before tucking them back into his pocket. Then she wrapped her hands around his neck and went up onto her toes so she could look him right in the eye. "Thank you for dreaming my dream with me. I would love to work in your conservatory." Her throat was tight as she continued. "I love *you.*"

A wave of smooth scales flickered over his cheekbones and then retreated slowly as Reece groaned. It was a sound of such profound relief that she would have worried if he hadn't lifted his hand to show her the claws slowly retracting.

His beast purred, deep and low, a soothing vibration between their bodies. And then he slowly, reverently, skimmed his fingertips over her cheeks, as if he was luxuriating in touching her. Soaking in the warmth of her skin.

His beast's low rumble vibrated through his voice as he spoke, as much beast as man, "I love you too."

Epilogue

DAENA WALKED down the rows of tables, enjoying the warmth and humidity, brushing her hand gently over the fine green shoots as they made their way toward the spring afternoon sunlight.

The new conservatory had taken teams of builders months to get right, and it was *perfect*. Reece had designed a complex system of pipes to bring water from the Tamasa into the greenhouses, while the glass roof let in and held light, heat, and warmth. Flowers, herbs, even small trees flourished in abundance, filling the air with the perfume of growing things.

Healers and herbalists had come from all over the kingdom; Mabin, Tarasque, Nephilim, and Apollyon, all working together, sharing knowledge and skills, and then returning to their homes with more knowledge and new friends.

The cost had been extraordinary, but, in the end, the reparations from the nobles who had supported Andred had paid for most of it. Lucilla had been careful to ensure that their families were left with enough of their original wealth that no martyrs were created. But the fines had been stiff enough to hurt, and the time the once-powerful men had spent in Gatehouse Prison was both an effective deterrent and an act of justice that made the people of Brythoria love their new queen even more.

Dionys and Pellin had been given a cell together. And as much as she detested their behavior and their attitudes, it was a relief for Reece—and Tor—to know that the two old men were together. Hopefully learning some wisdom.

On the whole, she and Reece stayed away from politics and concentrated on rebuilding instead. By working round the clock, they'd had the conservatory ready a week ahead of when Val and Alanna arrived back in Kaerlud—carrying the signed treaty and bags of carefully harvested Snow Lotus seeds. The very seeds that were now sprouting into rows of vibrant seedlings, their first leaves gently unfurling in the warmth.

Muted footsteps caught her attention, and she lifted her head to see Reece striding toward her. He'd filled out since she first met him, his already broad shoulders adding layers of muscle and a healthy tan from hours of hard outdoor work. His eyes were clear and bright, his scales gleaming deep, midnight blue.

"I found your note." Reece smiled over the worktop and its myriad of tiny plants. "Do you need help before we go?"

"No, thanks. I was just giving them a last once over...." And preparing. She tried to smile, but it felt tight, as if it was pulling her cheeks, and she resisted the urge to wipe her hands down her breeches.

He stepped up beside her, chuckling softly. "They'll be fine. We're only going away for a couple of days, and I know you've already got at least three people watching over them." Reece tucked a loose curl of hair behind her ear, eyes gleaming. "It'll be nice to have a holiday together."

"It will." She went up to her toes to kiss him softly. "And the wedding is going to be beautiful."

Nim and Tristan had waited for Val and Alanna to get back from Verturia and for Nim's childhood home to be fully restored after the fire that had devastated it. Now they would all be gathering there to celebrate Nim and Tristan's marriage.

Daena had helped arrange the flowers; irises for faith, wisdom, and valor; jasmine for grace; orchids for once-in-a-lifetime love, all woven through with ivy for eternal devotion. Blues and purples, like the color of Nim's eyes and the tunic that had been so important to the Hawks for so long. Gods and angels. She already felt emotional. How long was it going to take her to start crying when she saw her friend walking down the aisle toward the man she loved?

Daena gave the tiny green shoots one last brush with her fingers and then stepped away. The seedlings were small and new, but they were strong. Just like the Hawks. And she was a Hawk too. She could do this.

Reece frowned down at her. "Are you really okay?"

"I… yes." She let her half-smile fade. It was no use forcing it; he knew her too well for that.

Instead, she took his hand and led him through the conservatory, out the back doors, and down toward the river. Knowing he would follow.

Behind them, the castle walls threw long shadows over the newly planted gardens between the outer wall and the river. There were graveled walkways, benches for contemplation, pools filled with darting fish. Apple tree saplings were starting to bud, pale pink and white among the green. Crocus flowers, tulips, and daffodils waved in the slight breeze, a vibrant living tapestry, made even more beautiful by the fluttering of the first spring butterflies and the lazy drone of a bumblebee. It was a place of beauty for a kingdom at peace.

Daena led Reece down the gently winding paths and through an arch of woven jasmine to a small walled garden. He would know it was there; he'd helped draw the plans. But in the months since the building work on the conservatory was done, he'd turned his focus to the interiors of the barracks, and he hadn't been out here again.

His footsteps slowed as the first planted rows came into view. The heavy scent of rosemary filled the spring air, along with lavender, mint, and thyme. Rosebushes were just coming into bud, and lemon trees were covered in tiny star-shaped flowers.

The central path led through the rows to the back wall, where a small fountain splashed and bubbled. A little way to its side was a wooden bench, set perfectly to catch the afternoon sun. On the ground in front of the bench were the blanket and the overflowing picnic basket she'd left there earlier. And on the wall behind the bench was a gleaming bronze plaque.

They walked toward it slowly, Reece matching her pace, as he always did, and it took a few moments before he read the plaque.

The moment he realized what it said, he stiffened. His beast rumbled in his belly, scales flickering over his neck and up, onto his jaw.

His hand clung to hers as he read the words aloud:

> *Cateline Memorial Herb Garden.*
> *Rest here, and know that you are loved*

"Did you do this?" he whispered.

"I had help," she admitted.

Nim, Alanna, and Lucilla had worked beside her on the planting, while Keely kept them company from the bench. They could have had a team of gardeners do the work, but Nim and Lucilla knew the grief of losing a mother, and they had wanted to do it themselves. Gardening together, laughing together, sometimes crying—Keely blamed the baby every time—they had poured their love into the soil.

"Thank you." He turned to face her, eyes gleaming and soft. "This means… more than I can tell you."

Her eyes prickled, but she didn't dare swipe at them; she couldn't cry, not yet. She lifted his hand to press a soft kiss to his knuckles, and then slowly lowered herself to one knee, still gripping his fingers in hers.

"Daena," Reece murmured, his voice strained. "Why are you…? Your ankle…. I don't want you to hurt—"

She gripped his hand tighter, and he closed his mouth.

She swallowed, hard, knowing he could feel how her hands were shaking, how her body was trembling. Her mouth had never been so dry before in her life. But this was Reece. The man who'd trusted her with his past and his future. Who'd come for her. Who would *always* come for her. Who had supported her dream and worked hard to help her make it a reality.

She could do this. More than that—she *wanted* to do this. She wanted him to know that she chose him. That she would fight for him. That she was his, as he was hers.

"Reece, son of Cateline." Gods. She didn't mean to whisper, but she couldn't get the words to come out any louder. "I love you."

He lifted his free hand to cradle her face, his claws pricking gently against her cheek. "I love you too."

She looked up, into his eyes. They were almost entirely sapphire, his beast right at the surface, and somehow that gave her strength. His beast had always known.

"Reece," she murmured, "Will you marry me?"

His beast let out a loud, rumbling purr, and Reece dropped to his knees in front of her. The tears that had threatened earlier slipped out, running down his cheeks, and she brushed them away with her thumbs.

"Yes," his beast rumbled. "Yes," he said more clearly in his own voice. He wrapped his arms around her and hauled her against him, both beast and man. "Yes, I would be honored to marry you."

And then they were falling back to the blanket, the picnic forgotten, because he was touching her and whispering how much he loved her, and the sun was shining, golden and soft.

He gripped her hands, lacing his fingers through hers while his eyes never left hers. And everything she felt was real, and good, and right.

Reece lowered his mouth to hers and kissed her breathlessly. He tasted of salt, but mostly of warmth and truth. And, above all, he tasted of love.

Bonus Epilogue - Tristan

TRISTAN STOOD on the low hill, looking down toward the farmhouse.

Behind him, a stream gurgled and chattered, making its way down from the hills. If he climbed those hills, following the animal tracks and shepherds' paths, eventually he would reach an ancient hut where he and Val had played together as boys.

They'd taken pies and berries for their lunch and spent long days pretending to be warriors. Dreaming of the time they could finally become soldiers for real. Never once imagining the dark paths they would travel or how much light they might find at the end.

Once, long ago, Nim had run away and hidden in that hut, and when he and Val had found her there, the relief, the desperate rage pounding through him at the thought of how she could have been hurt, should have told him. Should have made him realize just how much she meant to him.

His beast rumbled inside him. It had known, but Tristan hadn't known how to listen. Not then.

Ahead of him was the farmhouse where Nim and Val had spent their childhoods—as had he. It was rebuilt and newly painted. No evidence was left of the fire that had decimated it less than a year before. He had wondered if it might not be better to pull the house down and build a new one somewhere else, somewhere far from the harsh reminders of those terrible days, but Nim had refused.

She wanted to keep her family home. The lands where her mama and her papa had lived, and the grounds where they were buried. Where the three of them had played together as children. Where she had fought for herself and triumphed. The catalyst that had finally brought them together.

But, gods, he was glad it had been painted over. He couldn't have borne to be here otherwise. And it felt right, to create something new on these strong foundations.

His eyes traveled from the house down to the front garden. Chairs had been set out over the lawn, and people were slowly settling into them, occasionally glancing at the bower of fresh flowers. Flowers grown in the new palace greenhouse and arranged by Daena.

While he watched, Reece lifted Daena's hand to his lips and then dipped closer to her ear and whispered something that made her laugh before leading her to sit beside Keely and Tor.

Keely's face was flushed, her belly large and lying low as she leaned back in her chair. It wouldn't be long before they had a new, tiny member of the Hawks. A baby that was both Apollyon and Verturian. A miracle.

Mathos had already started calling himself Uncle Matt and promising to teach the baby everything they needed to know about where to find the honey and the berries in the palace kitchens. Every time he said it, Lucilla blushed. Which, naturally, just made Mathos do it more.

Lucilla was sitting in the next row, Alanna beside her. The curvy, dark-haired queen leaned close to the willowy blonde Verturian princess as they chatted and laughed together.

Garet, Jos, Jeremiel, Rafael, and Haniel made up the next row. Garet's wing was fully healed, and he was back to enjoying his role as the best shot in the squad. He'd milked out the attention for far longer than he might have, but Tristan couldn't begrudge him the first true respite they'd had in years, especially not when he'd seen the look on Jeremiel's face when he heard Garet had been injured.

His beast rumbled, considering, and Tristan grunted his agreement. He needed to think of a mission that would throw them together, let them spend some time—

"I thought I'd find you here." Mathos chuckled behind him. "Always on the highest ground. And plotting something, by the look of you."

Tristan shrugged, turning to look at his former second-in-command, now Baron Mathos, consort to the queen. "I like to be able to see what's coming."

Mathos grinned. "And did you? See this coming?"

"Gods, no."

They both laughed.

"Are you ready?" Mathos asked.

His beast growled, a low hum of affirmation. Yes, he was ready—he and his beast. They had been since the moment Nim had looked up into his eyes, lying beneath him as his body covered hers, and told him that she trusted him. Gods. She had expected him to run, but she had offered her heart anyway. She had told him that she wanted him, and he had realized that he wanted her more than he wanted to breathe... and that he would never run again.

Mathos must have understood, because he didn't ask again, he simply dipped his chin in acknowledgment. "It's time."

They walked together, Mathos at his side, as he had been through so much.

Before they reached the bower where Ramiel was standing, Tristan looked over at his friend—his brother—filled with gratitude. "Thank you, Mathos. For everything."

Mathos looked back at him, face unusually serious as burgundy and gold scales flickered over his jaw. "It has been a privilege to serve under you."

They held each other's gaze for a long moment. Then Mathos grinned, insolent and carefree once more. "Now go put Val out of his misery."

They both laughed as they stepped up to the bower. Tristan nodded his greeting to Ramiel, while Mathos moved slightly to the side.

A light breeze ruffled over the audience, and Tristan took a deep breath of the cool air as it soothed the scales prickling up his neck. His claws had been half descended all day. Not because he had any doubts, but because his beast was fucking impatient. It had claimed Nim long ago, and it didn't see the need for anyone else to ratify its choice.

It did see the benefit in making its claim public though, and it wanted that done. Now.

Ramiel whispered something to Mathos, who nodded to Keely. Tor helped her up, and she made her way slowly to stand in front of the congregation. Conversations died as everyone turned to face her. And then she started to sing.

Keely had always had a beautiful voice, and it was slightly deeper now, making the ballad she sang even more hauntingly beautiful. It was a song he'd first heard on campaign in the Thabana Mountains, well known to the people of the north—both Brythorians and Verturians— part folklore, part legend.

She sang the story of Kaden and Ava, the last drake of all Brythoria and his soulmate. It was a story of danger, loss, and overcoming fear. It was a story of finding love and holding onto it, fighting for it. It was a promise, that when there were finally wings and scales behind the throne, when all of Brythoria was finally joined, all would be well.

In the front row, eyes gleaming, Daena whispered, "Truth," and the word floated in the air around them all.

The song came to a close as a flurry of scales climbed his arms, settling into armor.

Nim is here, his beast whispered.

Tristan lifted his eyes as Keely effortlessly transitioned into an upbeat aria and the audience turned in their seats to face Nim where she stood beside Val.

Nim was wearing a long, silver dress that gleamed like mercury as she moved. The bodice was shaped into a corset and covered in embroidered flowers and vines. Her arms were left bare, her long dark hair lying in loose curls over her shoulders. Her wings were back, loosely furled behind her, powerful and elegant.

Val offered her his arm and led her down the aisle toward Tristan, his own wings held back formally, his blue tunic with its silver fighting boars immaculate. He looked powerful and dangerous as he stalked beside his sister. But his lips twitched into a smile, his face relaxing just for a moment when he passed Alanna.

Nim and Val got closer, almost close enough to reach out and touch—Keely's voice rising to a bright, joyful

crescendo, before fading, leaving them all in rapt silence—
but then they stopped.

Val kissed Nim on her forehead and stepped back,
dipping his chin toward Tristan, his eyes full of warmth as
he moved to stand beside Mathos.

Nim took a small step forward, grinning as she closed
the last space between them. And then she slowly lifted her
heavy skirts and pointed her toes. And gods help him, she
wasn't wearing any shoes, only socks. And shoved into one
of them was the pewter dagger he'd given her. The dagger
she'd used to kill Grendel, setting them all on this path
toward freedom.

His beast rumbled a low purr of amusement as Tristan
grunted. "Fuck, I love you."

She stepped closer, her wings coming around him,
hiding them both in a cocoon of warmth and safety.
Somewhere in the distance, Ramiel chuckled at whatever
rude comment Mathos had just made, and Val cleared his
throat loudly.

Tristan ignored them all, because Nim had gone up on
her toes to wrap her arms around his neck and whisper, "I
love you too."

And deep inside him, his beast murmured, *and all is well.
All is well. All is well.*

Thank you!

Thank you for reading *Reece*! I have adored him since the very beginning and I'm glad he finally found Daena. I hope you've loved his happy ever after as much as I have!

If you'd enjoy spending some more time in Brythoria (and possibly learning a little more about where the Mabin and the Tarasque came from!) please join my mailing list at:
    www.jennielynnroberts.com.

I promise first looks, all the news, freebies, and bonus content including a **free Hawks novella:**

Kaden
    He has to leave. He can't take her with him. And he needs to go now.
    Kaden has always kept his true feelings for Ava hidden —he couldn't give her hope when he knew there was none. He must walk away even if it breaks her heart and destroys him and his beast.

Ava can't let losing Kaden stop her; she has patients to care for and a secret of her own hiding in the icy northern mountains. But there's danger on those lonely slopes—danger that could cost them far more than broken hearts.

Will Kaden walk away like he's always planned? Or will he risk everything for a happily ever after with Ava—and trust her to save him back when the time comes?

Kaden is a prequel novella set six generations before the events in The Hawks series. It's a hundred page (fully resolved!) sexy, steamy, adult fantasy romance with a guaranteed happy ever after.

Sign up for my newsletter and download for free:

Get Kaden now!

The Hawks Series

Kaden

*He has to leave. He can't take her with him. And he needs to go **now**.*

Tristan

*His redemption might be **her** downfall…*

Val

He'll do anything to save her. And then he'll say goodbye…

Mathos

All he has to do is find the princess, help her claim the throne, and not fall in love with her. Easy…right?

Tor

What is it about her that makes him lose his mind? Every. Damn. Time.

Reece

She's everything he doesn't want.

Honorable. Beautiful. Strong… wait, what?

Also by Jennie Lynn Roberts

Shadow Guardian

Blood Shadows – Book 1

Not all shadows are what they seem...

Kay swore an oath to use her Shadows to guard the light—an oath she takes very seriously. So, when a dark Shadow arises to terrorize London, she steps up and fights back. The last thing she expects is to find herself being patched up by a sexy paramedic who has no idea what kind of power he could control... or for her Shadows to recognize him as their perfect match.

Ethan doesn't trust easily—not in matters of love, and certainly not in... whatever supernatural secrets Kay's mixed up in. But the more time they spend together, the more he realizes he needs her with an intensity he's never known before. Accepting her crazy, Shadow-filled world will be difficult. Opening his heart to her... he's afraid that might be a step too far.

But the dark Shadows are growing. Their enemy is powerful—and closer than anyone realizes. Can Kay and Ethan claim their happily ever after? Or will the darkness take them first?

Shadow Guardian, the first book in the Blood Shadows trilogy, is an adult paranormal romance for readers who love fated mates, fast-paced adventure, and plenty of spice. Each book in the trilogy follows a different couple and has its own guaranteed HEA. The story will conclude in book three.

About the Author

Jennie Lynn Roberts believes that every kickass heroine should have control of her own story, a swoony hero to fight beside her, and a guaranteed happily ever after. Because that doesn't always happen in real life, she began creating her own worlds that work just the way they should. And she hasn't looked back since.

Jennie would rather be writing than doing anything else—except for spending time with her gorgeous family, of course. But when she isn't building vibrant new worlds to get lost in, she can be found nattering with friends, baking up a storm, or strolling in the woods around her home in England.

If you want to talk books, romance, movies, reluctant heroes, or just about anything else with Jennie, feel free to contact her.

Printed in Great Britain
by Amazon

10449052R00192